Red Sun in Morning

Rick Kemp

CR
Constant Reader Press

First Constant Reader Press Edition, August 2012

Library of Congress Cataloging-in-Publication Data Pending

ISBN: 978-0615678269

Printed in the United States of America

1 3 5 7 9 10 8 6 5 4 2

For
Mom and Grandma

To
My Loves
Tabitha, Tristen, Aiden,
Evan, and Linnea

Prologue

A dirt road ran right up to our grassless front yard. Some called it Wilder Road leaving me to often wonder what it was wilder than. It joined Hamlet Road passing fields of corn, cotton, beans, low shacks, and a brick house or two before connecting with State Road 9 by Bennettsville's water tower. The country folk called Route 9 by an older name— Cheraw Road.

There are things kids know and things they don't. I knew that the dirt path connected to Hamlet Road, which went east to the Atlantic Ocean and west toward Charlotte. I knew this, but I'd never been further than a day's trip from town—and only a few times then. State Road 52 went south, toward Charleston, but if a driver had the gumption to do it, that road kept on going all the way to Florida to find alligators and cougars and flamingos. I'd seen pictures of them in *National Geographic*. Just over from Bennettsville, U.S. Route 301 went as far north as Maine, but it passed through Washington and Baltimore and New York first. I knew because I listened to people who came and went and watched the cars and trucks pass by on those dirt roads. I read what I could and imagined. I looked at maps on walls, and peeked over people's shoulders as they read their afternoon papers in town.

As a little boy, I didn't know that people died. Kids don't understand death till they're older—till some type of experience lets them in on it. I thought that people were as permanent and temperamental as the rain, which came and went in docile droplets and hammering waterfalls allowing the cotton and corn to grow or be destroyed. We had it hard many winters and summers, but we never went cold, hungry, or unloved by Mama. Others had it much worse than we did. Some people farmed all year and still couldn't afford to eat more than what they grew in the field behind their homes.

Before the summer of 1944, I didn't know that life can enter like a trickle, but leave like a flood. I didn't know everything, but I always knew that I'd leave that farm some day because it wasn't in me to forever wash my hands with lye soap, and it wasn't in me to be a farmer, and it wasn't in me to not see the world.

I'd sit on the front stoop after I did my chores, while Mama washed dishes, and everyone else listened to the *Amos and Andy* show. I'd watch the road run along the farms toward the crossroad near the edge of the McCormick's fields. I'd sit and look at the packed dirt and listen to the crickets chirp and the radio's windmill flip-flip. From that front stoop a scent of manure and fresh cut hay, corn blowing in the breezes and summer rain, raccoons darting between the stalks and the twinkle of shooting stars at night, covered my world. I'd watch the road as it disappeared in a straight line away from our sharecrop farm: 160 acres of corn and cotton, a garden, a tool shed and barn, smokehouse, outhouse, a chicken coop, and a pigsty. We shared a spring with the McCormicks. And a cemetery.

The road brought, and the road took away. The road brought supplies and carried off our crops. It led to town and back, bringing and taking the sheriff and pastor and doctor and family and friends. Rain muddied it in spring and the sun turned it dusty in summer and the wind made it solid in winter. The road brought a young man to our farm and house and cemetery in the summer of 1944 and led us away from the dirt to Baltimore. Until I turned thirteen, I always wanted that road to take me away. To leave that farm, I would have done anything and I would have paid any amount to anyone. Except Death.

1

Bennettsville, South Carolina June 7, 1944

Lying on the floor at the foot of Lawrence and TJ's bed, stripped to my shorts, sweat covering me like a blanket, my heart pounding heavy in my ears, I wanted to hear about the war against the Nazis. The Big Ben on the mantle struck eleven. Then half-past. All the while I lay thinking and dozing, wanting to be listening to the radio rather than wasting time sleeping.

I inched myself off the floor.

Lawrence's snoring filled the black room.

I lifted the iron handle on the bedroom door. Earlier in the day I'd oiled the hinges with a little lard from Mama's kitchen while everyone else fed the chickens, milked the cow, and slopped the hogs. I pulled the door, the grease working to keep metal from metal; it opened without a squeak.

As I kept one eye on Mama and Daddy's door, I followed the path I'd mapped out that would make the least amount of noise. I stepped over the first three floorboards, slid along the wall, then over two more boards to the throw rug laid out before the Zenith radio, my eyes adjusting to the moonlight seeping through the house.

Only Daddy, Mama, and Lawrence, being the oldest, were allowed to touch the radio. As I turned the knob, it popped. I was sure it echoed through the house. Yellow light from the dial filled the windowless corner. I put my body between the glow and the bedroom doors knowing that even a little light could wake up Mama.

With my ear close to the speaker, and eyes on the bedroom doors, I tuned through static. Hissing came back to me as I ran the dial up to fifty megahertz, then down to forty-two, back to fifty. "You have to do it slow," Lawrence always said when he was searching for the *Amos and Andy Show*. The tunes and words to songs fluttered in and out.

I stopped at 43. "In a few seconds, we will take you to London for the first eyewitness account of the actual invasion of France by sea -- of the landing of Allied troops on a French beachhead. War correspondent, George Hicks, saw those landings from the bridge of an Allied warship, and thru the ingenuity of radio wire recording, the National Broadcasting Company is able to give you the story as witnessed by George Hicks in a pool broadcast. So, now, NBC takes you to London for the first eyewitness account of the actual invasion of Europe!"

"Hot, damn!" I whispered, covering my mouth, smiling, nearly giggling.

When President Roosevelt had announced that "Yesterday, December 7, 1941—a date which will live in infamy—the United States of America was suddenly and deliberately attacked by naval and air forces of the Empire of Japan . . .," I knew that I didn't want to be a farmer. I imagined following the roads to New York or Miami, Chicago, Los Angeles., and Boston. I wondered if I could drive a car right onto a boat so that when I got to Pearl Harbor I could drive off again. Years earlier, after I heard the slow, quiet tone of the man on the radio when he announced that Paris had fallen to the Nazis, I dreamt of looking over the world from the top of the Eiffel Tower.

The last time I went to school, during the winter when we had no crops, Mrs. Framlingham told us that Big Ben was the bell inside the clock tower and showed us pictures of fires burning in London because of the Nazi blitz. I drifted off to become a pilot flying over England, protecting it from the Nazis. Then I was a Marine fighting Japs in the Pacific, then an Army general in a Jeep in Italy. Sometimes I was a reporter or a photographer watching Churchill sip tea. I dreamt and thought and planned and was many people in many places, but I only ever pretended to be a farmer.

A lion's groan crept through the house making my feet tap the floor. My eyes pounded. The clock struck four. Four hours I'd lain there. The radio's battery, dead as a squashed coon, left the tattletale yellow light from the Zenith's dial black and empty. At first I thought the noise came from the radio, then I thought the wind had blown through the eaves where the bats kept house. I couldn't be so lucky. Daddy's mattress squealed and groaned as he got up from another bad dream or to get ready for the day's work. I tried to swallow, but my lips stuck to my teeth and my tongue felt swollen. I clicked off the radio so that when the windmill had recharged the battery it wouldn't suddenly start playing.

Somewhere in my head, the announcer's voice still called out to me. "Remember, loose lips sink ships." The announcer had changed voices. My head was sore from sleeping against the side of the radio. "Light along the shore is our Navy's toughest chore. Keep those lights out."

I paused on my knees hoping I'd be a mere shadow in the house. My knee came down on a nail head sticking up from the floorboards as Daddy's bedroom door chirped open.

He shuffled past the girls' door, then past ours where the floorboards took to groaning and popping. At the kitchen counter he lifted the dipper out of the water pail, and sipped. By the moonlight creeping through the window above the sink I saw the whiskers on his unshaven face. His lower arms were dark from the sun, but cut off sharply at the spot where his work shirt ended. His long johns hung around his narrow waist, the shoulder loops dragging the floor. His black hair shone and I wasn't sure if bits of gray dappled his whiskers or if the moon gave it an unnatural highlight. Daddy leaned against the sink and stared out into the lightening sky. I imagined I could see our Cherokee kin in him looking through the dark forest, stalking a buck or black bear. He turned toward me and I sucked in a breath holding it as it pushed to get back out. His dark eyes turned from the window and guided him through the kitchen door going toward the outhouse.

When he stepped down off the stoop, I checked the radio again to be sure it was off. Then I tried to stand up but my feet tingled and ached, dead numb. The nail head dug deeper into my knee. Another groan raced through the house. Bedsprings squeaked. Mama got out of bed.

Silhouetted in the doorway in her stitched-and-re-stitched gown, she wiped her eyes and went to the water pail. Her hair hung to her shoulders: Its blackness long since turning the color of shadowed snow.

My kneecap throbbed. If I moved, if I were caught, I'd have to clean out the pigsty. I might not be allowed to go to the fair with my Uncle George the next week when he came down from Baltimore for his yearly trip. Worst of all, I might not be allowed to listen to the radio.

Daddy whistled his way across the yard. As he climbed the stoop, his white smile seemed to glow at Mama. She patted him on the arm as she went and he came.

He passed into the black hole of his bedroom and bounced his way into a comfortable position.

I didn't move. Daddy would hear me slinking my way back to my room. "Please, lord," I whispered in a voice so low that only a mouse could have heard me, "they've missed me this far. Let them keep on missing me." I took my aching knee off the nail head.

Then I heard feet scrape on the dirt that had blown up onto the front stoop.

I looked toward the back of the house, wondering if Mama had come around front, but she shuffled her way toward the back stoop, her eyes half closed. There was a flurry of wings and a squawk as a wayward chicken got out from beneath her feet.

A shadow blocked the silver light coming through the front door's window. Someone, a blackness on the stoop, peeked through the glass pane.

Mama left the kitchen door open. There was a thump. "Dag-on-it," she said. She rubbed her knee and leaned against the counter raising her foot. Through the darkness I could just see a grimace and almost hear her counting as her pain slipped away. She slapped the corner of the sink stand, then hobbled back toward the bedroom.

I wanted Mama to see that someone or something was on the front stoop. Stillness. Frozen. A statue peered through the window. A Nazi? Had they finally invaded? An escaped POW from Palmer Field? Then Grandpa's old tales of the slave ghosts came back to me. He'd told them while sitting in this same room.

"No," I whispered. "It ain't the ghost, no dead slave coming for me, it ain't the ghost."

I thought it might be a burglar, lost from the town, thinking there might be something worth stealing from these farms, like a pile of biscuits or a tub of lard. I looked around wondering what a thief might want—the old iron pots, a few ragged pieces of furniture, my grandma's butter churn, the Big Ben clock, which Uncle George gave us kids the money to buy for Mama and Daddy. The radio! It could be anything but that. I thought about what I could offer the burglar instead of the Zenith. I would explain to him that it was too heavy to carry all the way back to town. I'd tell him to take the old Model-T Ford out by the barn if he could get it started. Take the Big Ben clock. I'd even offer him Lawrence. Anything but the radio! I couldn't imagine living without the radio that brought London and Paris, New York, music, Abbott and Costello, and Bob Hope.

I thought I'd yell for Daddy, but my aching knee reminded me of the whooping I'd get for messing with the radio, but only after he thrashed the burglar with the length of his belt.

A man, the shadow broad shouldered, the hair short, the face square, stood shadowed in the window of the front door. His silhouette, black as the fields behind him, reminded me again of the ghost stories. For a moment I was sure it was the Negro ghost of a dead slave come to return some justice. We ain't white, I thought, we're Cherokee. The iron latch clicked, coming out of the housing. Slowly, like the bending of wheat in a breeze, the front door opened.

My throat felt like I'd swallowed the cotton I'd been trimming that morning. Inside me, the soldier yelled, "Halt, who goes there?" The reporter told the soldier to shut up and just watch.

Black hair shining in the moonlight. His skin a natural darkness, but browned more from time in the cotton fields. In stepped my next oldest brother, TJ, his shirt hanging from his back pocket, suspenders dangling and swaying at his knees. Shoeless. Dried mud clung to his feet. I thought he'd been snoring when I snuck out of the room, but I guessed that I'd fallen asleep for hours while the wood grain of the Zenith left its mark on my forehead. I hadn't heard him leave.

Back in my dark corner where the moon hadn't shed its pale light, I let out a slow sigh, trying to remain invisible.

TJ lowered the latch into an oiled and soundless housing. Eyeing Mama and Daddy's door, he stepped over the first two boards, tip-toed over the next ten, stepped over two more, slithered along the wall, then stepped over three more boards stopping at our bedroom door. He knew the map of the house as well as I did. His muscled back, grass and dirt stuck to it, gleamed in the pasty light. With a last look toward Daddy's door, he slid into our bedroom.

I stood, my teeth clamping shut around a moan. I rubbed my sore knee and wiggled my numb toes, wondering where TJ had been. I couldn't believe I hadn't heard him leave. He had to have been sneaking around at least for a while to know those loose boards so well.

Trying to skip over a few of the floorboards, dragging the prickling and stinging dead leg behind me, I went into the kitchen to wet my sticking and crusty mouth. I dipped and sipped from the pail. There weren't as many stars in the east field where the corn was green and tender. Just above the trees along the McCormick's acres, the clouds were lighter; a shade of gray.

From the back stoop, I saw a pack of raccoons dashing into the cotton beside the house. "Dogs ain't worth a spit. I'll be damned if they're any kind of coon catchers," I said. Crickets chirped and a locust buzzed a long message.

Halfway back from the outhouse, I kicked at the flapping hen, watched a pair of eyes glowing from beneath the house, hurled a rock at a passing coon, and went on up the two steps. As I turned toward the water pail, my body jerked to a stop. Daddy blocked the path to the bucket.

"Boy, what you doing up this early?"

"Going to the outhouse, Daddy." I didn't look right at him.

"I can see that. You been listening to the radio?" He seemed to be looking at my forehead where a wood grain indent likely stood out.

"I . . . ." Mama always told me that being honest was the best policy. I knew what I'd lose by telling the truth, but if I lied it would be worse. "Yes, sir," I said, stepping back.

"Come here, boy." His sledgehammer of a hand landed on my shoulder. I turned my eyes up to the man. "What I tell you about messing with that radio?" I stared into my father's dark eyes wondering if I was going to get a whooping. I didn't know why Daddy took everything so hard, but he did. It wasn't so much me touching the radio, it was disobeying him that was the real problem. I feared the beating I'd received before and seen my two brothers and two sisters get, but it was almost always for something serious when he used his belt. One time Daddy beat Lawrence for letting the mule run off. Lawrence, laid up for two days, went back to work while the bandages were still red with blood. This wasn't that bad.

"I ain't talking to myself, boy. What I tell you about the radio?"

I looked at the floor with the weight of my father on my shoulder. "You told me not to touch it."

"How old are you now, boy?"

"Thirteen."

"Well, boy, you're old enough to know better. Instead of going to town Saturday night, you'd better stay here and clean out under the house."

I'd forgotten about that punishment. I wanted to tell him I wouldn't do it. That I couldn't do it because I had to go to town or I'd end up twitching the way one of the rabid dogs did after a bout with a coon. I had to hear news from the soldiers in town. Before the war, everyone was just farmers or town's folk. Now, there were people who'd been places and seen things. The soldiers were life beyond the corn and cow and cotton. I had to go to town. Besides, the Captain America cliffhanger couldn't be missed at the Carolina Theater. I was going to town.

"Yes, sir," I answered looking Daddy in the eyes. Complaining would only make him angrier, I knew, and I couldn't refuse—though inside my head, the familiar "No" popped up.

"Get to bed now. About another hour before you're supposed to get up." I kept my head straight and my footsteps quiet, but solid, as I returned to my bedroom. "Don't forget to clean out the tool shed, too." I paused and nodded my head before lifting the latch. I'd forgotten about the tool shed, the stench of chicken pee from the attached coop so thick that I always had to put my kerchief over my nose just to get a hoe. The last time I cleaned the shed, I'd planned to build a new one across the yard, away from everything, especially the stench.

In the bedroom, TJ and Lawrence's faces glared at me, lit up by the colorless light flowing through the door. I stepped on a shirt, covered in flakes of dried dirt, and knew that TJ had wiped his feet with it. I climbed up onto the bed as Lawrence whispered, "What happened?"

"He caught me."

"Yeah. We know he caught you," TJ said. "What did he do to you?"

"Got to stay home Saturday night and clean under the house."

"You'd better not mess up us going to town on Saturday night—" TJ said.

"—Shut up." I pushed him so he had to grab the wall not to fall out of bed. "Probably you he heard anyways. I ought to tell him you were out all night."

"Shut up both of you. Boy, I swear if you mess up us going to town Saturday nights, I'll whoop you myself. Get to sleep." Lawrence rolled over pulling most of the covers with him. "TJ."

TJ didn't say anything, but he lay on his back with his eyes open.

"Boy, don't be staying out so late. Hear me?" Lawrence said.

"Yeah."

Our little house in the middle of the cotton fields grew silent. I thought of the adventures I'd make of cleaning the crawl space. It would be a Nazi nest and I'd be an American Army sergeant ordered to go in and flush out the Kraut-eating bastards. I dreamed of the beach somewhere in France as I fell asleep between my two older brothers.

2

I said to Frances in the cotton fields the next morning "Got something to tell you." She looked around to see who might be listening. Lawrence stood off two-dozen or more rows.

"Irene, go get some water for us, honey." Frances patted Irene on the head. Irene tossed down her rag doll and stood up.

"I'm not thirsty yet." Irene crossed her arms.

Frances nudged her toward the water bucket at the end of the row. "I am, honey. Will you get me a jar full?"

When Irene had stomped off far enough, I told Frances, "TJ was out tomcatting last night." Frances' black hair reached to her waist when she let it down, but in the field she wore it under a corn-leaf hat that kept the sun off of her.

"How you know that?" Frances pulled a dozen cotton worms off a plant and shoved them into a canning jar. Her hands were like stone from years of working the cotton. The thorny leaves could no longer cut through her tough skin. At harvest time, she could out pick everyone except Daddy.

"I was up listening to the radio when he came in and—"

"—Jimmy!" Her brown-red forehead squinted, her mouth grinned. I knew she wasn't mad, but had to protest anyway.

"Daddy caught me . . ." When Mama wasn't around, Frances was our mother of the fields.

"Oh, Jimmy boy." Frances' "boy" was gentle and sweet. Her "boy" understood and lashed with gentle prodding. I liked to hear her "boy," even if I'd done bad. "What'd he do to you?"

"Wasn't too bad. I've got to stay home Saturday night and clean out under the house."

Her skin darkened. "James Quick! If you mess up us going to town on Saturday nights--" She straightened. I was catching up to her height. At seventeen, she was pretty much done growing.

"—You'll whip me good. Get in line because TJ and Lawrence are way ahead of you."

"Uh huh." Frances went on, pulling cotton worms faster than I could see them. "I work my fingers to the bone in that netting factory. Getting caught by Daddy. Damn it, boy. Sorry, Lord. I take you all to town every chance we can. Not to mention having to take care of you if he beats you to within an inch of your sorry life."

"I'm sorry."

Truth is, I didn't get too many beatings. The ones I did get, I deserved, like the time TJ and I wandered clear over to the Pee Dee River without telling anyone. Mama had near about the whole county out looking for us. Daddy was certain our Negro neighbors, the McCormicks, had taken and killed us. After we got back and Daddy took us to the tool shed, we stayed in line because we feared the whooping. Mama asked Daddy every day for a month to apologize to the McCormicks. After church one Sunday, on the rare times Daddy stepped across the holy threshold, he came home and went stomping off across the field. "Suppose I'll apologize," Daddy said as he went. Since then, they've been good friends with us. Mama always said that the Lord works in mysterious ways, so even though I didn't know anything about the Bible, I figured that my whooping and Daddy making friends with the Negro folk must have been one of those mysteries.

Worse than Daddy's tool shed was when Mama would make us get a long stem off a young tree. She called it a "switch." "Go get me a switch," she'd say. It had to snap when she whipped it. If we brought something back too small or too brittle to be useful, the licks would be longer and harder. One time TJ brought back what was near about a limb. I could see that he meant it to be funny and impossible to use, but Mama got in two or three hard licks with it sending TJ out the door crying. After he rubbed his rear a few times, we laughed so hard we fell off the fence.

When Frances finished the row, she drank the water Irene brought her. "Now, bring Jimmy some water, please."

Irene rolled her eyes toward the sky and huffed off toward the bucket.

"TJ and Lawrence ought to whip you. It took a lot for Daddy to let us go to town." She took off her corn hat and wiped her forehead. "What time did that stinking brother of mine get back here?"

I dragged two sacks of cuttings used for slop through the plants to the edge of the dirt road before I answered her. "After four."

Frances grabbed my shirt and yanked me towards her. She looked toward Irene who was spilling water along the row back toward us. "—You mean to tell me TJ was out till near day?" Her teeth clamped together, her throat rasping. The green brim of her hat overlapped mine. Her breath still stunk of the fried potatoes we'd had for dinner. "I'm going to whip him good." She let go of me and opened the lid to the jar. A cotton worm wiggled from the top, stretching and pulling itself along. Frances poked it back as she dropped in two more.

"What you think he's doing?" I said, sucking on a cut from a leaf. If the fair had a cotton-picking contest, Frances would win.

"Well, I don't rightly know." She stopped picking and looked up at me. "Why ain't you asked? You two like a couple of peas in a pod."

"I'll tell you." Lawrence's deep voice shook us, making me quiver. Frances's whole body shimmered. I stepped back from the fright thinking I should run across the field.

"Lawrence!" Frances punched his arm. Broad across the shoulders and chest, tall like Daddy, he reminded me of a tree.

"Sorry. Didn't mean to scare you." Lawrence rubbed

his arm. I knew Frances' little hit couldn't have hurt him. His arm, big around and as hard as an oak limb, could lift anything I'd ever seen him try to lift. "Good thing I wasn't a lion, you'd be dead." Lawrence lifted one sack of cuttings onto his shoulder.

"Ain't no lions in America, except the zoo," Frances said, wrinkling her forehead. "And the carnival."

"Circus, dummy, they got lions in circuses not carnivals, but you go on believing what you want." Lawrence grinned, showing his broken front tooth, now dull and smooth edged. "Besides, you ain't never seen a zoo anymore than I've seen a lion."

"What were you going to tell us?" I said.

Lawrence raised his dark eyebrows. Though farm smart, he would never be city slick. He could lay out the fields as well as Daddy, but couldn't keep the books no matter how many times Daddy showed him. Lawrence lived for farming. It showed in his brown eyes. He could talk about corn the way Mama talked about God and I talked about war. His excitement came from good growth, his pain from failed crops.

"You said 'I'll tell you' when you came up. About TJ?" Sometimes we had to fill in or finish thoughts for Lawrence.

"Oh." Lawrence scratched behind his ear. "I bet he's got himself a girl." He smiled so that his teeth were big, crows feet extending, his high Indian cheeks forcing his eyes into slits.

"A girl!" Frances slapped her knee, then chuckled, deep and heavy, the way a man does—years of being in the fields with three brothers and a father. "Maybe it's Liz from down the Breeding place."

Out in the distance, too far for me to tell what kind of plane it was, an Air Corps fighter rose and dove, darting about, twisting and turning.

I don't know why, but I didn't say anything about TJ sneaking in without a shirt, dirt caked to his back and feet. It wasn't much like me to tattle. I didn't tell Frances to get TJ in trouble. We always watched out for each other. If cornered, we'd have to tell, but we didn't offer much. Irene couldn't always be expected to keep her mouth shut, but that was just her way. She was the baby. Nothing she did ever got her in much of a fix. TJ could be out after a girl or he could just be out wandering the night to get away from the matchbox-sized house we lived in, the summer heat hard to breathe, the rusted roof dinging and pinging in the rain. It could have been anything. I wanted to be anywhere but this farm, why not TJ?

3

On Saturday, before leaving to catch the bus to town, Frances came to me. I had my hands on my hips, imitating Daddy, deciding how I'd go about cleaning the crawl space.

"I don't think we should go." Frances had on her yellow print dress. A little tattered about the collar, it was the best one she had.

"It's all right. Go on to town. I wanted to hear the music, so I have to pay the fiddler." Grandpa told me that, among a hundred other sayings. I meant it. I almost never had any time to be alone, punishment or not. Besides, I had an entire Allied invasion of France planned and the crawl space worked well as the enemy headquarters.

"Are you sure?" Our Saturday night treats made Frances smile and dance down the streets of Bennettsville. I don't know how much of her pay she saved, but she never failed to share what she earned.

Daddy had been whistling "The Battle Hymn of the Republic" the day Frances asked if she could go to work in town. Frances must have felt safe and sure that Daddy's anger had stepped out for a rest and that he might listen instead of talk or yell and that he might agree. She'd managed to talk Daddy into letting her get a job at the camouflage factory. When she came back from her talk with the foreman, she had the whole plan together. She'd work on the farm every day to keep up her share of the load. Then she'd go to work on Mondays, Wednesdays, and

Fridays from three in the afternoon till midnight. Frances had found another girl from a farm the other side of town who wanted to share a job. She'd work the other three days of the week. During harvest, the factory man knew that some would have to work the fields, so others took double shifts. Frances gave Daddy most of the money she made. He told her to keep it, but she insisted and every time she gave him the money, he'd walk out of the house with his head low and his hands stuffed in his belt, looking humble and sorry that she'd given it to him. "Thanks, Fran," he'd say and kiss her on the forehead when he returned from his walk an hour later, the shame wiped from his face.

Fran said she'd saved most of what she had left, but every Saturday night off to town we went. At first, Mama and Daddy didn't want us going to town on Saturday nights, but Frances explained that we'd eat ice cream and look in the store windows at the toys or talk outside the drug stores. On other Saturday nights we'd see movies at the Carolina Theater. Mama and Daddy listened and set conditions. "Never walk that late at night and if the bus don't run then you don't go," Mama insisted.

"Don't go to The Gulf," Daddy ordered. "Them nig--" Daddy glanced at Mama, "I mean Negroes might skin you alive soon as look at you."

"Be polite," Mama said to us, but meaning Daddy, too.

"If I have to get you out of jail, you might not ever see the light of day again," Daddy added.

We all loved Frances for doing this for us. I thought that she would always give while most other people would always take, but she didn't do it just for us. The war brought boys to town, and Frances liked to flirt.

Not to mess up Frances' happiness in town is why I wanted to stay and do what Daddy told me—to smooth it all over. To get him to forget my misdoings.

Under the house, narrow boards supported the floor above and connected to wide beams that rested on posts that sat on cement blocks keeping the house more than two feet from the ground. This became the Nazi bunker.

From above me, I heard Mama and Daddy settling in at the table. Some nights, Mama would read the newspaper to Daddy while he leaned back and listened, grunting and nodding. She had a pair of rusted scissors that she used to cut out recipes, photos, and stories. "Listen to this one," Mama said, and then read an article about a Cherokee man being lynched for getting in a car accident and killing a soldier. Daddy grunted.

From beneath the house, I hauled out a forest full of elm and beech leaves, piled them up, ran through them, jumped into them, used them for cover against bullets. Then I burned the dry leaves. Fire lifted into the still air. As they popped and sparks jumped off of them, I packed slimy and cold wet leaves around Mama's tomato plants. When I pushed them around the garden, the rotting leaves smelled of the spring, where the leaves lay like a thick carpet. I pretended that one pile of leaves was my best buddy killed by a Kraut sniper and I had to bury him.

I expected plenty of rabbit, mouse, and coon droppings under there, but found little, so I decided to give the hounds a little more respect, forgiving them for the spat of coons the night I'd earned these chores. Still, some critter had hauled in twigs and branches to build a nest.

Small dogwood stems became my rifles while I turned witch hazel limbs into temporary forts and Jeeps. As the flames from the pile of leaves glowed and the sun dropped low in the sky, I broke all the dry branches into kindling for the wood stove.

When almost finished, my knee caught in a shallow pit, tumbling me forward, my chin striking the dirt. I lay there, not moving, feeling my teeth and jaw ache. TJ had not refilled the potato pit last time Mama sent him to get the last of them. It reminded me that Mama would want me to bring the early potatoes down and bury them in the cool ground.

The tool shed I feared in a whole other manner. Scythes and sling blades, awls, hammers, pitchforks, shovels, rakes, hoes, more and more hoes, axes, empty wood crates, piles of rusting nails, a family of field mice, barn swallows dropping white streaks, all leaning and piled and stacked, none where they belonged, all used, reused, shoved in, pulled out, careless and quick. I gagged when the acid stench from the chicken coop crept through the burlap I used as a mask. Hen houses always stunk, no matter who had the chore of cleaning them. Sometimes, Daddy had everything in order, and other times he didn't seem to care if things looked like a tornado had struck it. The tool shed became a supply depot for a German Panzer unit.

With everyone gone and Mama cooking hoecakes and succotash, and Daddy down at the McCormick's talking about the next fish fry, I found time to invade France and capture a squad of Nazis.

I sat on the front stoop looking down the roads. Something that sounded like an Army truck passed down on Wilder.

"You finished?" Mama said from the kitchen sink.

"Yes, ma'am."

"Why don't you listen to the radio for awhile? I don't suppose your Daddy will be home for a few more hours."

I didn't get up because I worried that Daddy might come through the door as soon as I put my hand on the radio's knob, his body appearing like a misty ghost.

Mama sang, "Go tell it on the mountain, over the hills and everywhere." She slapped a mound of dough on the counter, flattening it.

I waited at the doorway.

"Jimmy. I'd like to listen to the radio," she called.

I stood up and went inside. The house seemed to glow with the sunset. "What do you want to hear, Mama?"

"Anything. Whatever you want is fine."

With the twilight seeping away, I listened to the message from General Eisenhower. The announcer reminded everyone that this was recorded earlier. "A landing was made," the General said, "this morning on the coast of France by troops of the allied expeditionary force."

When all I could get to come through was the popping and hissing of distant static, I read from a *National Geographic* that my Uncle George had sent. One of the stories, about searching for the North Pole, showed pictures of sleds and thick coated dogs. After I read it, my head heavy, my muscles twitching, I found somewhere in my twilight sleep a team of Huskies and I dreamed of being cold and snowy.

4

Sunday morning, the heat pushed down, frizzing Frances' hair, keeping the dogs and cats under the shadow of the stoop.

Mama said, "Jimmy? You coming with me today?" She wiped the biscuit pan, blackened and hardened from thousands of turns in the fire.

I glanced at Lawrence and TJ. They kept their eyes down, pretending to see only their grits and sausage and biscuits, hoping they wouldn't be called to go with Mama to church.

"It's Sunday, Mama."

"I know it's Sunday, boy. That's why I'm asking you to go with me."

"We're going down to the plantation," I said. Sundays we had off from the farm, but not from our chores.

"To play? You'd rather mess around them old huts then go with your Mama to the house of the Lord?"

I wanted to stick to her policy about being honest, so I went back to my eggs and peeked at TJ who had his mouth full. He glanced about the room without moving his head, and then mouthed, "Shut up" to me. A grain of grits stuck to his lip.

"I'd like it if you went with me." Mama's back was still to the table.

My sausage went down hard. I chased it with milk, warm in the morning air. Daddy, Lawrence, TJ, and Frances snickered at me, their eyes darting between me and Mama, making fun that it was my turn to go.

Several times each year, Mama pestered each of us to go to church with her. When I was still a kid, she'd pull us along on Easter when the minister gave us chocolate and the women got mayapple flowers or sandhill lupines and the men received a lecture about bringing the families to church more often. For a while, Mama's trip to the clapboard sided church with her children moved to Christmas Eve. That became the only time that I enjoyed going to church because I loved the songs and the feel of the cool winter air brightening our noses and cheeks and spirits. The smell of burning swamp cypress or pine floating into the sky from each farm house and shack's chimney hinted at the thin layer of snow that often promised to come, but rarely did.

When I was younger, Mama went alone, sometimes with Irene, but more often she left the farm after breakfast, Frances doing the final dishes of the morning, and walked the four miles to the congregation that serviced those who were poor and migrant and sharecropping.

"Well, boy?" she said, putting down the holey dish rag.

"Yes, ma'am," I said, wolfing down the last sausage, an offering to those condemned to church.

"Now, get changed. Frances, will you finish the dishes for me, dear."

Mama put on the only hat she had. In her handbag, she stuffed a Mason jar of water and her good shoes. On her feet, she wore the moccasins I'd always seen her wear for these walks.

I creaked my way into the bedroom to change. I wore my good hat, the best white shirt with the pocket coming loose, and my shoes strung across my shoulder.

Big Ben bonged a quarter till the hour, fifteen minutes earlier than we used to leave. She took my hand. I liked it for the first quarter mile, but our steps were uneven—Mama's short and choppy, mine long and bouncing. I pulled my hand away to swat at an imaginary bee, and then never put it back within her reach.

The morning sun curled my hair, tingled my scalp, burned the tops of my bare feet, forcing me to take short breaths. Mama said, "Whew," every few feet and wiped a clean kerchief across her forehead. We walked without word until we reached the end of the property we called ours, but which belonged to Old Man Patterson.

"Got a surprise today," Mama said.

I watched the beetles dart between stalks along the cornrows.

Mama looked at me. "For you."

Still taller than me, but not by much, I looked up to her, the sun glaring over her head. "For me?"

She nodded. She seemed to watch a crow dart between field and tree.

I thought that there might be a church holiday I knew nothing of that came in the middle of the summer, and, like the Easter and Christmas trips before, would come for now and go later. "What?" I said.

"A guest at the church. Someone to talk to us all."

I nodded and pretended to watch the beetles again. I wanted to say, "So what?" but I didn't want to hurt her feelings and knew that at least a whack across my head would follow if I said what I wanted. I felt that I should tell her that I would miss a great day at the plantation wandering through the old slave quarters and climbing down into the cellar of a building that had no purpose we could understand. The great house had lost its roof, but the stairs still went to the second floor. I would miss drinking from the deep well that still had a working pulley, though someone had put a new rope and bucket on the spindle. I wouldn't have the opportunity to play with the large black-and-gray cat, petting its matted hair, its haunches rising up with each stroke. For someone I ain't never met, I thought I'd miss a heap of fun.

Mama watched a crow lift fibers from the cornfield and land in a tree where it worked on a nest. "He's from the Army," she said.

"The Army? Why didn't you tell me before?"

"Because I wanted to surprise you."

"A soldier?"

"Yes." She swatted at a fly. "And a pastor."

I thought about those two jobs, but couldn't see where they fit together. I wasn't sure why a pastor was a soldier, at least not like the soldiers I knew, or how a soldier could be a pastor since they all seemed to drink, curse, and pet too much. I decided that he must have been a minister who, for some reason, went off to war then returned to speak of the Bible.

A few feet further on, after Mama said, "Whew," again and blew air from between her teeth a dozen more times, she said, "He's coming to talk about the war. Seeing how you've been so interested in it, I figured you might like to hear him."

"Yeah," I said, pleased to be going, forgetting the plantation that would always be there.

Two miles into the walk, Mama slowed, her right leg a little gimpy. We stopped so that she could rest and I thought about what the pastor might speak of. I wanted to know about battles and tanks, Europe, people who spoke fast so that some of the words sounded familiar but most of it was gibberish. I'd heard the Greek who owned Sanitary Café talking in town once to his wife. Their words reminded me of when someone in the church spoke in tongues and the deacons and pastors came over to speak in tongues and lay hands on. I hoped no one spoke in tongues while the pastor, also a soldier, visited us there.

A quarter mile before the church we stopped again. She drank from the Mason jar and offered it to me, but I refused it. She pulled off her moccasins. Her right foot looked swollen and a bit blue and purple, darker than the skin above the ankle.

"What's wrong, Mama?"

"Getting old," she said, rubbing her foot. She tried to put on her good shoes, but the foot was too swollen, so she gave up and put the moccasin back on while I tied on my pair of Uncle George's old brown Oxfords.

Outside Brother Frankel's whitewashed church, drivers had tied a few mules and buckboards to posts and trees. Two cars parked near the steps—an Army Plymouth and a brown Cadillac—shimmered in the heat. I'd never seen either skimming about the roads of Bennettsville.

Inside, benches made of stray lumber lay across bricks, and where they sagged, sticks and milk bottles propped them up. At the front stood two pews, one on either side of the aisle. A piano, a lectern, two chairs, and a table sat on the low stage. The windows, though wide open, let in only a slight gust of air.

We arrived after everyone else was seated, but before Brother Frankel had made his way to the pulpit. I looked from bench to bench in search of the man in uniform, but could see no one I didn't know. Mama waved to a few of her friends. The hall reeked of sweat and bad breath, despite everyone wearing their best. Several people had summer colds, their coughing and sneezing heavy in the heat. Two babies cried in a competition.

As we sat, the members stood and the congregation sang "How Great Thou Art." I mouthed the words as I tried to read from the hymnal, but I didn't have the tune nor could I follow the high pitches and the low drawls that the congregation took.

During the prayer, I fanned my face and wiped the back of my neck with my kerchief. Then we sat.

Brother Frankel preached about Hell and the Devil. He spoke about the hardships of farm work. He talked, and hand fans flipped, men using their hats to cool their faces. I dozed in the heat, sweat running down my back following the bumps of my spine and contours of my muscles. We rose and sang and I leaned my calves against the wood bench, my head heavy, tired from the walk. Brother Frankel pounded on his Bible and held it out to the congregation and they raised their hands and said, "Yes, Lord," and "Praise be to Jesus," and "Glory be."

I dozed.

Out of a dream where I swam in the spring on our farm, while a fly buzzed by my ear so that I swatted at it in what seemed like exaggerated motions, I heard Brother Frankel say, "Now let's welcome our guests."

"I see that Novaline Quick was able to convince her youngest boy, James, to come today," Brother Frankel said. He extended his hand toward us. The congregation chuckled.

We rose and I felt my face heat up to have these people look at me, whose names Mama expected me to know, but I could never remember. I grinned and through tight lips whispered, "Mama," angry and red.

"And the Hoopers." Brother Frankel stretched his arm to a family in the front pew. We sat as they stood. A

24

man with thick glasses rose. He wore, unlike everyone else, a suit and tie, both brown. His wife wore a Sears catalog dress with a flowered print. A girl, young like Irene, four or five, her hair gleaming, stood next to two boys, one younger than me and one older, both in blue Sears trousers, white shirts, and open collars. They looked even unhappier at being there than I did. "Hank and Mary Hooper, and their daughter, Ella. Their sons are Justin and Mike." Hank waved, Mary kept her head down, Ella fidgeted, Justin, the younger boy about my age, rose and sat, quickly, Mike, the older boy, blinked, then blinked again, he rubbed his eyes, then blinked again. Even from where I sat I could see that his eyes were red, puffy, tearing, a summer cold taking him over. The family sat. They were from town. Since we arrived late, we had no time to hear the scuttlebutt about their attendance. The town folk were not Pentecostal. They had their own churches, many of them going to the Catholic one, red brick with a bell tower and clock, across and down the street from the courthouse, on Hamlet Road.

"And our esteemed guest," Brother Frankel said, "Pastor Norman Myers of the United States Army."

Everyone applauded.

I stretched my neck and inched from the bench. Peeking through the crowd, I saw a young man stand from the end of the same pew where the Hoopers sat. His uniform, the color of dry cornhusks, made it look like he could hide in a field dressed like that and no one would find him till harvest. Strips of colors shone from his chest. Two silver bars, indicating his rank as captain, sat atop each shoulder. Attached to his collar, on each side of his tie, were two silver crosses.

He wobbled as he moved forward. Brother Frankel stepped down from the two steps to help the pastor up. His left leg was encased in a metal framework. He grimaced at each stair. He was stiff when he turned, but when he faced the silent and watching congregation, he smiled.

"Good morning," Pastor Myers said.

"Good morning," the congregation said in a practiced chorus.

"Well, the sermon Brother Frankel just gave was very inspirational . . ."

"Praise the Lord," several members said.

Others said, "Amen."

". . . So today, I won't be going on with any more of that."

Praise the Lord, I thought.

He drank water from a glass. After wiping sweat from his forehead, he said, "I'm here to let you know that there's another minister in your community to help you whenever you need it."

The congregation mumbled to each other.

"I'll never replace Brother Frankel, nor would I try, but I'm here if you need me." He looked about the hall to people who nodded and fanned, and fanned some more. He patted the metal frame on his leg. "I'm here at the Army Hospital recouping from a wound I received in North Africa." I nearly stood, but Mama pulled me back down. Africa. I'd wanted to find someone who'd been there, but I never asked the soldiers where they'd fought, I just listened and waited to hear. "I'll be ministering to the hospital, the POW camp, and to Palmer Air Field, and I'll be making my rounds to most of the local churches."

A man sitting in front of us whispered to his wife, "Even the niggers?" She hunched her shoulders. Mama shushed him.

"Now let me tell you," Pastor Myers said, "war ain't no picnic . . ."

"No, sir," some said. "Amen."

". . . If you pardon my language, ladies, war is hell."

"Yes, it is," Mama, and others, said. "Amen. Your granddaddy fought in the Great War."

"However, it is necessary for this war. If God ever wanted war, it is this war that he wants . . ."

"Yes, yes," some said, quiet, unsure. "Amen."

". . . for it is this war that will drive evil from the earth."

"Yes, Lord, yes," almost everyone said. "Amen. Praise the Lord. Glory be."

" . . . for if there is evil, certainly in resides in the bowels of Hitler and his Nazis."

"Amen," they said, louder.

Pastor Myers wiped his brow.

It bothered me to think that God wanted there to be

war. I thought God should be working toward stopping the war. As I looked around, the congregation understood what he meant, and I'm sure, supported any mention of driving evil from the earth—whatever evil that was.

"Let us pray," Pastor Myers said. The congregation bowed their heads. I looked about, off through the windows, into the fields. The heat in Africa had to be hotter than this, but maybe not by much.

When the prayer finished, Brother Frankel stood and whispered something to Pastor Myers. Pastor Myers tried to turn, stiff and awkward, but Brother Frankel put his hand on the pastor's shoulders, continued to whisper and motioned to one of the windows. Pastor Myers nodded and returned to the lectern. "Brother Frankel expressed that I'd be speaking about the war."

Several people mumbled. People nodded and shook their heads. Mama and Mrs. Applethorpe shushed the crowd.

"But considering the heat, let me finish by saying that I served in Africa and I know that all that you suffer, every bale of cotton, every bushel of corn, every drop of oil you work so hard for is needed and appreciated over there. Over there."

The heavy man in front of us started humming the song, "Over There."

"And this here humidity has got the desert beat hands down."

The people laughed. He seemed to have answered my question.

I chuckled, but I thought that he would talk more about the war, and though interesting to see and think about, I'd missed a day at the plantation for really nothing.

When the chatter stopped, Pastor Myers said, "But I'll be around and you'll see me and if you want to talk about anything, I have an office at the hospital." He turned back to Brother Frankel. "If I may, I'd like to say a prayer for all the men in uniform," he said.

Brother Frankel rose. "Of course, of course."

Some paused their fanning to fold their hands. Others slowed, but didn't stop. Everyone's face was down, eyes closed, except Pastor Myers. He looked about the room, then at me, his eyes brown and unblinking, his face pale and shining from sweat. He lowered his head, raised his hands, and prayed.

"Lord, bless the men in uniform wherever they may be, but in particular, bless those men who have undertaken the end of this awful bloodshed along the coast of Normandy. Lead them through the many perils of war and rigors of combat and through the Valley of Death. Show them the light that they might follow it back to our shores and our families and our farms." He looked up, saw me staring, then looked away. "In the name of the Lord, Amen."

"Amen," the congregation said.

Mama waited at the foot of the steps talking with other members. I heard the word "lynching" at some point as she passed on word from the newspaper. When the Hoopers went by the preachers standing at the door, they nodded, shook the hands of Brother Frankel and Pastor Myers, and walked off toward their Cadillac. Mike rubbed his eyes, Ella pulled her mother along. When they'd driven off down the dirt roads back toward town, the whispers began.

"Why're they here?" a woman standing with Mama said.

A man, who I thought must be her husband because of how close he stood to her, said, "Come to see how the other half lives?"

"Don't belong here," another man said.

I ignored them. I watched a duck waddle up from the church's pond, one wing damaged and wayward. It walked fast, wobbling back and forth, until it passed through a hole in the lattice around the bottom of the church.

When the steps finally cleared, Pastor Myers struggled down a step, then paused as if catching his breath. I went up the stairs.

"Mind if I lean on you, son?" Pastor Myers said.

He didn't wait for a reply, but pushed down on my shoulder as his stiff leg and metal frame lowered to each step.

The crowd retreated. Some went off across the fields

of cotton and corn while others meandered down each road passing north and south and east and west. Mama and Brother Frankel spoke in another small group of adults.

I didn't know what to say to Pastor Myers. I wanted to know what happened to his leg and what the war was like. I didn't understand how a minister could also be a soldier. I noticed that his shoulder patch had a red "1" within a white field and I wanted to know what it meant.

When the pastor reached the ground, sweat dripped from his nose and I could smell the exertion coming from him. Thin and tall, he looked down at me. "Thank you," he said. He wiped his brow with a kerchief. "James Quick, right?"

I wondered how he knew my name, but then recalled that Brother Frankel had called it out like he was auctioning a steer. "Jimmy Quick, sir," I said. I starred at his metal brace, then out across the fields. When the wind blew the corn to one side, I could just make out the courthouse tower down in town.

"Jimmy, why did you visit today?"

I looked up to his face, then back across the fields. "Mama makes us come once in awhile."

He smiled. "Oh, she makes you come."

I feared this might sound rude. I wasn't trying to be hurtful. "And you."

"Me?"

"I didn't know it at first, but Mama said you'd be here to talk about the war."

"Oh, well, I'm sorry I didn't talk more about it. Anything particular you want to know?"

I didn't mean to, but I looked at his leg, then toward Mama.

"You want to know what happened to me?"

I nodded.

"Nazi land mine. I was next to a man who stepped on one out in North Africa, Libya. Nearly took the bottom half of my leg off, but they saved it and the hospital here put the bones back together with metal sheets and screws. I hope I don't walk past a strong magnet."

I nodded again, not exactly sure what he meant.

Mama waved for me to come to her. She stood with

her right foot off the ground, the big toe keeping balance.

"You heard what I said inside? You can come and talk with me anytime. My office is in the hospital in town."

"Yes, sir."

I shook Pastor Myers' hand and ran after Mama who had hobbled off toward home.

A quarter mile up the road, I turned to see Pastor Myers lift his leg into a green Army staff car, a white star on the door, the heat glimmering off the roof.

5

With my dues paid for breaking Daddy's rules about the radio, I thought all was forgiven and I wouldn't miss going somewhere with Uncle George the next week and that I had my Saturday nights in town back.

Chugging down from Baltimore in his 1941 DeSoto breezer, our Uncle George took us somewhere every summer for a day or three so long as we'd weeded ahead. Mama would pick up feeding the stock and Daddy would milk, they'd eat leftovers or cold meals so Mama didn't have to cook so much, and to them, they got a little time away too, though they never left the farm. Frances told me that Mama and Daddy made Irene during one of our trips, the time we went up the mountains and met our people on the reservation. For the longest time I imagined Mama sewing an arm onto Irene. Mama and Daddy could spare us.

Uncle George, his black hair standing on end from the wind, his Cherokee red skin shining, burnt from the sun, drove fast down the dirt roads, plumes of dust trailing behind him, a cloud encircling the car when he stopped. Mama's brother, who left the farms to fight in the Great War, then afterward went to the University of Maryland, settled in Baltimore to teach. Big for his age, he'd joined the Army too young, probably at fourteen or fifteen. When he went off to college, he looked no older than anyone else. He'd earned a scholarship for him being so smart.

Frances leaped from the front stoop and met Uncle George before the car had even stopped moving. "Uncle George," she said, bouncing like a baby.

Irene ran behind Frances, yelling, "Uncle George, Uncle George," though I think she still had trouble remembering him each year.

Uncle George provided a form of safety when he came down. Unlike the toiling on the farm and the too often boring town and the routine of brothers, sisters, Mama and Daddy, he became the difference in our lives, the reason for Mama to bake sweets and Daddy to shave and dress nice and for all of us to be extra clean and put on our best, often handed down to us from Uncle George. Mama would giggle thinking of her childhood brother and Daddy would hum and whistle to have someone to jabber with. I think Frances loved him so much that if they weren't uncle and niece she'd have married him. It would be best of me to say it wasn't the gifts, or his car, or the sweets he'd bring, or the trips he'd take us on. But I can't. It's how I knew and why I loved Uncle George.

Daddy came out the door, wiping his mouth, and extending his hand, walking down the long yard, arm out, till Uncle George took it. "Hey, there, brother," Daddy said, though Uncle George was Mama's brother. The two had known each other most of their lives.

"George," Mama said, coming from around the side of the house, drying her hands on her apron, patting down her hair. She waited till he came to her, then they hugged and kissed, and she whispered something to him that they laughed about, an old joke, the same thing every time.

"Jimmy," he said. "Heck, you're too big to be picking up anymore." He shook my hand and I laughed and felt the heat of his palm, as if our blood mixed together right through the skin. "Where's Lawrence and TJ?" he said, picking up Irene who had her arms extended, begging like a kitten.

"Down the spring splitting wood," I said. "They'll be ready to go."

"Well, maybe we should just go down to see them. Novaline," he said. "Okay I go down to find them boys?"

"And give them a lick or two when you do. I told them to be back quick, but they've been down there all morning," she said.

Uncle George put Irene down and she started to twitch and jump, but he bent and whispered something that made her giggle. Frances walked close behind him as we went off toward the spring, but Mama said, "Frances, get back in here to help me pack up these here things."

Frances looked as if she wanted to jump and twitch too, but stomped off toward the house, muttering over her shoulder, "I'm sitting in the front seat then, you boys off doing stuff without me."

From the backyard, going around the smokehouse and curving behind the barn, a dirt path, beaten and narrow, the grass long gone, the stones sticking out and crumbling, meandered toward the spring and thicket of trees. The air stood hazy, thick with humidity.

Uncle George said, "What do you think of the war? About time we got into Northern Europe, huh?"

"We're going to win. Beat 'em last time, we'll beat 'em again," I said, then told him about Pastor Myers and about some of the soldiers I'd met in town--Matthew the MP and Felix the medic. "Say, how's a pastor also a soldier?"

"Well, soldiers, maybe more than most people, need a lot of ministering to. Heck, they could die any minute, so they want to be close to God. There's a saying—there aren't any atheists in foxholes. Get what I mean?"

I nodded, but then said, "But it don't make much sense that a pastor is a soldier. He get a gun?"

"Well, I never saw a preacher carrying a gun when I was in," he said.

We walked and I pulled at some raspberries along the path.

"Did you finish that book I gave you?" he said. He'd either give me books when he came to see us, or, sometimes, he'd mail some to me. After telling me about *Time*, *Life*, and *National Geographic*, he let me pick one that he'd pay for the subscription. I chose *National Geographic* for us, which was quite something because I knew that it was likely no one else in all of Marlboro County had that little yellow magazine delivered to them each month. The last two books he gave me, Hemingway's *For Whom the Bell Tolls* and *A Farewell to Arms*, were about war, which I liked to read.

"Yeah. You gave me two."

"Oh, that's right. Well? What did you think?"

I thought about it for a moment or two. I could have talked to him about what I read and even that I might get into hot water if Mama knew that there was sex in them, but she didn't read them, so she didn't have to know. "I liked them," I said.

Uncle George laughed. "You liked them? That's it? Well, we're going to have to work on your analysis a bit."

I had no idea what he meant. I thought books were for liking or not liking, and I did like both of Hemingway's books. I was going to ask him if Hemingway had written anything else, but I wasn't sure if he was making fun of me because I certainly didn't know what *analysis* meant.

Not far from the spring, I heard the sound of an axe thumping into wood. There was only the sound of one, so I knew someone, TJ I thought, had ditched his chopping. The thunks came slowly, one, then another.

Growing beside the spring that stunk of old eggs, a grove of willow and laurel oaks, a lone magnolia, a thick cluster of holly trees, longleaf pines, and red cedar shaded the water. On nights when lightning bugs flickered and crickets hummed a tune, we'd swing from a tattered rope tied to an oak tree and splash into the cold waters. Scarlet tanagers, red-headed woodpeckers, goldfinches, flycatchers, towhees, sapsuckers, wood ducks, and screech owls darted through the grove. Thick patches of sunflowers and goldenrod, ragweed, blue and pink flax, cranesbill, and orchids bordered the little place set away from the farm. The rocks and water bubbling up, pouring over, flowing down to the Little Pee Dee river, kept the farmers, for as long as there'd been farmers there, from plowing everything over and cutting everything down.

At the edge of the grove, etched stones, piles of rocks, rotting wood crosses marked the cemetery where decades of people like us lay buried. Leaves covered the place a foot deep.

Lawrence, his white shirt laid across a boulder, brought the long axe up, then down onto a knotted limb. The wagon, piled only half-full, would anger Daddy because the boys had been out here for days chopping whatever trees had fallen. Whenever Daddy could, he'd come out and help get through the trunks, but Lawrence and TJ had the job to whittle it all down to burning size. We needed the wood for the stove and for the smokehouse, and preparing for the fireplace took all year. The grove was thinner than when I was a child, but it still looked dark and full and we mostly took only what fell or needed chopping before it fell and the McCormick's, who bordered this little place with us, did pretty much the same.

"Hey, Lawrence," Uncle George said.

Lawrence looked up, the axe missing the limb, sparking off a rock and digging into the ground.

"Hey, there," Lawrence said, coming toward us with his hand out, imitating Daddy.

"What have you been eating?" Uncle George slapped Lawrence on his thick arm. "You're as big as a moose."

"Ain't got much, but we got Mama's cooking." The two laughed.

I saw TJ floating in the middle of the spring. He was stripped naked, his nose, hands, feet, and willy breaking the surface.

"Where's TJ? Your Mama said he was down here with you," George said.

Lawrence tossed back his head, motioning over his shoulder.

Uncle George raised an eyebrow. I shrugged.

"Uncle George," TJ called. He was treading water and waving. Light bounced off the cool, still surface, TJ making tiny ripples. Just feet from the shore the water turned dark blue, then almost purple, and then black. TJ swam out in the darkest part, where the deep water turned the light dark.

On some Sundays, when Mama walked to church, she'd make us a picnic of leftovers. We'd lie out on the hot boulders and eat potatoes and tomatoes, fried chicken or sausages. Whenever we finished swimming in the spring we smelled a bit like eggs. Uncle George told us it was because the spring water brought sulfur up from deep in the ground.

TJ swam toward shore, at first on the surface. Then he dived down and I could see him, like a frog, still shallow, moving, his arms and legs out, then back, out, back. Then he disappeared into the deep, indigo water. Gone. I didn't see him anymore. The water took him, eating him like popping in an acorn.

I could feel the seconds tick by.

Uncle George's smile dipped, then dimmed. "TJ? Uncle George looked around. "TJ!" he yelled.

A breeze blew across the spring. The water stilled, not a ripple until a leaf fell from a tree.

"Oh, God," Uncle George said. "TJ!" Uncle George yanked off his shoes, ran across the pebbles and sharp stones, one of them cutting his foot, but Uncle George didn't stop, though I could see the blood coming from his heel, and splashed through the shallows, then plunged into the water. The wind picked up a drop or two and sprinkled it onto my face, cold.

"Daddy!" I yelled, knowing that we were too far from the house. "Daddy!"

Lawrence stood there, not moving, his jaw slack, his eyes unblinking.

Uncle George splashed about, dived, came back up, dived again, surfaced. "Where did he go down?" he said.

"Further out! Out there!" I pointed.

"Get your Daddy," Uncle George said, diving beneath the dark waters.

I turned, Lawrence ran toward the water, leaping into it.

Then, I heard the surface explode. A gasp, gurgling water, spitting and spewing. TJ seemed to leap up from the depths. "There ain't no bottom," he said. Thin blood trickled from his nose mixed with snot.

Uncle George and Lawrence swam out to him. TJ spit red water and then the three stroked back in, casual.

"What the hell was that, TJ?" Uncle George said.

"I don't know. I was swimming and it kept getting darker and colder and I knew it should be getting lighter. Then I felt my ears pressing in." He climbed onto a little rock island.

I ran down to him. "You all right?" I said.

"It was good. I looked up and could see the light way above me. It was really dark. Wow. I thought to myself, 'Am I trying to swim into the darkness? It's so cold.' It felt good. Peaceful. Then I knew that I'd better get the hell back up, so I started pulling myself back toward the top. It was a long way."

I put my hand on TJ's shoulder. His skin felt like the winter flurries that often sprinkled the farm and spring and grove a light cover of white. He trembled a little.

"You scared the hell out of me," Uncle George said.

"You better not do that mess again, boy," Lawrence said, swatting him on the head.

"Yeah. It was good," TJ said again.

"You're bleeding." Uncle George pulled his soaked kerchief from his pocket and handed it to TJ.

"You, too," I said. I bent to lift up his leg, the heel cut, but already healing.

"Damn," he said. "Oh, sorry. Shoot. I'll have to patch that up."

"Don't tell Mama and Daddy. Don't tell them or they won't let me go," TJ said, pressing the kerchief to his nose, leaning his head back.

"Jesus, TJ," Uncle George pulled off his shirt and wrung the water from it. "Don't be doing crazy stuff like that."

Mama held up both of her hands like she was trying to stop a runaway wagon. "Don't be bringing that blood into my kitchen," she said. "Your nose will be fine, TJ. Georgie—you might need a stitch."

"I don't think so," Uncle George said. "You ain't butchering me like Frankenstein's monster."

"I don't know nothing about no monster, but I know a heel that needs a stitch when I sees it. Sit here," she said, grabbing Irene's hand and pulling her up off the back stoop. "Not inside. That blood'll spoil my fresh-cleaned floor. Devil's work." She'd gotten into her head that blood spilled from a chicken's wrung and split neck or the corpse of a hog, then later, even the blood from inside her own children, was somehow from Hell and she did all she could to keep it out of the house. "Frances, bring me a needle and thread."

She rammed cotton up TJ's nose, not too gentle, and covered Uncle George's heel, saying, "Okay, you're lucky you won't need a stitch or two."

"You still don't use a doctor for this stuff?" Uncle George said.

"Shoot, don't need no doctor for most stuff. Been stitching up gapped skin for most of my life. I stitched plenty of spots on you when you were a boy."

Uncle George picked up his arm and showed a long pink scar on his forearm. "Fell off the roof and landed on a board with a nail. Bled like a stuck porker." Irene reached out and followed the trail of pink flesh.

"What you boys doing down there?" Mama said.

"Just messing around, Novaline," Uncle George said.

"Well, next time, toss Jimmy in. Ain't right three of you wet and he comes back like the King of England." Everyone laughed.

"Speaking of wet, they've never seen the ocean," Uncle George said. "I was thinking of taking them over to Myrtle Beach."

Mama looked up from tying off his bandage. Her face questioned Uncle George. Everyone sat quietly. I prayed she'd say he could take us.

"Never heard of it," she said.

"Used to call it New Town," Daddy said. I could tell he stood on our side.

"Over in Oh'-ree County?" Mama shook her head. "Too far. Too dangerous."

"It's only three hours," Uncle George said. "Down Route 9 all the way. Ain't nothing dangerous about it."

"Big wash of water come in and take my child away, that's dangerous. I know, I've heard, even read about people yanked out to sea." Mama pushed away, wiping her hands onto her apron. A tiny speck of blood dotted the string that went about her waist. "Look there," she untied the apron and balled it up.

"They don't know how to swim," she said.

Lawrence and I looked at TJ. Lawrence said, "Mama, we've been swimming in that spring and down Pee Dee River for most of our lives."

"Yes, boy, but a spring ain't no ocean."

We didn't protest. Though I wanted to plead, and Frances and Irene both looked as if they wanted to bounce a little, and TJ had already looked to Mama, his eyes begging, we said and did nothing. This debate happened every year, whether we went off to the mountains, up to Fayetteville, over to Charlotte, down to Columbia, on any trip Uncle George took us, it started this way.

"Too far," Mama said.

"Just a little farther than Charlotte. Not nearly as far as the reservation," Uncle George said.

Mama looked to Daddy, who nodded his head. Though the final answer came, the discussion was never over at that point.

"Irene ain't to go in that water."

Irene deflated a little, tears popping into her eyes. Frances gave her a hard look. Irene wiped the tears slowly.

"And I know you boys are going in no matter what I say, so no more than up to your bellies. And Frances, you keep an eye on everyone. You too, Lawrence."

Then we jumped. We all kissed Mama, thanking her. We boys slapped Daddy on the back. Frances picked up Irene, both of them kissing Daddy on his cheeks.

"But," Mama said, everyone quieting, "if you get eaten by a shark, don't come crying to me."

6

*U*ncle George bought his DeSoto convertible the week before the Japs bombed Pearl Harbor. Yellow like a sunflower, with white-walled tires, dirty from the road dust, the bumper and grill like the cattle scooper on the front of a locomotive, the engine roared like a freight train. He'd covered the headlights with black tape, leaving a narrow slit. The car's top was pulled down, tucked behind the rear seat. I imagined it was expensive, $1000 or more, I'd heard Mama say. "He's working out the track," she'd told Daddy, "Pimlico, as a side job." I had no idea what she meant because Uncle George was a school teacher and I didn't know what a track was.

Lawrence squeezed into the front seat, but Frances stood with her hand on her hip, glaring at the eldest brother, until he gave up, not a word or twitch, and clamored into the back with me and TJ. Irene sat upfront with Frances and Uncle George.

Uncle George drove down the back way toward Wilder Road, where he pulled over. "Who wants to drive?" he said. We each looked at the other as a breeze blew by, then everyone yelled, "Me!" at the same time. Irene put her hand in the air like asking a question at school.

"Next time, honey," Uncle George said, patting her head.

Lawrence, TJ, and Frances drove the car, each a few

miles, down Wilder, back to Hamlet, on toward Bennettsville, then down Cheraw Road toward the ocean. When it came my turn, I sat in the driver's seat with my eyes peering through the steering wheel. "I can either see the road or reach the pedals."

"Short stuff," Lawrence said.

"Big car," Frances defended.

"Use the tips of your toes," Uncle George said.

He showed me the fancy Simplimatic gear shifting, and when I pushed the pedal, we buzzed off like a tornado. Rounding a corner, I looked for the brake, took my eyes from the road, missed the pedal, Frances squeaked and Uncle George grab for the wheel from where he squeezed between me and Frances. We rolled off the road, bounced across a narrow irrigation ditch, Irene's body flying into the air, and stopped in a pile of hay, fresh cut, splintery and stinging as it filled the car.

As the hay that had been tossed into the air drifted back down, no one said a thing. Then Irene giggled and said, "That was fun." Then we all screamed, laughed, clapped, and hollered.

When Uncle George got back in the driver's seat, he said, "Okay, let's get to the ocean."

We drove down 9 through Clio where we had to slow to get around a truck waiting to get gas at a pump placed alongside the road. We passed a sign that read "Little Rock," but except for a vegetable stand, there weren't any other buildings that I saw. At Dillon, long lines of Negro men with hoes over their shoulders, walked into bean fields. Aunt Gertrude lived in Dillon with Uncle Willard, a man who once sold moonshine and still stank of the corn-mash whiskey. Then came Lake View. Though I looked hard for water, I never saw a lake. Nichols, Green Sea, and Longs all passed the same way—places with names, but little more than a Pepsi sign or a crossroad to tell it apart from the fields around. Between this scattering of towns, miles of corn, cotton, hay, hedgerows thick with willows, a field of orange milkweeds that pushed aside as the DeSoto passed, stretched across the land.

Hours passed with Frances talking the whole time, and TJ and Lawrence sleeping, and me looking. Just beyond

Longs, the road bent a bit one way, then the other, the ocean, blue and white, the sun splintering off of it, appeared.

"Wow," I said. I poked my brothers. Everyone oohed and awed.

"There's the Atlantic," Uncle George said.

Until I saw the ocean, I'd thought that the mild snow we got during the winters, just enough to quiet the farm, coat the trees and land, make the ground just hard enough to crunch, the spring just cool enough for a thin layer of ice to form, was the most beautiful thing. I'm sure I didn't breathe for a full minute as I watched the distant movement, up and down, of the water.

We turned onto a road that ran beside the beach, south. Along the horizon, a dozen or more ships sat, unmoving, in the afternoon haze.

"What they out there for?" TJ said, to anyone.

"Guess they're transports," I said.

"Out of Wilmington and Charleston waiting to build a convoy to cross the Atlantic. They need escorts," Uncle George said.

We drove past the Seaside Inn and the biggest building I'd ever seen, the Ocean Forest Hotel. I thought how I'd like to have Mama and Daddy stay there someday, when I could pay their way.

Just past the Army Airfield, built right up to the beach, Uncle George pulled off and parked beneath a tree, the front wheels resting in the sand. The little town ended just across the street, where Sea Cliff Market's *Open* sign waved in the ocean breeze. On the front porch, a gathering of men leaned against posts, their brims pulled down shading their faces from the hot afternoon sun.

We jumped from the car, ran down onto the blazing sand, the tiny grains stinging my feet. We yelled more wows and ahhs and oohs. Lawrence, TJ, and I ran faster, into a race, heading for the water, past a tower, splashing in the shallow waves, then chased back, frightened from what Mama warned when we saw another wave, tall, rushing, crashing, coming toward us. The warm and clear water hit so hard that white foam plumed up. A tiny crab walked sideways away from us. Shells rocked in and out with the moving water. Irene picked one up, sniffed it, said, "Eeee," then tossed it back down.

"It's okay, honey, we'll get some clean ones for Mama and Daddy," Frances said.

"But they're stinky," Irene said.

"Wash them off and dry them, they'll be fine," Uncle George said. "Got to watch for the ones that still have something alive in them. A few might be rotten, too."

"Now you guys all listen to me," Uncle George said. "Your Mama wasn't just paranoid about the water. There's something called a riptide that will pull you out to sea if you're not careful. If you start getting pulled out, don't swim straight for shore—swim along it till you stop feeling the water pull. Understand?" We all nodded, even Irene.

We stripped down to our one pair of boxer shorts each, spread out our dungarees and overalls to dry, and plunged into the water. Something ran across my foot. We learned that we could float and ride the waves. I saw Frances help unpack the car with Uncle George, while Irene sat in the sand, piling up the wet muck, tossing handfuls of it into the rushing water. Salt stung my eyes, the sand made my nipples sore as I rushed ashore with the breakers. At one time, Uncle George, Irene, and Frances walked across the street to Sea Cliff Market and returned with a sack. When the sun had passed way into the west, Lawrence, TJ, and I had drifted far down the beach and near a long line of dark rocks laid out into the ocean, on purpose, as far as I could tell, but for what reason I didn't know. Uncle George called for us, and we ran back, the sand slipping beneath us, our legs pumping hard, but not moving us much.

Uncle George had built a fire in a shallow pit of sand. Over top of it he'd put sausages on sticks so that the grease ran out of them and popped and hissed as they dripped onto the flames. It smelled of the farm and made my stomach grab.

"Had to do a little dealing to get those," Uncle George said.

We sipped Cokes slowly, careful not to gulp it down, saving it a little at a time.

I sat beside Uncle George. He said, "Jimmy, what do you see yourself doing in five years?" I loved him for asking these questions. He made my head ache a little when he did, but it always ended with me having new ideas. He used to ask where I wanted to go, and I'd always say Europe until he told me about Hemingway going to Africa, so then I wanted to go there. I'd go anywhere.

"Here they go again," Frances said. "Same thing every time. Come on Renie, let's wash up these things. I saw a spigot back next to that market."

"I'll go too. I ain't interested in them clamoring about this stuff," Lawrence said. "Only one place for me in this world—the farm."

TJ stayed, sitting the other side of the fire, his back to the ocean. His face was lit orange, and the smoke drifted toward him, but he didn't move.

I wasn't sure how to answer Uncle George. "Well, it ain't often a matter of what people want, rather what just happens to them," I said, "especially on the farm."

"Oh, yeah?" he nodded. "Well, let me say it a different way. England's up there." Uncle George pointed out to sea, beyond the waiting ships, almost north. "Those ships will be heading that way. And Africa's pretty much that way." He pointed straight out to sea. "Morocco, maybe the Straits of Gibraltar are right across there. And Antarctica is down there an awfully long way." He pointed south along the coast. "You said you wanted to travel, now what's it going to be?"

I thought for a second or two more. "I ain't going to be no farmer," I said.

"Oh, yeah? I had those same thoughts before the Great War. So, where do you want to go? What do you want to do?"

I nodded. I liked the color pictures I'd seen in *National Geographic*. Girls swimming in the Gulf of Mexico, a woman with her hair made to stand up, planes landing on the water. "I think I want to take pictures."

"Oh, yeah? Take pictures, huh?"

"For *National Geographic*." I had my head down, playing with the sand. When I raised it, looking past TJ, out to sea where the orange setting sun shined off the sides of the ships, the sky heavy and purple, I said, "They get to go so many places."

"Sometimes dangerous places," Uncle George said.

"I ain't never even seen a camera up close." I felt the

44

nonsense of what I wanted. I'd never held a camera, but somehow that's what I wanted to do. Uncle George didn't look surprised. His face had a grin, he listened and concentrated on what I said. "But I could learn to use one."

"You sure could. My experiences as a teacher tells me that most people can learn just about anything they set their mind to."

"Mama says that, too," TJ said.

Frances, Irene, and Lawrence came back, wiping their hands on a blue kerchief. The sunlight dimmed more. Above our heads, pink and orange streaks of clouds stretched into the blackness of the dark east. A warden on a green drab bike peddled through the town, stopping at the edge of the road, near the bumper of the DeSoto.

"Time to put that fire out. Douse it down with sand, all the way. Not a flicker," the warden said. "Even a little fire might let a U-boat see too much." His red and white Civil Defense triangle patch reflected the color of fire.

"Yes, sir," Uncle George said. TJ took the heels of his feet and pushed sand into the pit. The wood and flames moved sideways, so I pushed sand in from my side. Flames crept around, but dwindled and died.

"You all just visiting?" the warden said.

Uncle George nodded. "It's okay, ain't it?"

"Like popcorn. Just want to warn you about razor back hogs running the beach. One ain't too bad, but a couple of them can cause just about anyone a heap of misery. Course, town folk have hunted most of them. You watch out for that little one," he said, pointing toward Irene.

"Well, thank you, sir. We'll keep our eyes open."

A slither of smoke drifted up from an unseen hole in the sand. Without the fire, cold air dropped from above, the breeze coming from shore seemed heavier, the darkness pushed down and around us. The warden yelled, somewhere in the town, to douse a light. The blackness seemed to be all there was.

We lay on blankets that Frances brought out from the trunk of the DeSoto. Uncle George showed us Venus. Steady and clear, it shone brighter than any of the millions of other stars. The smell of salt filled our noses. "That's the constellation Leo," he said, pointing north. "There's the Big Dipper."

"Where? Where?" Irene said.

Uncle George pulled her close, pointed into the sky, and outlined the handle and cup for her.

"Wow," she said. Lawrence seemed just as interested as Irene.

Uncle George tried to outline Hercules for us, but I couldn't put all of the points together.

We shivered a little without the warmth, but we sat close together, Frances and Irene leaned against each other's backs. We sang "Row, Row, Row Your Boat." TJ tried to sound like Perry Como singing "White Christmas," but he couldn't get his voice as deep. We looked at the stars, sang, ate the pecan-molasses clusters Mama had packed, and slipped into sleeping, then back, then into it again. I thought I heard something heavy, big, fat rustling through the brush the other side of Uncle George's car.

A flash jumped off the sea along the horizon.

"What the hell?" Lawrence leaped to his feet.

Uncle George put up his hand. "Ssshh!"

Another burst, brighter, more explosive than the first one. Red and yellow flames bobbed on the dark water. A ship stood clearly outlined in the flickering below the flames. Somewhere in the dark town behind us, a bell rang a dozen quick tones. Then the boom from the explosion rolled onto shore above the crash of the waves. Frances jumped to her feet at the sound. Lawrence ran down to the water's edge.

"U-boat!" I said. My stomach felt weak. I stood, unblinking, my hands dangling at my sides, tingling. Flames leapt up from one of the ships. From the distance, the whooping of its alarm came across the sea. Men were dying. My shoulders slumped and I felt heavy in all of my muscles and bones. Sorrow crept into me. My hair tingled, I could feel my face flush. Strange to be safe and know others aren't, to see it, hear it. Flames lit up black smoke charging into the sky. I thought of the Hindenburg and the reporter crying.

Irene walked down to hold Lawrence's hand, water swept over their feet. Frances wiped tears from her face as the light show grew bigger in the otherwise pure blackness.

46

Another eruption on the ship sent flames even higher than before.

"Wow!" Irene said.

"Ssh, honey," Frances told her.

Then a boom mixed with a wave as it crushed the sand beneath came ashore. We all wandered down to the water line. I wanted to be closer to the ship, to swim to the side of the boat, to reach out and say, "Jump, swim, I'll lead you to land."

Frances put her arm around me. "Oh, Jimmy," she said, crying. "How many men do you think?"

"I don't know. If it was just a cargo ship, maybe only a hundred. A thousand if a troop ship."

Lawrence held onto Irene.

"If it was a troop ship, it could be thousands."

Uncle George stuffed his hands deep into his pockets.

TJ was gone into the darkness.

Sulfur floated in with the breeze, stinking, but I inhaled it, deep, smelling.

Town's folk ran down to the beach. A truck, its lights off, pulled onto the sand behind us. They gawked and pointed at the distant flames as if a fireworks shows on the 4th of July had gone off.

From the Army Airfield just down the beach, an engine choked and puffed, then clamored to life.

Another flare lit the sky. Another plane throttled to life. Another streak left the deck of another ship. "That a U-boat too?" Uncle George said.

"One of ours, I think. Destroyer coming to help!" I said, my excitement rising.

"How do you know all this?" Uncle George said.

"I heard it all in town. U-boats hunting along the coast. Haven't been too many in recent years, but back in '42 there'd been more than 140 ships sunk this same way. They look for any possible light—a cigarette, a flash light, or sometimes the moon but there's no moon tonight. Possibly, a light on shore." I thought that maybe our fire had done the ship in, but it had been at least an hour or more since the warden ordered it out, though I didn't know how long we'd dosed.

"What time is it?" I said.

"Near midnight." Uncle George picked up Irene.

Another flash from the destroyer.

"What's our guys shooting at?" Lawrence asked.

"Trying to scare away the U-boat," I said. Another flash, another boom, snapping. "U-boat must still be near the ship."

Two planes climbed into the night from the airfield, flying above our heads toward the burning, sinking transport. More flickering as the destroyers rushed to help the sinking ship. All night, planes took off and landed. We stood and watched and listened to the towns' folk. We wandered back to our blankets. The flames in the distance looked as if someone was kicking sand onto them until they went out.

7

*B*efore the sun peeked its body over the horizon, the darkness turned to ash, pale blue, dungaree. I went down to the water's edge to watch dolphins go by, the air blowing from their heads. I wanted to wake everyone, but didn't, so I just counted the dolphins and thought that I'd never been to such a wonderful place as the ocean.

When the sun broke the horizon, it glowed golden in long streaks.

Two yellow Civil Air Patrol planes circled out at sea where the ship must have gone down. As they turned toward land and passed overhead, I waved to them. Their engines buzzed making my ears tingle, everyone else woke up.

Sometime in the night, the smoking hulk slithered beneath the waves. TJ sneaked back. We slept, waked, watched the flames out at sea grow, fall, grow, then sometime late, when the dew had settled wetting my thick blanket, the cold ocean doused the last flame.

With the morning light warming the air, TJ and I stretched our arms above our heads, picked the sand from the corners of our eyes, chewed on some sassafras leaves, and walked down the beach. I don't know if all brothers are buddies, but TJ was my best friend. It couldn't be helped. Whether we were killing rats or chasing coons or planting corn or hauling hay, most of our chores were done side by side. Brothers get to know each other pretty well working so close to them. He knew me as well as I knew him. His certain grunt meant he was upset, another meant he was happy. If too many teeth showed in his smile it really meant he was angry, while just a smirk where white showed through pink lips showed his cheerfulness. When getting sick, he smelled a certain way--musty and dry--which meant I knew when he faked being ill. A laugh that bent him at the waist was true, everything else was a lie. I knew when he wouldn't look at me that he'd just been cuffing the carrot, but it was similar to the look when his stomach hurt and he couldn't eat.

I thought I knew just about everything about TJ, except I didn't know why he sneaked off so often.

"Where were you last night?" I said, when the sunflower DeSoto and made-up camp lay far behind us. "I won't tell Daddy, you know." He picked up a shell, gray and smooth. The waves rumbled. I wondered if I'd just thought the words and not said a thing, but I knew I hadn't. TJ tossed the shell; it skipped between waves.

As we walked up the beach, picking up rippled shells and glittering rocks, the first sheen of oil, a rainbow in the morning sun, came ashore with the white foam, covering the sparkling sand. It looked like the ship's blood oozing about, refusing to sink. Wreckage bobbed in the surf just behind the oil. A wooden crate, one corner sticking out of the water like a pyramid, rose and fell with the swells. A scattering of papers, pieces of wood, cushions.

"Jesus, TJ, look!" I said, pointing up the beach. Empty Mae West lifejackets, bobbing and orange, banged against the long line of dark rocks that stretched away from the shore. We ran toward the breaker.

I heard the grunting above the booming waves and seagulls screeching. For a second or two I thought the grumble and snorts was a sailor hurt and needing help. Up the beach an olive drab truck pulled onto the sand.

On the other side of the breaker, where a rip tide tore in, beat up the sand, then raced outward along its edges, a Mae West clung to a rock like a limp flag on a rain-beaten pole. A head without much of a face glared at us, the eyes gone, the nose a giant hole, the cheeks torn off. Two boars ate into the bowels, pulling at the clothes, ripping the

50

lifejacket. Their attack was harsh and quick. Their tusks tossed blood into the air, dotting the sand. It ran down the shore and mixed with the froth.

"Jesus Christ," TJ said, looking at the wide, empty sockets where eyes should be. Flies crept along the teeth.

"Oh, my God," I said. A crab tugged on the fingers dangling in the water. A gull sat on his shoulders picking at the man's ears. "Get away from him," I yelled, picking up a dimpled oyster shell and tossing it toward the body. The wind caught it and dropped it without harm into the foaming waves. The boar stopped its pulling and snorting, looked up at me, huffed, shoved sand with his toes, then went back to eating.

"You son-of-a-bitch. Come down to the farm during slaughter and we'll carve you up into hams, damn it!" The sow turned, not liking my yelling, I supposed, and charged two or three yards, kicking up sand behind it, before turning back to its meal. TJ and I scurried away; behind trees near the road we watched.

I'd never seen a dead man before. I don't think TJ ever had either. We'd handled the innards of swine and wrung the necks of chickens, lobbed off the heads of turkeys, hammered rats with pitchforks, and even pummeled coons with rocks till their bodies burst, but none of that cruelty needed to run a farm was like the stink of the inside of a man being eaten by hogs.

An Army deuce-and-a-half rumbled down the beach road and stopped at the breaker.

I felt that invisible weight pushing on me again— down on my shoulders, on my brain. I felt sad, but I didn't cry. I imagined a mother waiting for her son to return, her flowered frock blowing in the breeze as she stood on a street corner looking both ways.

TJ plopped down onto the sand and ran his fingers through shining grains.

"Jeepers creepers," a soldier said, leaping down from the truck.

"Oh, for crying out loud," a sergeant said. "Wilkie, shoot that futz."

Wilkie, standing in the back of the truck, shoved a long copper bullet into the top of an M1 rifle, and fired. He hit the boar in the head, knocking it over in one flat slap. I'd never heard the clap of a gun before. The sow took one more bite, then turned to run down the shore.

"Get it," the sergeant said.

Another shot and the sow stumbled, crashing into the surf. My head and ears hurt from the gunshots.

"What a fucking lollapalooza," a soldier said.

A half-dozen town folk ran down the beach from the porch of the market across the street. One of them looked like the Civil Defense warden. He pulled out a knife and slit the throat of the sow. Another man took the knife and headed for the boar. They carved into the two hogs with knives and tossed the meat into buckets, fast and bloody. Blood poured into the surf, foaming up pink.

"Going to be some bacon frying tonight," the sergeant said. He carried a blanket down to the sailor's body. His men followed with a mesh stretcher. "This gives me the heebie-jeebies," he said.

8

"**Y**ah, Yah there Yah!" Daddy shouted at the mule. Though Daddy allowed us to go with Uncle George, the day after we returned our chores came back with double force. Daddy broke the ground using our mule and plow, and Lawrence used the McCormick's. Most of the fields had been plowed, but one remained beyond what the few of us and two mules could do. Though not something the war effort wanted, this field would have to be pumpkins. Grandpa would have said, "Planting in June, do it soon." It was June, but it wasn't soon.

I heard the distant buzz of an airplane. Its noises floated about the morning sky first from above, then behind, then in front. Two blue Corsairs passed overhead, low to the ground, the earth shaking from their roar as they rushed toward Palmer Field.

Irene walked far before the plows clearing little stones and tossing aside any branches along a line Daddy had made with his foot. TJ came behind putting fertilizer in the furrow. I dropped in the seeds. We stopped at the end of each row while Daddy turned the plow and mule onto the next line. Frances came behind with a hoe refilling the ditch with the rusty-colored soil.

TJ's back popped as he stood his long, bronze body upright. "You know what, Jimmy?" He groaned, pressing in on his lower back. "I ain't going to stay on this farm all my life."

I grunted. "If you make it off this farm alive," I said. His wanderings worried me. I think Lawrence knew, which likely meant Daddy knew, too. Though I saw no change in the amount of work TJ put out, I knew that his late-night wayfaring would eventually drag his load down. Daddy wouldn't be too happy with that.

He didn't say anything right away. He scooped the fertilizer out of the sack, his nose curled up, teeth pulled back, his lips cursing beneath his breath. We went down almost an entire row before he said, "What you mean?"

I wanted to talk about it, then I didn't, even though I'd brought it up. I counted the turkey vultures circling above the trees way off near the McCormick's farm—twelve of them, their wings wide, floating and circling, waiting for a feral hog or dog to stop kicking out its last breath. "How long you think it'll be before Daddy finds out you been sneaking around?" I asked, shifting the burlap sack slung across my shoulders, a half-dozen or so seeds spilling into the trench.

"What?" I could tell his lies by where his brown eyes looked—somewhere beyond me, into the distance.

"Don't be saying you ain't been doing nothing. You have. I seen you. You snuck out at Myrtle Beach." I wiped the sweat from my forehead.

"I—" He still looked off into the distance.

"—TJ! I saw you sneaking in the other night. You going to get a girl knocked up and get into a heap of trouble with Daddy." I sounded like Our Mother of the Field more than myself, but I couldn't help it. I didn't want to see TJ in a jam. Selfish it was, but trouble for him meant grief for all of us.

Daddy looked up from the plow in our direction. "Need help with that?" I yelled to him. He shook his head as the mule took to digging another trench.

"You sounding like them soldiers in town. Mama wash your mouth out with lye soap she heard you say 'knocked up,'" TJ said.

"We ain't talking about me, here, brother."

He rolled his eyes to the heavens, closed them, peeked toward Daddy, then whispered, "I ain't going to get no girl knocked up." He glanced toward Frances. "That's for sure."

"Who is it?" TJ's eyes stayed on the trench. Sweat soaked his shirt. His hair stuck to his head as if he'd been in a rainstorm. "Is it Liz?"

TJ stepped over a pile of mule crap already gathering flies. I covered my mouth and nose until the smell passed.

He chuckled and grinned. "Naw. Ain't Liz." TJ put more fertilizer into the furrow.

"Who then? Maybe you drinking or smoking." I never smelled anything on him but cow and pig and dirt. Drinking might be covered up with a twig of sassafras, but smoke clung to a person like scales on a flounder.

"Hey, Daddy! That old nag's got the craps!" TJ said, moving his eyes away from me. He primed the line another few feet and stepped over another pile of dung before answering. "Ain't no one."

"Then what you sneaking off for?"

I didn't think he was going to answer me this time. He dropped to his knee to tie his tattered shoes. "Ain't nothing," he said. As he straightened up, he pretended he was looking me in the eye, but really he looked past me.

9

*T*hat next Saturday night, instead of the movie we chose to get ice cream from Breedon's Drug, which had put in a lunch counter when the war business came to town. We'd gone from a one horse show to the whole Ringling Brothers Circus in just a few months. Soldiers and sailors filled the streets, drove by in Jeeps and trucks and cars, even flew planes overhead. Late at night, so I'd heard, military police would bring Nazi prisoners through town and out toward Palmer Field to the prison camp there.

Soldiers, dressed in olive drab, forest green, khaki, and blue denim fatigues, packed the front corner of Breedon's, leaning against the glass window, where Mr. Breedon had removed the card racks to put in more tables. In the back, near the bathroom with running water, sat, stood, and leaned the town's kids in their jeans, sloppy Joe sweaters, and sneakers. It seemed more crowded than usual because *Ziegfeld Follies* had been running for several weeks at the Carolina Theater and everyone had already seen it.

The place buzzed like a high-speed fan and smoke hung low making the overhead lights dull. At the counter, some adults wore gray Chesterfield and plaid Norfolk jackets, their ties absent having been saved for the war effort. They sloshed back coffee and ice cream. Most of the ladies wore slacks, while some were in dresses ending just below the knee. They sipped sweet horsemint and goldenrod tea and finished off pecan pie covered with honey and topped with nuts Breedon bought off farmers instead of the rationed sugar. We stood near the front of the store where noise from the tavern on Market Street across the square surged through the open windows and mingled with the clatter in the drug store. Outside, leaning against the windows, children from other farms gathered, laughing, screeching, and talking.

"They got a new flavor," Irene said. Frances pushed her way to the counter. Lawrence carried a ten-pound sack of pecans we'd pulled from the trees and gathered from the ground to sell to Breedon. He squeezed through the crowd toward the end of the line of stools. TJ slid through the wall of brown-shirted soldiers. Irene followed Frances, ducking beneath the crowd, tugging on sleeves to get attention.

More soldiers came in. They overflowed the store, spilled onto the sidewalk, talking, laughing, yelling. I worked my way to a place where I could hear the head speaker, who I knew would be Matthew, an army MP, one of the first soldiers I'd met. He seemed nice.

"Oh, she was a bombshell. Real goddamned cheesecake," Matthew said. The other soldiers laughed. Many of them wore MP armbands and worked at the POW camp. "She had headlights like a fucking tank." His friends laughed louder. One fella blew milkshake out his nose.

I leaned against the wall, having made my way through a screen of brown, green, white, and blue shirts. I didn't see my brothers and sisters anywhere. Other crowds of soldiers bent over tables, listening, shouting, throwing cards, chugging back whatever Breedon had acquired on the black market or through ration book oversights or by buying extra from the farmers.

"Hey, beat it, kid. This ain't no conversation for a fella your age," another MP said, stepping in front of me.

"Whoa. You're all wet, you New York wop," Matthew said. "That's little Jimmy. Let him through, he's on the up and up."

"Yeah, I'll wop ya," the New York wop said. I thought they might fight, but Matthew stood and slapped the wop on his shoulder. They laughed. "Hey, kid. I'm Frankie." We shook hands. "Hey, save my space here. I've got to see a man about a dog."

"Come on, Jimmy, sit next to me," Matthew said. A sailor, dressed in light blue shirt and dark blue pants, already sat there. "Get up, up, up. You sailors are all alike. Give the kid a break." The sailor got up and took my spot. "Everyone, as I already told my Italian partner, this here's Jimmy. He's on the level and I want you goons to treat him like your own kid brothers—except you . . ." Matthew pointed to the next booth over, where, when another sailor stepped aside, I saw TJ sitting. A soldier in olive drab sitting next to TJ raised his head, smiling. He looked as if he'd not yet gotten out of high school, much less joined the army. He was tanned from the sun, his teeth white as cotton bulbs, his hair neither too dark nor too light—like wheat. Matthew pointed straight at this soldier and said, "You, you three-letter-man, you leave this one alone, unlike your brothers." The guy extended his middle finger, the sailor stepped back, and I could no longer see either TJ or the three-letter-man. "Fag," Matthew said.

"Hey, what the fuck?" Frankie said, pushing aside the sailor who gave up his spot for me. "Hey kid," Frankie put his hand on my shoulder, "I thought you were going to save my spot."

"Did you even wash those hands? Keep your paws off the kid, wop," Matthew said.

I looked up at Frankie, his face had a sheen on it, his hair dark. "What kind of dog you looking for?" I asked Frankie.

The crowd burst into laughter.

Frankie's scrunched up his face. "Huh? Oh, the dog. Yeah, a long one."

Everyone chuckled. Matthew poured half a vanilla milkshake into a glass and slid it to me.

"You hear about that Liberty Ship sunk off the coast last weekend?" a sailor said.

Everyone turned toward him. "No fucking way," Matthew said.

I stopped sipping, the paper straw collapsing.

"Those Nazi bastards," Frankie said.

"I thought we'd kicked the U-boats clear back to da faderland already," Matthew said.

"Ah, he's full of hooey. We'd have heard before now," Frankie said.

"I saw it," I said. TJ turned around in his booth and leaned into ours. The three-letter-man was gone.

"We saw it," TJ said.

"Oh, Applesauce, I don't—" Frankie said.

"—We saw it," I said.

"That where you were last week, Jimmy?" Matthew said.

I said, "Our Uncle George took—"

"Duh, George?" a Marine said. No one laughed.

"You should talk, jarhead. Clam up and let the kid yammer," Matthew said.

"He took us down Myrtle Beach—"

"Yup, that's where I heard it was," the sailor said.

"Look, you futzes grip my cookies. Shut up and let the kid tell the story," Matthew said.

They did, and I retold how we'd gone to the beach and witnessed the sinking of the ship. Everyone listened quietly, turning to TJ every so often. TJ nodded, but didn't interrupt. The sailor, unable to control himself despite Matthew's threats, confirmed it was a Liberty Ship, that the Navy, Army, and Civil Air Patrol hadn't sunk the U-boat, and that it was the escorts, gathering off the coast for the run, that came to help.

When I finished, no one said a thing. I sat up in the booth. One of the MPs told the soda jerk to bring me a Pepsi. I'd listened to many of them talk most of the summer, but now they all looked at me, as if I had something more to say. I hunched my shoulders and sipped on my soda.

"Wow, Jimmy. Some fucking story," Matthew said.

"Hey, we going to cut a rug tonight or what? I want to hear some boogie-woogie before the sun comes up," Frankie said. "No offense kid, but this place ain't getting me any closer to blotto."

"Yeah, yeah. We'll go. The joint down on Broad Street should be jumping by now," Matthew said. He motioned for me to get out. The soldiers and sailors filled the street, followed by the town folk. "You coming, Jimmy?"

"Nah, we ain't allowed to do that?"

"Says who?"

"Mama and Daddy."

"Mama and your pappy, huh? Well, I'll see ya next week. Unless, you going to take up my offer to come out to the camp. I'll show you around swell. You ain't afraid of them Nazis, are you?"

"I ain't afraid. That's for sure."

Frankie rushed back through the door into the thinning drug store. "Come on, Matthew. I got to get me a charity girl before they're all gone."

"Yeah, yeah. Dummy up. That reminds me, kid, who you come in with tonight?"

I looked around. TJ was in the back near the bathrooms talking with the three-letter-man. Lawrence spoke with Mr. Breedon. Frances and Irene weren't inside; I imagined, as usual, that Irene had dragged Frances up to Main Street and was looking at the toys in Kurtz's 5, .10, & .25c Store window. "My brothers and sisters."

"That was your sister, huh? Hey, I'd like to meet her some time."

I first thought he meant Irene, then realized he meant Frances.

"I've got to amscray. Next week, kiddo."

TJ smiled as the three-letter-man shook his hand, holding the shake for a long time. Between the drug store's clatter of "Pepsi Cola hits the spot," and "Mr. Breedon, hey, Mr. Breedon," and "How much?" and the ringing of the register and the passing of the cars on the streets and the soldiers laughing and shouting and the teenagers pushing through the doorway, I couldn't hear anything from where TJ leaned. He and the soldier chuckled about something. "Europe . . .," the soldier's mouth seemed to say.

The soldier seemed without companions. TJ usually avoided the uniforms, preferring to talk with the kids from the other farms who mostly stayed outside, sitting on the curb. I wanted to know what they spoke of and I felt jealous that TJ was getting news and learning about the war. He'd walked in on my thing to do on Saturdays.

Breedon's Drug quickly became almost empty. A few adults remained at the counter. I heard Lawrence's deep voice talking about corn.

TJ and the soldier's conversation seemed private. They did not speak loudly, they did not stand near anyone else. When people passed them to go into the bathroom, they stopped talking. I thought that I could hear a word or two matched with watching their mouths move.

"Saturday night . . .tavern . . ." he seemed to say.

They broke the long hand shake and the soldier headed for the door, not looking at me as he went by. He seemed very young up close—perhaps one of the soldiers who'd lied to get in early.

TJ leaned back against the wall. Lawrence sat in an empty booth while Mr. Breedon cleared dishes from the lunch counter. Frances and Irene returned and sat with Lawrence. Outside, the farm kids waited for the bus that would take us back into the fields. I looked about the empty drug store, my ears ringing from the gumbo of voices.

Outside, the bus screamed to a stop. Lawrence stood up as a signal to us that it was time to go.

10

Whenever the sweet corn seed was gone, Daddy had us start planting dent corn. Sometimes this came early, but not this time—we were pretty late getting the feed corn into the ground. The sweet corn already stood high and rocking in the summer breezes, when Daddy came into the kitchen, a handful of cotton between his hands. Planted in March, the creamy blossoms appearing in mid-April turning into pink and dark red flowers, the cotton bolls opened later in May and we let them dry and fluff until July.

"Early?" Mama said.

"Damned early." Daddy tossed the cotton onto the table. "They're ready to go now. Damned weather." He pushed his hat back far on his head and scratched his forehead.

"What about the peanuts?" Lawrence asked.

"Damned if they ain't ready, too." Daddy pulled a handful from his pocket.

"We got a lot of work to do, huh?' Mama said.

Daddy nodded. I went on down to the barn.

During harvest, breakfast came before the rooster crowed, the stars full and drowsy. As the eastern sky turned first blue then moved on to pinks and reds, Daddy doled out our daily requirement. "Frances, two hundred. Lawrence, two hundred. TJ, one fifty. Jimmy, one twenty-five." I always wanted to ask Daddy how many pounds he would pick, but I knew I'd get slapped and I had no reason to doubt that Daddy hadn't picked 250 to 300 pounds or more.

Pulling as fast as we could, ignoring the barbs on the leaves, the cotton bugs, and cotton boll worms, we'd fill our burlap sacks, then dump them onto burlap sheets, tie up the four corners, and pile them alongside the road.

We pulled as the sun rose turning the coolness of the fields into fiery hell. We pulled into dinner when Mama brought pork-chops and biscuits out to us. We pulled into supper when Mama hauled fried chicken into the field to feed her children. We pulled all day because Daddy had given us our requirements and we would pull all night until we'd stacked up all the cotton alongside the road waiting for the wagon. Daddy stomped and shouted when supper came and went and we weren't finished because it would be too dark to weigh the sheets and too late to take them to the Miller's gin, so Daddy would have to do it in the morning and miss pulling time. "Damn it," he said, huffing off toward home.

TJ and I stretched out on top of the tied cotton sheets waiting for Lawrence to come back with the wagon so we could load the bales. Sweat still dribbled down my forehead. My shirt clung to me, damp and heavy. Stink drew the flies.

"Red sky at night, farmer's delight," I said as the last of the purple and red clouds turned dark. Mosquitoes buzzed around my ears. Lightning bugs lit, went dark, then lit again. The wind brought in the salt smell of the sea, reminding me of our visit to Myrtle Beach. "Red sun in morning, farmer's warning."

"It was red last night. I don't think I'd call this day a 'delight,'" TJ said.

"Proverb don't mean it'll happen right away," I said.

TJ swatted a mosquito on his leg. "Yeah."

My eyes flickered. I forced them open, but as soon as my thoughts turned to the sky again, they flickered shut. When I opened them, TJ sat humming a song I didn't recognize and the stars seeped through the thinning clouds. "Where's Lawrence with that wagon? I want to go to bed sometime today."

"Uncle George says them there stars are being looked

at by people all over the place at the same time." TJ brushed his hand across his eyes.

"Yup." I heard myself talking, but I was floating in the clouds, reaching for stars. "Think they see them in London?"

"Yeah. I think so." TJ rolled onto his side and threw a piece of grass at me.

"Where else?" I rolled onto my side facing TJ. Crickets chirped as the temperature settled.

"I want to go to New York."

"I saw a picture where the Nazis dropped a bomb right onto Buckingham Palace." We were just talking. Each thing had something to do with the other, but we didn't really care how they connected. We'd sheeted cotton all day. We thought cotton all day. We sucked on cuts from cotton leaves all day. It was good to talk about anything but cotton.

"Yeah. I wonder what the stars look like from top of the Empire State Building." TJ rolled back and put his hands behind his head.

"Yah, Yah, get on there," Lawrence's voice floated across the harvested field. Wheels rattled and the blubbering snort of the old nag clearing her mouth mixed with the crickets.

"They look the same," I said.

"Huh?" TJ brushed grass and dirt from his shirt and britches. He'd dozed off in the second or two since he'd laid flat.

"Them stars look the same from the top of the Empire State Building." I stood, stretched, and shook the dirt out of my hair.

TJ wrinkled his forehead at me and then shook his head. "Well, I'd like to see them from up there anyways."

"You think they'd let just anyone go up to the top of the Empire State Building?"

"You think they let just anyone go to London?"

Lawrence stopped the wagon next to the first tied up burlap sheets. "Alright boys, lets get to it." I never liked Lawrence calling me "boy." It wasn't the "boy" Mama used when she felt happy or frustrated and couldn't remember the name of one of her five children. Nor did he say his "boy" like in "paperboy" or "bag boy." Lawrence didn't say "boy" the way people used to call a nameless child. He called "boy" the way slave owners used to address their property. His boy was the "boy" Mama didn't want us using when talking to a Negro man. It was the "boy" the Sheriff used for crooks. He got his "boy" from Daddy, who used it to weaken the knees, flush the faces, and ball up the insides of his three sons. I didn't like to hear Lawrence's "boy," but when Daddy wasn't around Lawrence had charge of us. "Let's haul them up, boys."

I dragged the bales, the burlap digging into my skin, my fingers feeling as if bees stung them, across the dusty ground to the side of the cart where TJ pushed and shoved them onto the gate. Lawrence then flung and tossed the bales into piles. I leaned against the wagon wanting to rest. Pale light covered the fields. When we'd finished stacking the first pile, Lawrence got down and between the three of us, we pulled ropes taut across them. I did this senseless, only thinking of sleep, forcing my eyelids open. At the second pile, sweat dropping from our foreheads, our pace matched the rhythm of the crickets.

"I know what you been doing," Lawrence said, tossing a bale onto the pile.

"Huh?" I asked, drifting back to the farm.

"Yeah. Hmm," TJ said. Lawrence hadn't been talking to me.

I'd been wondering for weeks when Lawrence would say something to TJ about his disappearing. Lawrence usually stayed quiet about anything when it came to Daddy possibly whipping him for not being in charge. He had a "bushwa mouth," as Mama would say. Yet, he'd been silent despite the possibility he'd get punished for letting TJ wander. Lawrence had been aiming his slave-days "boy" at TJ.

"You going to get in trouble, boy." Lawrence tossed another bale.

"Yeah? Nah." TJ pushed a sheet onto the wagon.

"When you get caught, you're likely going to get us all in trouble. Especially me." Lawrence pulled the bale from TJ. They moved from one bale to the other. Stiff.

"Ain't no trouble," TJ said.

What was good for the wandering gander was good

for the flock. If he got whooped bad enough so he couldn't work, we'd have to pick up his share. Either way, no one wanted to see anyone punished for being stupid.

"Uh, huh." Lawrence tossed the last bale.

I went around to the other side of the wagon to receive the tie-down rope.

"Ain't no trouble." TJ looped the rope in his hands.

"Boy, how can you stand there and say there ain't no trouble?" Lawrence wiped his head with his kerchief.

"You don't know."

"I know." Lawrence pulled the ropes running the length of the cart so tight that the top bales eked out a deep place for the coils. I could feel the boiling. These two glowed, their faces bright in the rising moonlight, jaws locked.

TJ tossed his rope across the pile. He turned and looked at the black shadows beneath the brim of Lawrence's hat where brown eyes should be. "You don't know nothing."

"I know you been out at night."

"Yeah." As he pulled on the ropes, his hands and arms shook. Fear. Anger. I thought that this might come to blows. Lawrence snorted like an unbroken horse. TJ breathed fast and heavy. Lawrence's temples throbbed. TJ's forehead turned red and dots of sweat dripped down. The two looked like they wanted to jump on each other, but TJ wouldn't start it because he was too timid. Lawrence would.

"I know you wandered off down the beach for most of the night."

"Yeah." TJ pulled the next set of ropes.

"'Yeah.' 'Yeah.' Is that all you can say, boy."

"Yeah." TJ yanked the two ends of the rope into the first part of a knot. "You don't know nothing."

"I know plenty."

"You know I've been out and not with you all the time," TJ said, his teeth grinding. "You don't know!" TJ barked.

The two stepped toward the nag's head. The glared at each other across her back. Lawrence's whole face lay deep in shadow beneath his hat. TJ's chest rose and fell heavy and fast.

Lawrence pulled on the nag's bit. "I'll find out," he said over his shoulder.

"Yeah." TJ looked back toward me, then across the silver field. "Dandy. You find out."

"I will." Lawrence stopped, dropped the lead, and stomped back toward us.

TJ turned and faced him, Lawrence wider and taller, a tree, TJ, a sapling. "When I do, I'll . . . " TJ just stood there.

I waited for the first blow to come from Lawrence. Humid night air clung to them, sticking their shirts to their skin. Wind blew across the field throwing chaff and dust into the air. "I will," Lawrence said, then wheeled on his heel back toward the mule and wagon.

I don't know what was different, but I could tell something had changed by the way Lawrence kept his back straight and the distance his voice held when he spoke at TJ.

"You don't know nothing." TJ's words were lost in the gaining breeze.

11

We worked well into the night all week, our pace quickening as Saturday night grew closer. On Friday, Daddy told Frances and Lawrence to do 250 pounds of cotton each, TJ to do 200, and me to do 150. He didn't need to say it—we knew that he meant do it or no going out Saturday night. Lawrence and TJ nodded, not looking at each other. TJ had taken to sleeping on the floor at night.

On Saturday night, our fingers sore and stiff from picking, we tramped toward the theater down the dusty streets of Bennesttsville. Frances pulled out ahead of the rest of us to walk next to Lawrence. "Can I sit in the balcony tonight?" she said, quietly, her eyes on the sidewalk.

"What in tarnation for?" Lawrence didn't look up when he said it. He had his hands stuffed deep into the side pockets of his dungarees.

Negro folk sat in the balcony, if they came over from The Gulf, just the other side of the courthouse square. Soldiers liked to sit up there, too.

"Hey, yeah. Can we all sit upstairs?" I said.

Frances glanced back at me, stretching her eyes, begging me to be quiet. Those who sat below the balcony smelled of perfumes and store-bought soap. Upstairs smelled of sweat and smoke, the stench falling over the balcony wall and sinking into the main seats.

I whispered to TJ, "Why she want to sit up there?" He

looked around, into corners, at every face that passed. He hunched his shoulders.

Irene strayed behind, stopping to look at the toys in Kurtz's window, then running to catch up.

Frances and Lawrence whispered to each other. I couldn't hear. I watched the patches of every passing service man, looking for new ones, for anything different because I knew that new patches meant new units and new units meant the soldiers, who had begun to blend in my mind, came from different places. I looked for someone who had been in the Pacific fighting the Japs.

Irene caught up and took TJ's hand. "Stop it, Irene," TJ said. "I ain't holding your hand."

"Come here, baby," I said. She looked up to TJ, who still peeked into corners, up alleys, and kept glancing behind us. She dropped his hand and ran to me. She was getting too big to pick up. Her hand felt gritty and tiny. "Ahh, Reenie, you been leaning against something." I stopped and wiped brick dust from her palm.

Just as we got to the ticket booth, drizzle started falling. Frances took Lawrence by the arm and pulled him to the wall. "Ya'll go on. I'll get the tickets," she said.

When we went through the door, a man in a brown hat glanced over at Lawrence and Frances. He watched for a moment, then went back to looking at a lobby card for *National Velvet.*

Her whispering done, Frances said, "Lawrence Quick! I pay for these tickets and I'm a grown woman now and I want to sit in the balcony and--"

"--What you want to go up there for?" Lawrence looked through the doors at us, but I kept my head down while kicking a piece of thread on the red carpet of the lobby.

The man in the brown hat looked at them again. He looked as if he wanted to say something, glancing between them and the poster and the usher just inside the door. I wondered if he knew they were brother and sister, because they looked like they were fighting like man and wife. TJ and Irene counted their steel pennies, the metal clinking together, by the candy jars counting how much peanuts or walnuts or honey sticks they could buy. Frances gave us all pennies and when Uncle George came, he handed out dimes and quarters and always a dollar or two just before he left.

Frances looked up at Lawrence. I thought she turned her head toward me, then back to him. "Because." She tried to keep her voice low. "Because I just want to."

"Stop this foolishness." Lawrence took a step toward the doors, but Frances touched his arm. He stopped.

"I . . . Oh, please, Lawrence."

I don't know if she had tears coming up in her eyes or if her face was flushed or if her teeth were grinding, but I could feel Lawrence deflate as a cool breeze blew up the wide theater entrance. "Tell me what for?"

"No." Frances took a step toward the street as if she might leave.

"Then come on. Woody Woodpecker will be starting soon." Lawrence stepped toward the doors, but stopped when Frances didn't follow.

Irene sat against the wall beneath a lobby card advertising *Lifeboat*. I leaned against the jamb of the exit door, but they'd forgotten I was there. "Please." Frances said. "I just need some time alone. Don't you understand?"

I felt sorry for Frances. Until she went to work in town, every hour of her life had involved taking care of us. Then, with the little money she earned tying mosquito netting and camouflage netting, she spent much of it on us. She'd made friends with those who worked in the factory and spoke of them around the dinner table. She began to know as much about the uniforms and the war as I did. Like the late pumpkins we planted that had only a slim chance of flowering for harvest, Frances took a late interest in the world outside of us kids.

They didn't know I could hear them. They didn't care. They weren't mad--just determined. "What are you talking about?" Lawrence said.

The drizzle had turned into a heavy rain. A car splashed by sending a rooster's tail of mud onto the sidewalk. "I just need some time."

"What for? You sick?" Lawrence touched Frances' shoulder, but she stepped away into the cold rain. She looked into the gray sky. With clear drops covering her face, she stepped back beneath the overhang.

Me, TJ, and Irene stood in the doorway, stepping

aside to let the town folk in, then returning to our positions like a fleshy door. When Frances saw us, she went to the ticket booth and bought our tickets. "Ya'll go on inside."

"The cartoon--," TJ said.

"--We'll be there. Go on." Turning her back to us, she handed Lawrence a ticket. "Go on," she said to him. "I'm fine."

Lawrence just looked at her. Something electric buzzed above their heads. I knew he wanted to be the boss over her, to make her shrink beneath him, to make her beg, to give her permission, to call her "girl," and laugh within his mean self when he got his way while she didn't get anything she wanted. Lawrence's face seemed swollen, but his temples weren't throbbing from his jaw clenching and releasing. "Who'll help me with them?" he said, tossing his head toward us, as if we were the hogs ready to be herded for slaughter.

"Jesus, Lawrence. That's the point. They ain't kittens. Irene's only one needs any watching. Christ, watch them yourself for awhile." His temples and forehead throbbed, the high hairline red and glowing. "Stop being a bully." Frances wiped her hand across her face as if she were removing wet mud. "Come on."

Lawrence nodded. Frances turned, saw me staring at them, and winked awkwardly and stiffly. Then, when she passed me like a breeze moving through the corn, a real smile covered her face. She bought two popcorns to share and each of us a Pepsi, plus a bag full of maple peanuts. She kissed Irene, who looked like she might toss a fit, but Lawrence took her hand and went into the hall, Woody already laughing and bouncing about the screen, Irene forgetting about missing her sister. Frances slapped TJ and me on our shoulders and went up the stairs to the balcony while we found our regular seats in the back against the musty red curtains.

By coming in so late, we missed the newsreel that I was sure would be about the Allies landing in Normandy, but rather than being sore, I figured I'd have to ask someone what had been said while waiting for the bus after the movie. When Woody finished bouncing off across the screen laughing, the trailer for *Gaslight* passed by; all the

71

while I wondered why Frances wanted to sit in the balcony so badly. I kept turning around, stretching my neck till I felt the muscles popping, looking up hoping to see her through the smoke and flickering lights of the movie. I figured she must be with Mary, the girl who shared the job at the factory, because she was near about the only person Frances knew in town. Irene sat on one side of Lawrence, me on the other, and TJ against the aisle. Each time I turned to look, Lawrence poked me.

Lobby cards had told of the coming of a Hitchcock movie called *Lifeboat*. For what seemed like years, I'd look at that gray and black scene, a ship half sunk in the back, a U-boat drifting away beneath the waves, people in a little dingy, a hand reaching out of the water for help.

"From the master of suspense," the announcer said, "comes the most important movie of the war." From deep inside the picture along a horizon of gray water, gray clouds, gray sky, taller than the town's clock tower "Alfred Hitchcock's" followed by "Lifeboat" raced toward us. The teaser, like a little movie, told just enough to get the kids quiet, the boys leaning forward shushing the girls who didn't care much for the war picture and wanted *Arsenic and Old Lace* to get started. I said "Geez," low and quiet, thinking they shouldn't let girls come to the movies if they're going to be all fidgety.

I'd hoped that I would find answers about the sinking of a ship that had been with me since Myrtle Beach. I wondered what drowning felt like. That night, the sky roaring with airplanes and flashes of light, the stench of gunpowder floating in-land on the wind, I thought that someone out there had been a hero, someone had been a coward, and many had died quiet and simple. I wanted Alfred Hitchcock to answer my questions, but the teaser only added to my suspense.

I knew Matthew really good, but he was a soldier. I didn't think it was right to find a sailor who'd been on a sinking ship to ask him about it. Living through it once must have been bad enough—weren't no sense repeating to a farm boy what must have been tough.

While *Arsenic and Old Lace* played on, I fidgeted worse than the girls during a battle scene. I looked back for Frances, smelled the popcorn and butter, wished people didn't smoke in the theater, listened to soldiers laughing in the balcony, saw Irene suck her thumb while sleeping next to Lawrence. I dozed and tried to watch and scratched some rash on my leg. That's what happens when a person gets too used to something—they take it for granted and don't appreciate what they got, and it was a shame because Frances spent good money on those movies.

We didn't much match the town folk. Our clothes were hand-me-downs, patched with burlap, flour sack, and stitching. We'd always wash before coming to town, but people looked at us as if they could smell the hogs or the farm following us in a cloud. We stuck together and tried to sit away from everyone, but getting there late left only a few seats in the back. Red curtains hung from the walls and at the edges of the silver screen. The chairs padded, covered in cloth, showed dark stains where hundreds of bodies had sat. Ceiling fans whirred, forcing warm air down and hot up.

Just as I caught on to the movie, Cary Grant making everyone laugh, the two old ladies killing people, burying them in the basement, hiding what they'd done, Lawrence got up and whispered to me, "Get Frances."

He had Irene by the arm, still groggy and unaware, stepping past me. TJ had slipped out. I understood Lawrence's anger. Wherever TJ had gone off to this time, Lawrence would find him.

Two Marines and two town girls stumbled down the stairs leading to the balcony. I stood aside and could smell the heavy cigarette smoke seeping down from above, a light cloud of it drifting along the hallway. The carpet along the step edges was frayed so that the brown backing poked through. I thought there might be a guard on the first landing, but I saw only spilled popcorn. I thought there might be an usher at the top of the stairs who would tell me I was too young, not a Negro, not a soldier, too smelly, that I'd have to turn around and go back, but no one stood there. The hallway behind the balcony stunk of sweat. Two sailors sat on a bench by the entrance to the toilets, smoking and talking. A Negro girl leaned on a counter selling cigars, boiled peanuts, and popcorn. Another staircase exited the other side; I could hear cars passing on the street and a draft sometimes blew the smoke around. A sign hanging above those stairs read, "Coloreds Exit Here" with a giant hand, finger extended, pointing down. I didn't know another stand sold cigars. I had never thought to myself that I'd never seen Negros in the lobby downstairs, but knew they sometimes came to this theater rather than the one over in The Gulf.

Besides the girl behind the counter and the two sailors, it was empty and dark, the overhead lights turned low.

I waited at the closed double doors, my hand on the knob, the balcony forever a mystery to me about to be revealed, the ending of a Hitchcock film. When everyone laughed at something else Cary Grant must have done, I pulled the door, light spilled down the dark aisle and onto the screen below, a Negro man turned to me, then the door closed killing the light and I stood again in the darkness waiting for my eyes to get used to the haze and flickering.

"Hey, kid, sit down," a man's voiced whispered.

From the last row came murmurs and chuckling. A girl squeaked, but nothing funny was happening on the screen. Then I heard Frances say, "Jimmy boy? That you?"

I nodded, not knowing where her voice was coming from. I heard her whisper, "Excuse me, sir," then she stood next to me, having come from the back row.

A man said, "Sorry, bub," and appeared as Frances had.

"Where you going?" another voice said.

"SNAFU," the man's voice said.

Frances took me by the hand and pulled me into the balcony's lobby. Back into the dim light, I blinked and rubbed my eyes. Standing beside her was Matthew.

"Jimmy, what are you doing up here?" she said. I wondered the same. "Lawrence said--"

"—Lawrence told me to come get you."

Matthew combed back his hair with his hands. "The dogs are howling," he said, and walked off toward the toilets.

"TJ slinked off again. I think Lawrence is going after him."

Frances looked around, walked to the men's room door, cracked it and said, "Matt, I'll see you later." The

Negro girl and the two sailors gazed at Frances, then went back to doing nothing. She came back, taking my hand, and we headed down the stairs.

"You better not say anything about Matthew to Daddy. Or to Lawrence."

"Uh huh," I said.

"He's a really nice guy."

"Uh huh."

"He's from Baltimore, just like Uncle George. We met when I got the job." I thought back to Matthew asking about her and knew she was lying. "If Daddy knew, he'd can that job of mine. He's a really nice guy. He's my friend."

"Uh huh," I said, thinking of the friend idea because Matthew seemed to be my friend, too. "I know him. He's one of the fellas I talk with so much."

"Uh huh," she said, a little air letting out of her puffed up chest and shoulders. "You ain't going to tell, are you?"

"Tell? Heck no. You're old enough."

"Uh huh," she said. "Thanks, Jimmy boy."

Out front, heavy blackout curtains were pulled back from the front doors of the theater. Lawrence stood outside next to the ticket booth, his hands on his hips, looking up and down Clyde Street. Irene sat along the wall eating from the brown bag of nuts. Soldiers, sailors, and Marines mixed with town folk, farmers, and the civilians who worked for the War Department walked about the town. Their clothes lit up when they passed a store, then they disappeared into the darkness between. No lamps burned over the streets. The theater did not boast a bright marquee. Most places had their blackout curtains drawn, but a few let the light shine through.

"Where'd he go?" I said.

Lawrence hunched his shoulders. Pointing at Irene, he said, "Watch her. Come on, boy."

"Lawrence, you don't hurt him when you find him," Frances said, picking up Irene.

Next to the theater, Mr. Richardson's drugstore stood dark. He'd never taken to staying open late, and unlike Mr. Breedon, never put in a lunch counter or fountain.

The Ford dealer had the windows boarded, a sign painted across it read, "Reopen after the war." Around the corner on Main Street, Sanitary Café, run by the Greek, had no one in it but the cook and the Greek waiting for the movie to be over. Thompson's Drug closed and dark, having picked up the crowd before the movie. Lafayette Café, lonesome, its front door open, old couples eating, flies swarming in and out.

Lawrence strode from place to place, his legs stretching out, pulling him along faster with each step, me almost running to keep up. His head swung and looked into the empty lots and dark stores, peeking wherever he could. I looked where he looked, seeing nothing but the darkness that war brings to a town that waits for the enemy.

Across from JC Penney's, Breedon's Drugstore and Soda Fountain looked like something right out of Hollywood. Light fell from Mr. Breedon's windows splashing brightness across the street—the warden not minding so long as the store had curtains ready to be drawn. We ran between the few cars passing down Main Street, plumes of mud behind them. A few town kids sat on the stools and in the booths, but no more than half a dozen. TJ wasn't among those bathed in light.

Across Marlboro Street, opposite the courthouse, along McCall's Block, the Strauss Company Store just being locked up by the owner, its blackout curtains pulled and its doors shuttered.

Lawrence didn't pause for the cars, their headlights taped over so that only slits allowed a sliver of light to guide the drivers. He walked behind them, sometime in front, not waiting, a driver honked his horn, a bumper brushed his leg, me running, nodding, apologizing as I tried to keep up.

The corners where school friends and farmers gathered to talk and smoke and tell dirty jokes stood empty. Everyone was inside the theater or the drug stores or the cafes or home in bed or in The Rendezvous Saloon behind the courthouse, next to the fire department, its single truck locked up waiting for a blaze.

The Rendezvous Saloon, the only beer joint in the town, sat well inside the Negro part of Bennettsville, only no one called that part of town Bennettsville despite there being no barrier, no change in streets, no difference in sidewalk. Negro Bennettsville was called The Gulf, though I never knew why—I always thought because the Gulf of Mexico must have black water.

Sinatra's smooth voice singing "Stormy Weather" wavered through the noise of the crowd crammed into the bar. An air raid warden leaned against the window on a barstool, his helmet propped against the building, his armband rolled down covering the "CD" stitched in felt. Someone had painted "The Rendezvous" on the window in red letters half a foot high. "You think he went in there?" I said. I knew TJ had better not have. If he had, Lawrence would have to tell. If someone saw TJ in there and told Daddy there'd be a whooping coming Lawrence's way.

Lawrence squeezed past two sailors on the stoop.

"Amscray," someone said.

"Hey, hey," others shouted, as Lawrence tried to work his way in.

Shouts and jeers, "Give him the bum's rush," came from the compressed crowd as they shot him back out the door like a cannonball.

I laughed a little as he stumbled toward the street. He looked as if he'd been in the bar all day and was ready to tumble over, but he caught himself on a signpost, turned like a bull, then, as if only a balloon, the air went out of him. His face looked strained, the vein in his temple and forehead visible even in the dim light. He stomped over to the window.

We pressed our faces against the glass on either side of the warden's body. Only a small gap existed between a paper sign saying, "Soldiers and Sailors Welcome," and the dark curtain held against the wall with old hemp rope. Olive drab and khaki pant legs and black shoes mingled with the red light. A lady's leg, the heel of her shoe splintering, the painted fake stockings running with sweat, crossed our path and then disappeared. I could see little else.

"What now?" I said, but Lawrence was gone. The air raid warden snored. I looked both ways up the street. Darkness filled the road. The slits from taped-over headlights made the cars look like giant cats. Smoke seeped from the bar, glowing red.

Up the alley next to the saloon, I could see the ends of a dozen cigarettes burning in the night. Sinatra sounded mute in the dimness.

"Hey, boy," someone in the alley said. This "boy" didn't sound like any I'd heard before. This "boy" had no face or name. I would find this "boy" in nightmares, the "boy" heard in dark alleys on Saturday nights. I turned toward the voice, but only a shadow, somehow darker than the night, stood against the wall--faceless, nameless.

Between piles of crates, figures moved beneath khaki trench coats like chickens in a burlap sack. Old urine, stinking somewhere in the dark, stung my nose, human stench worse than cow or pig smell. Stale, old beer and the acid reek of vomit caused me to gag. Smoke from cigarettes smelled welcoming, less offensive, as men appeared, glowing from matches and cigarette ends. A silence lingered in the air, spreading into me. Something more than drinking went on in that alley—love and sex and something rough.

Passing the tavern's alley door, red light eked out of it and Sinatra belched and hummed "Close to You" through the garble of voices. I imagined the entrance to Hell must be similar to this. Glasses clinked. Darkness ate the light, the smoke, the sounds. Everything but the smell.

Behind the door, deeper in the alley, men held glasses of beer. Red flames burned tobacco. Like a fence, these men living in shadows, spread across the alley. Their attitude said, don't look here. I wondered why the quiet seemed so full. No one spoke. Unlike the bar, no one laughed or chuckled. No slapping of backs or dirty jokes. These dark shadows of men stood one hand in a pocket, the other around a mug, or a cigarette, the tip moving from face to side, the uniforms glowing. Sipping every few seconds like the tick of a clock.

"Lawrence?" I said, my voice hissing.

"Shut up kid," someone answered from a deep shadow.

Behind the dim and fleshy fence, a scuffle of feet and unheard whispers escaped. "Lawrence?" I wheezed. "TJ?"

"I'll be your Lawrence," another shadow said.

Sinatra screeched to a halt as someone pulled the

needle across the vinyl killing the violins. A roar of protests shook the night air. Those in the alley ran toward the main street. "Quiet! Quiet!" shouted the air raid warden. Main Street filled with people looking toward the sky. "Put those lights out!" the warden yelled. "Draw the shades." The town disappeared into veiled darkness.

Cigarettes and the red light of the bar extinguished, the alley's darkness was complete. I heard a thump. Silence settled over the town. A distant thrum grew louder. Bombers and escorts. I knew it. Everyone who stopped talking and looked toward the sky knew it, but the game had to be played. Just in case. Pearl Harbor and rumors about other attacks kept people ready for another enemy surprise. One soldier once told me that a Jap bomber had made it all the way to Oregon, but he was the only one to ever mention it.

I heard feet scrape across the ground, then running toward me. A dark shadow, a face, a head, just a moment before my legs flew out and my head thumped something hard and my eyes filled with bursts of white. For a second I thought one of the planes had dropped a bomb, but as I fell to the ground, I looked into a dark face and recognized the black outline of the jaw and the short hair as the boy-soldier I'd seen in Breedon's talking with TJ. Then he sprung up, stepped on my hand, and ran down the alley.

The thrum grew loud above us now. No one moved. Everybody held their breaths. "They're ours," the warden said. At once, the air rustled as everyone exhaled. The dark alley filled with green light, once, twice, three times as the warden raised his lantern. "All clear! All clear!"

"You alright, Jimmy?" Lawrence asked from the darkness. My hand ached and I felt blood seeping from my knee. A lump would likely grow on my forehead where the other guy's head hit mine.

I pushed myself off the rough alley. "Yeah, I hope this is only water," I said, wiping my hands on my pants, I smelled it stinking of piss and beer. As the lights flickered back on in the bar and the curtains were pulled back, I could see Lawrence holding TJ up around his waist. "Holy crap! What happened?" I took TJ's other arm and draped it across my shoulders. "What happened?" TJ pushed away from

Lawrence and put all of his weight on me; my legs groaned as I almost fell over.

Lawrence looked at TJ. As we came to the end of the alley, I could see blood leaking from TJ's nose. "I guess someone beat him up," Lawrence said. I grabbed TJ's arm and slung it over my shoulder as we sat him on the curb. TJ squinted up at Lawrence, then looked away. Blood seeped down his face, dripping from his chin, running down his neck, soaking his shirt. A slight cut above his eye had dribbled but seemed to be already closing up. Bruises around his eyes already forming looked like deep bags of dirt.

"Lawrence!" I gritted my teeth together. "Damn it Lawrence. Damn it! Now we're all going to get in trouble. Damn it!"

TJ sat on the curb, his feet in the gutter. He groaned, put his forehead in his hands, and spit blood, a red stream of dribble hanging down from his swollen lip. I thought he might lose a tooth.

Frances rounded the corner at Clyde and Main, running down the street so that her flower-print frock flew out behind her, Irene jostling in Frances' arms.

I strained to hold Irene as Frances passed her to me. "Oh God, dear God! TJ what happened? Lawrence, Lawrence, what happened? Oh, oh!" Frances said. She took the bottom of her dress to mop away some of the blood.

A Negro woman came up the street from The Gulf wringing the water from a dripping cloth. "Here, you'll need this there," she said.

I sat Irene down and took the cloth, "Thank you," I said. I held it to TJ's nose. He flinched, pushing my hand away, held the cloth himself.

A crowd stood along the streets talking about the planes that had passed and the rumors of bombing and how they knew it couldn't be Nazis and a mumble started as they noticed us healing our brother.

Lawrence stood back, his hat brim rolling and unrolling in one hand, the other shoved deep into a pocket, his hair stuck to his head with sweat that continued down his forehead, a drop falling from the tip of his nose, the knees of his overalls muddy, the way mine were, a mix of vomit, beer, piss, alley crap. His knuckles showed signs of redness and rawness.

"You going to be okay?" Frances said to TJ, kneeling in the street, bending to look up into his down-turned eyes.

He shook his head, whispering, "No."

Frances sprung up, marched toward Lawrence, pushed him back with her hands. She hissed, "What happened? What happened?"

"I found him up that there alley. Someone beat him up. Don't like it too much that we're Cherokees, I suppose," Lawrence said, his voice low and slow.

The Hunter and Usher Farm Bus came to a stop up the street by Breedon's Drug, operated by collecting gas rations from farmers whose ragged Model T's and ancient Model A pickups, regardless of the availability of gas, were too expensive, too old, too beat up to run without spare parts and rubber for tires.

Frances and I got TJ to his feet. He walked all right, but drifted here and there like the men who wandered from The Rendezvous and fell down beneath the Confederate Soldier Memorial.

When Lawrence tried to help TJ get onto the bus, TJ said through swollen lips, "Don't touch me." I knew he hurt. It looked bad. People sometimes say it looks worse than it feels. Not for TJ, not this time, I'm sure it hurt.

Frances sat on the bus with her arm around TJ's shoulders, moping at the blood, kissing the side of his head. I sat behind them, Irene sleeping against my ribs, drooling onto my shirt. Lawrence stood in the back, rocking side to side along the lumbering roads.

I wasn't sure just what I'd seen in that alley. Fight or not, drinking, smoking, carousing, whatever went on, there'd be a heap of hell and high water to pay.

Daddy wouldn't be there when we got home. He'd be at a fish fry where the men sat around talking about what things needed help with that season—some chopping, the hog slaughter, borrowing each others' mules and plows. Daddy told us that morning we'd have to do something about Old Lady Copper since her husband went down ill and the boys had gone off to the war but the crop stood tall along their land. Then they'd play cards, so I guessed, because I never figured it took all night to talk about a couple of things like that.

12

"*O*h my, oh my," Mama said when the pale candlelight fell across us. She pulled the end of her apron up to her mouth and then dabbed tears from her face. "What happened?" I supported TJ on one side while Frances had his arm on the other. We stepped onto the stoop, Mama said, "No, no. Don't bring him in here bleeding like that. No, no."

"Mama," Frances said, pushing the word out fast.

"No, no." Mama brushed the sand off the stoop, her hand rasping away the grains. "I can clean him up just as good out here. Oh, my."

She went inside and clattered together some pots. "Jimmy, run and fetch me some water," she called out. She stopped for a second and wiped her eyes and head with the lace-edged apron.

"Lawrence. Run over and get Daddy from the McCormick's," Frances said.

Lawrence held Irene in his arms. His face seemed lost. His skin ticked just near his eye.

One of the hounds charged up and licked at the blood on TJ's arm. "Get," I said, kicking at it as I hauled back a bucket of water. It stepped away, tail wagging, and sat on its haunches.

"Lawrence?" Frances said.

"I'll go," I said.

"No. Your Daddy will be home before long," Mama said, coming through the door. She sat a pan of water down. "What happened? Oh, God above."

"Some sort of fight," Frances said.

Lawrence stepped past us, Irene still in his arms. He carried her into the girls' bedroom.

Most of the blood had stopped eking down TJ's face. It was dry and flaky. Dark, like spilled ink, shadowed in the dim light. A few spots opened up, shining. Mama dabbed at them, slathering Thompson's Balm. TJ winched with her prodding.

"TJ, honey, why you in town fighting?" Mama said.

TJ lifted his shoulders a little.

I went into the house. The only light came from the radio's yellow face in the living room. I heard the faint trumpets of Glenn Miller. I felt the air pushing on me, wet, heavy. All the windows stood open. The girls' room black and deep, facing away from the moon, not a candle or lamp lit. I smelled Lawrence's musky sweat.

"Night, night," he said to Irene.

He stepped out of the girls' room and closed the door, it squeaking, me thinking I should oil the hinges.

As he came into the living room, I got up close to him. "What was that?" I said. My low voice came out as if I were gargling. "What the hell happened back there?"

"Ain't for you to question me, boy," Lawrence said. "And watch your language."

"Lawrence—" I said. He grabbed me under my arm. His fingers squeezed tight, my skin pinched, I opened my mouth to scream, but didn't. He dragged me toward the front door, shoved me onto the porch, then pulled the door shut, the panes vibrating.

"Listen here, boy. I went up that alley and found him . . . I found him fighting with some fellas. I don't know what the hell happened, but I ain't too happy that I'm about to get a whooping because of him."

"Lawrence—"

"—Shut up, will you? I should have told Daddy already about all this sneaking around."

One of the dogs barked just before I heard from the backyard Daddy say, "What in the hell is going on here?"

My bowels jumped and I thought I might crap myself

84

as I stood there.

Lawrence stepped down into the front yard. He looked as if he might take off across the field. He flung his hands about a couple of times, cursing in a whisper. "Horse shit," he said.

"Lawrence Quick!" Daddy called.

Lawrence stopped flinging his arms.

"See? He's going to tear me up."

"Just tell him what happened. You ain't the one sneaking off."

Daddy stood in the frame of the backdoor. "I ain't calling you again, boy. Get your ass up here now!"

"You know it don't matter, Jimmy." Lawrence pulled the front door open. Though the evening had become cooler, sweat leaked down the back of his neck. His collar was wet, his hair laid down flat and shiny. "Here, Daddy. I'm right here."

Lawrence stepped through the house in a few strides. I hadn't been called. I stepped in and slipped the hook onto the door so it wouldn't bang about if a breeze came up. I turned off the radio, then crossed through the kitchen and stood in the backdoor frame. Mama and Frances sat next to TJ. Daddy and Lawrence stood in the backyard. Lawrence stared at the ground.

"You supposed to be watching them, boy," Daddy said.

"Yes, sir," Lawrence said.

"You're the oldest."

"Yes, sir,"

"I ain't there, you in charge,"

"Yes, sir."

"Yes, sir? Yes, sir? That all you got to say about this?"

Lawrence put his hands deeper into his pockets. I don't know if he carried anything in there, but when he shoved down deep, he seemed to roll around a stone or a coin.

"Exactly what happened?"

Lawrence rolled the thing in his pocket. He didn't move. His head hung down. As big as Daddy, maybe bigger, it looked sort of funny to see the big man, Lawrence, cowering like a hound. If Lawrence had a tail, it would have been between his legs. I felt sad, because I knew that what came next would be a trip to the tool shed, and it had been some time since Daddy had taken Lawrence there.

"You planning on answering me, boy?" Lawrence turned his head toward TJ.

TJ looked in their direction, but I could tell he saw past them, perhaps at a distant star.

Lawrence nodded his head. "Yes, sir. Was some folk I ain't known too much. Was dark."

"Dark? Ain't no lights in that town?"

I stepped down from the stoop. "Air raid, Daddy," I said.

Daddy's forehead wrinkled, "Air raid?"

"That warden shuts down the lights if a flock of dragon flies go by," I said. "They were our planes."

"So during this air raid, when the town went dark, TJ finds himself in a scuffle?" Daddy shook his head. "That right, there, boy?" He said to TJ.

TJ's eyes refocused. His lips were swollen. His face seemed the color of candlelight. His cheeks were loose and turned down. His eyes darted toward Lawrence, then back to Daddy. "Was the Cranbull boys, I think, Daddy. Jumped me out the shadows calling me . . . ." He looked down at his feet, and I knew he was acting. ". . . called me half-breed, no good injun."

Daddy put his hands on his hips. "Where were you?" he said to Lawrence.

"I couldn't find him in the dark—" Lawrence said.

"—But he pulled him off of me," TJ said.

Daddy turned and walked toward the chicken coop. He kicked at a rock, tapped his forehead, disappeared beyond the reach of the pale light from the house, then came back. "This all happened in Bennettsville?"

We all nodded.

"I ain't never heard a word about anyone giving two cents about anyone being off the reservation." He tossed his hands into the air, and they slapped down to his sides. "Well, if that's the story you're sticking to, so be it." Lawrence's back seemed to relax. TJ returned to looking at the ground. "Nobsey," Daddy used Mama's nick name, "if you're done with him, they all need to get to bed."

Everyone but Lawrence and Daddy went inside. The two big Quick men walked down toward the tool shed and pigsty. They stood on the line where light could no longer reach and the black night pushed in toward our house.

I don't know what they said, but Daddy slapped Lawrence across the face. Lawrence didn't move much, but he stopped staring at the ground. He looked at Daddy straight on. It could have been that Daddy said, "Look at me," but something told me, by the way Daddy got angrier, his arms moving more, that Lawrence was trying to stare down Daddy. The last I saw before Mama shooed us off to bed, Daddy pointed toward the tool shed and Lawrence turned.

I lay on the bed next to TJ. "What happened?" I said.

"Shut up," TJ said.

"TJ, what happened?"

"I said, shut up!" He rolled over to face the window. I rolled to face the door.

I don't think TJ slept. I know I didn't. Sometime in the night, I think the Big Ben had struck one, I thought I heard, muffled and distant, the weak and rusty tool shed door squeal open, then slam shut. Then, there came the dampened sound of a whack, like when I took a shovel to a snake. A whack, like clapping hands. A whack. Another. Then another.

I dozed for a moment sometime in the night. I heard Daddy open the girls' door and say, "Frances, come out here."

Irene cried and Frances told her to go back to sleep.

Mama, Frances, and Daddy talked, but not Lawrence. I'd long known each person's whispers as they gathered around the kitchen table, not wanting to wake me or Irene. Mama would stand most of the time. She'd make tea with week-old leaves and grounds. She'd refill the Mason jars each time they went empty. Daddy would talk to Frances and talk to her and keep talking until she would wish, because she told me she did, that he would beat her instead of listening to him talk more.

At some point, between dozing, but never real sleep, TJ sat up, leaning against the wall. He cried, with his arms crossed. I could smell something different in the room.

Fart and sweat, mixed with the smell of tears and whatever happens when someone shivers too much. Some say that a person can smell fear—I thought that must be the smell coming off TJ.

"That's it. That's it," I heard Daddy say, the whispering gone for a moment.

"No, Daddy, please,"

"No more Saturday nights," Daddy said.

Frances pleaded more. TJ cried harder, but covered his mouth. I rolled over and hugged him, but after a few seconds he pushed me away.

I got up, leaned against the windowsill and watched a barn owl skim across the silver shining fields. I could have just hopped down out of the window and left. Gone to Baltimore to be with Uncle George. Gone somewhere not to be here. For a second, a plot came into my head to sneak into Daddy's room while he was sleeping and take the wood axe to him, landing it right into his skull, then I pushed that thought away and pounded the window sill a few times. I wanted to go to town. I hated TJ for messing up everything. I would miss seeing Matthew, and now Frankie. All I wanted to know about the war was not yet finished—really just begun.

The alley bothered me. It felt so strange. I remembered thinking that my image of Hell had always been somewhat like that alley. Something had been going on there. I thought gambling, but the men I'd always seen tossing dice bellowed happiness and shouting and having fun. I didn't know what else to make of it. More than anything, I couldn't figure why the soldier-boy in the drug store that TJ had been talking to would run from the alley so fast and so hard as to knock him and me to the ground. I touched the swelling bump on my head that no one else seemed to notice.

I sat down against the wall beneath the window. Cool, middle-night air fell onto me. As I dozed, in and out, I knew that Lawrence wasn't coming to bed, and I thought that maybe it hadn't been that same soldier-boy because it had been dark and I couldn't see all that well.

13

Mama stood at the back of the yard, near the edge of the garden where we grew peppers, melons, pumpkins, tomatoes, and other vegetables. Town folk called them "Victory Gardens," but we called it life. She scrubbed the red-stained rags she'd used to wipe up TJ with, then hung them across a hemp line strung between two saplings

In the barn, Frances pulled the stool off its peg and stroked the cow's head. Irene called the dumb cow "Ham," so we all did. "What happened last night, Jimmy boy?"

I went to the barn door, looked about the yard, and then closed it so no one could hear or walk in on us. The stench of manure and piss reminded me to clean out the stalls.

"I was going to ask you the same thing. Lawrence didn't come to bed."

"I didn't see him when Daddy called me out last night neither."

I hadn't slept much, except for those minutes between three and four a.m. when the world from the previous day dies and the next one is born. Big Ben chimes off those hours, but everyone's used to the clamor. "I thought there'd be more shouting," I said.

"Me too. Sorry if Daddy and I were too loud."

"Guess we ain't going to town no more." I dragged a bale of hale into Ham's stall.

Frances sat the stool next to Ham. "Maybe he'll let us after awhile. Got to keep TJ out of trouble, though." She pressed her cheek against the cow's side and closed her eyes before she pulled on Ham's teats. "I'm still working at the factory, though." She tugged at the cow like ripping cotton off the boll. Ham whacked her with her brittle tail.

I watched her pull at the cow for a minute or two, wanting to tell her I'd do it. It looked like she was hurting the old cow. "That when you'll see Matthew?"

"We're just friends, Jimmy."

"Up in the balcony?"

"Just friends." Frances pulled and Ham stomped. "I need some company." Ham swapped her, turned her head, bellowed a long sorrowful note. "We ain't talking about that, now are we?"

"Then what should we talk about? Whole world seems crazy to me."

Frances stopped and patted Ham's side. "Don't make no sense someone jumping TJ and calling him names. Ain't no one ever bother us in that town. They don't much like the smell of farmers, but they ain't never said nothing like what TJ said."

I wanted to milk Ham. Milking comforted and warmed me. Nuzzling up to Ham and listening to her stomachs churn and heart rumble reminded me of laying next to Mama's side in the living room while everyone listened to *The Bob Hope Show*.

She tried pulling again, but Ham whapped her twice and stomped her hoof. "What you see up that alley?"

"It was weird," I said, while dragging another bale of hay. "Quiet, smoky, dirty. Strange. Like walking in red fog."

"Red fog? Sure you weren't dreaming, boy?"

"That pink light they got in The Rendezvous made the smoke glow. I don't know what to say." I rolled the wheelbarrow over and shoveled a little before continuing. "Things were moving in the shadows. I swear, Hell must be like that alley." Unlike the inside of the bar, the alley seemed soundless. Faces glowed as the ends of cigarettes grew and died. I had the sense that people watched something, but I couldn't tell what. A wall of men seemed to guard a treasure. "I don't think it was just someone . . ."

Frances stopped milking and looked at me through the dim lantern light.

I shoveled and scooped manure into the wheelbarrow. "Well, go on."

"Lawrence was—." I shook my head.

"Lawrence?" Frances blinked at me a few times.

I tore apart a bale and spread it around Ham's stall. The rooster crowed as the sky turned to gray. "I didn't see anything." But, I knew.

"Nothing? What do you mean? Make sense."

"I didn't see Lawrence actually hit him."

"Lawrence hit him? Jimmy, stop stalling. Come out with it."

"There were a bunch of men strung across the back of the alley—"

"—Watching the fight."

"Let me finish." I flung a handful of straw at Ham's chewing jaws. Her cud smacked and slurped. "I don't know. They weren't watching anything. Smoking. Drinking. No talking." I turned the wick down as light seeped through the slats. The men in the alley hadn't frightened me, but they seemed scared of something. Or maybe not scared, but waiting, looking, wanting something. People tapped their feet. Glasses went to mouths for tiny sips of beer. Cigarettes grew red in the dark, flung to the ground, and others lit. No one touched in the red light, but something or someone moved in the dark.

"Jimmy!"

"Okay." My heart felt like hot water ran through it, warming all the pipes and chambers. "When the planes came, it got really quiet. The music stopped." I rested my arms on top of the stall door. Frances couldn't keep her rhythm and listen to me at the same time. Ham swatted and stomped each time Frances tugged like a boxer.

When Ham swapped Frances on the head again she pushed away from the cow, knocking the little stool over. "Guess this is why I don't do this chore much." She wiped milk off her arms and hands. "Go on, Jimmy. What are you saying?"

"Everyone waited to hear from the warden. Those men just rushed out. I thought it was because of the planes, but now I think it might have been to get out of Lawrence's way."

"You ain't making no sense, boy. What's Lawrence got to do with this?"

"He went down the alley looking for TJ." Whatever TJ was doing, he shouldn't have done it in town where Lawrence could catch him. "You know Lawrence would be angry enough to hit hard if he caught TJ doing something we'd all get in trouble for." Frances nodded. "I heard some feet moving. Next I know, I'm lying on the ground staring right at the soldier who knocked me down."

"You knew him?"

I pulled at a string sticking out from one of the buttons on my overalls. "Same fella was talking with TJ in Breedon's last week." Frances slapped my thread-pulling hand. "Next I know, Lawrence is helping me up and TJ looks like he'd fallen off a roof. Ain't nobody else in the alley but us, near as I could tell. And I don't think that soldier fella beat up TJ. They looked like they were getting along just fine in the drug store. Besides, looked like TJ could have whipped that boy's skinny butt here to the river and back."

"TJ was drinking and smoking. I'd bet my buttons he was."

I'd never smelled any alcohol on him, though smoke stuck to his clothes after we'd been in Breedon's. It stuck to everyone's clothes. "I don't know." I shrugged. "I don't think so."

"Then why . . . " The barn door clattered open and a morning breeze flung straw into the air. TJ stood in the opening, the morning shades of gray and pink behind him. He held a bundle in his hand.

"TJ, you ought not be up today. You oughta stay in bed and heal." Frances met him in the midway and took a rag and biscuits from him.

When he came in closer, I could see his swollen and black right eye. "Mama says ya'll can have these, but to come on. Breakfast's almost ready." His split lower lip and inflated nose blended blue and yellow. Lawrence's back and butt were indigo and violet and blistered the time he lost the mule and Daddy whooped him. Irene's teeth went through her lower lip when she fell while chasing a white-tailed rabbit across the yard, a jagged white scar still there.

But I'd never seen anything as bad as TJ's face—at least not on anyone living. His swollen upper lip, pulled back from his mouth revealing his teeth, which reminded me of the dead sailor hanging from the breakers down Myrtle Beach.

"TJ, you ought to be in bed." Frances pushed TJ's hair back revealing a long scuff across his forehead. The blood we cleaned the previous night seemed real and natural, but the splits and scrapes on my brother's face were not something I could recognize. I thought that if I'd passed TJ on a long deserted road, I wouldn't know him by looks alone.

"What?" He attempted a smile then shook his head. "Ain't no excuse I got tangled up last night; now I have to pull my share."

"Sunday, TJ. You can rest today. We'll take care of your chores." I'd fallen off a cart once when a hawk spooked the nag and my back felt sore and tired for a few days; I knew TJ must have hurt far worse.

"Already fed the chickens and slopped the pigs."

Frances turned toward me, then went to the barn door and pulled it shut. A gust of wind rushed down the midway, making the barn creak at the other end.

She put both hands on TJ's shoulders. "TJ, who did this to you?"

He looked at my eyes before looking past me. "I don't know."

"Come on." I put my arm across his shoulders. "Was it Lawrence." There, I'd said it. The air seemed thick with morning humidity.

TJ looked at the ground and pushed Frances' hands and my arm away. "I don't know. It was too dark." The blackout curtains had doused even the red bar light, shading the alley, but the fight must have begun before the curtains came down.

"Was it Lawrence?" Frances reached for TJ's hand.

"I don't know."

"Did he do this to you?" She pulled TJ's chin up. It hurt me enough to see the damage torn into my brother, but the tears trying to eke out of his swollen eyelids pressed on my heart and lungs. A rush of sad air escaped me in a quiet groan.

"It was Lawrence. After the boy ran out of the alley, there wasn't anyone else there," I said.

"I didn't say that." TJ turned back toward the barn door. "I told you, I don't know anybody who would do that to me. I don't know. It was too dark and I'm not sure what I did and I don't know." He pushed open the barn door. "Mama says come to breakfast," he called over his shoulder. His step and the way he didn't slam the barn door said that he wasn't mad, but he hurt somewhere we couldn't see.

Frances turned toward me. "What's going on, Jimmy?"

"It was Lawrence. I know it."

14

*A*t first, no one spoke at breakfast. TJ first sat on the rear stoop, where he broke apart a buttermilk biscuit and worked it between his swollen lips. He chewed, very slowly, only on one side, so I figured maybe he'd chipped a tooth.

After Daddy had eaten two biscuits and drank a whole jar of milk, he sat back in his chair and stretched his long arms toward the roof. "TJ, come in here and sit at the table."

A rooster chased after a flapping hen across the yard.

TJ stopped eating. The plate in his lap dangled and slid a bit. Then he stood up, bringing the plate with him. He marched in, put the plate down firmly on the table so that the milk in the Mason jars rocked. Then he pulled the chair out, screeching across the wood, and sat hard, like a sack of dry wood let down from a tall shoulder. He didn't eat, even though Daddy pointed at TJ's plate with his fork.

Frances ate, her head down. Irene hummed, but stopped when Mama lowered her brows in Irene's directions. I chewed fast, coughing on the spicy sausage patty, wanting to not be there.

Lawrence wasn't at breakfast and no one asked where he went.

As Mama washed up the pots, and everyone else had gone their Sunday ways without word, and Irene played with her wood blocks before the Zenith radio, I cleaned myself up, put on Uncle George's hand-me-downs, and said to Mama, "I'll go to prayer with you today."

She put the pot onto the narrow counter, knocking off one of Grandma's old plates. It broke on the floor, shards dashing about the wood planks.

"Oh, Lordy," she said. She bent and picked up the large pieces. I fetched the cornhusk broom and the wide wooden shim we swept mess onto. As I swept up the tiny sharp shards, I saw Mama's leg, purple, spotted, and swollen.

"You going to the Lord's house with me today?"

"Yes, ma'am."

"And I ain't got to ask or beg or threaten or nothing?"

"No, ma'am."

She leaned back on the sink, her hand on her hip, and raised one eyebrow. "Uh huh," she said.

"Pastor Myers going to be there?"

"Yes."

"What time we leaving?"

She ran her tongue along her teeth, then smiled and said, "Alright then. We'd better leave by half-past. My legs been bothering me more and more."

"I'll get the water," I said.

Though we left a half hour before we used to, we still got to church late. Mama walked a few yards, then stopped, then walked a few more, then stopped. The heat didn't press so badly, light dew hung to the leaves, a low fog meandered in the dips of the fields and trees. Mama's feet and lower legs looked swollen, spotted, purple and blue. She leaned against a fence, then a holly tree, and then sat on a rock. I held back from saying, "Come on, Mama, we'll be late," because I could see that her leg hurt by the grimace on her face. When I thought back about breakfast, I realized that Mama might not have been planning to go to church.

Irene trudged behind, running fast, squatting to play with leaves and watch a troop of ants cross the road from one hill of red clay to another hill of brown sand, then running fast to catch up.

"Don't eat that," Mama said to Irene when we stopped at the holly tree and Irene looked as if she might pop a row of Christmas-red berries into her mouth.

Mama said, "It's a shame, shame, shame what happened to that boy in town."

I wanted to tell her that I supposed Lawrence had done the beating, but like the cycles of the crops growing along those dusty fields, things came and things went and TJ's beating would pass just as sure as the cotton would be harvested.

When we did get to Brother Frankel's church, the congregation had already finished the first hymn, but I didn't much care that we missed it. Two people stood outside, watching, and waiting I supposed for the right time to go in so as not to disturb the singing. Mr. Hooper, and his son Mike, town folk who wore nice Sears suits and store-bought clothes, leaned against the side of the clapboard church. The father had his arm across his son's shoulders. Mike had a kerchief out dabbing his eyes. I wondered why he was crying, but then he blew his nose, long and runny and hard, and then I recalled he had a summer cold likely caused by the cotton pollen in the air, or maybe corn smut.

They went in as the congregation sat. Mama pulled herself up the steps, me holding her other hand. Some of the folk nodded at the Hoopers, a smile or two, but no glances this time that seemed to question what town folk were doing out in the fields of corn and cotton. They took the second to last row while we sat in the last, the bending bench, this one supported by half a cinderblock, flaking and dry.

I'd come to see Pastor Myers, to talk with him, to learn. I'd decided at breakfast, as I watched TJ walk out the back door and across the field toward the spring, and Frances go out the front door down the dirt path toward town, and Daddy cross the yard toward the McCormick's, and Lawrence nowhere to be found, that sometimes a day in church might not be too bad.

Brother Frankel preached about Cain and Able and told the story about one brother who "Slew the other with vengeance and anger." I thought about the alley and decided that Brother Frankel had heard about the fight and had blended it into his sermon and that he knew, like I did, and like Frances suspected, but like only Lawrence and TJ could really tell, that it was brother fighting brother in that dark place that smelled of piss.

Then Pastor Myers rose to speak. His leg extended by the metal brace, he rocked as he made his way to the podium. "And like Cain and Able, this great planet of God's now engages itself brother against brother," he said.

"Amen," the congregation said.

He went on to talk of struggle, strife, and calamity. I understood the first two words, but had no idea what "calamity" meant. That was how I could start our conversation, "Pastor Myers, what's 'calamity'?" I'd say.

During the prayers, I looked at Mike Hooper, sitting before us, his tan-colored shirt reminding me of the uniforms in town. His very short hair, as if an Army barber had cut it, ended at a tanned neck. I suspected he'd gotten it by running around town or swimming in the Pee Dee River, but not by working in the fields. He sniffled, and sucked snot back into his nose. He used his own kerchief, then his Daddy's. From inside the brim of his fedora he pulled out another kerchief, with lace and an engraving of pink thread—his mother's I presumed. I recalled that Mike had worn a white shirt and blue trousers last time. I brushed at the same clothes that I'd worn every time I'd come to church or gone anywhere important enough to put on something nice. The nape of his neck where his buttercup-colored hair ended was bordered with pimples.

Brother Frankel didn't pass baskets at the church the way I'd heard they did at others, like the Catholic one in town. People gave what they could, when they could. Often, someone might tie up a pig to the porch, found when Brother Frankel arrived. He'd use it as he saw fit, so I heard, sometimes for himself and his family, sometimes sold to pay for something at the little white clapboard building, and sometimes, really most often, butchered and given away to those still poor despite the riches of war coming to town.

I waited at the top of the steps, standing opposite the pastors, while they shook everyone's hand and Mama leaned against the corner talking and laughing with all that would listen and talk.

I said my greetings to Brother Frankel, then helped Pastor Myers down the stairs by letting him lean on me and the railing. "What's 'calamity' mean?" I said.

"'Calamity?' Oh, my sermon," Pastor Myers said. "Calamity is a tragedy, great woe, something terrible. Like the Hindenburg, or war."

"Like the sinking of a Liberty Ship?"

"Attaboy, like the sinking of a ship. That's right."
We reached the ground. Pastor Myers sweated heavily,
giant drops standing on his forehead, his beige shirt wet
beneath the arms. "I was told you Quick boys didn't come
around these parts too often."

"Yes, sir," I said.

"James," Mama said. She took a few steps, slowly,
her body pitching from side to side.

"What's wrong with Mrs. Quick?" Pastor Myers said.

"Her feet ain't no good no more," I said.

"Mrs. Quick," Pastor Myers called. Mama stopped and
turned, Irene far ahead chasing a butterfly. "Would you like
a ride home?"

I ran to her and took her hand so she'd say "Yes,"
because I knew that Mama would say "No, thank you." I
whispered to her, "Nice to have him for dinner."

She looked back to Pastor Myers, who'd made his way
to his olive drab Plymouth, the large white star on the door
peeling and chipping.

"Will you stay for dinner?" she said.

"Any time it's offered," he said.

"Then I'll take that ride," Mama said.

Pastor Myers pulled his braced leg into the car. A
cane, the bottom covered in a great ball of tape, leaned
against the front seat. When the car started after coughing
and spitting a few times from the cheap war gas, Pastor
Myers used the cane to push on the gas peddle and his left
foot to press the clutch and brake.

Before we'd lost sight of the whitewashed church,
Mama said, "Shoot," beneath her breath. More a rasp.

"Is there a problem, Mrs. Quick?" Pastor Myers said.

Mama leaned against the glass window for a moment.
"Just remembered something," she said. "Never you mind,
though."

"Yes, ma'am," he said. "If me coming to dinner is a
problem—"

"Oh, ain't no problem, pastor. We've got plenty of
food."

Pastor Myers nodded.

Irene kicked her feet out and back. Her legs thumped
on the backseat.

"Hush there, child," Mama said. "Stop fidgeting."

Like Mama, I'd forgotten already that our little family wasn't usual. There was no telling if everyone would wander back for dinner or supper. The pastor seemed to be a good man, but it would be hard to not at least talk about TJ's torn up face. Daddy would be sulking, Frances ill tempered, Irene nervous, and Lawrence might not even be there.

Turning off of Hamlet onto Wilder dirt road, I thought I heard a scream. When we'd cleared the cotton growth across from our shack, Mama's hand sprung to cover her mouth as she said, "Oh, my Lord."

In the front yard, dust floated up into the afternoon sky. Daddy stood hunched over beneath the weight of TJ on his back. Frances lay in the dirt pulling on Daddy's legs. From where I sat, I could see Lawrence standing around the corner of the house, peeking out. Daddy twisted quickly, flinging TJ from him. Frances rolled away, and Lawrence charged Daddy like a mad bull. When the two men collided, they both fell to the ground, and rolled about.

"No, no!" Mama said.

Pastor Myers stopped at the foot of the front yard. Irene jumped out, almost knocking herself over with the door, and ran to where Frances had Daddy's legs pinned while TJ pulled on Daddy's arms and Lawrence laid across Daddy's chest. They all laughed and shouted to each other, "Get him, get him."

Irene screamed, "Leave my Daddy alone! Leave Daddy alone!"

They laughed harder.

Mama's shoulders relaxed. I took off my good shirt and dashed into the pile of family, where I pulled on TJ, who flung me away, then I pulled on Lawrence, who flung me away. All the while, Irene cried louder and louder, "Daddy, Daddy! Leave Daddy be!"

"We're just playing, honey," Frances said.

I don't know what happened among those four people while we had gone to church, but by the time Pastor Myers made it up the to the house, through the well-swept and grassless yard, we were all covered in dust, and muddy streams of tears streaked down Irene's face. We all laughed hard, and wheezing, me so much that my chest and cheeks and temples hurt.

Daddy looked surprised to see a man in uniform, a metal brace laced across his leg, looking down at him. "Good gracious. Alright, I give up."

After I helped Frances up, her knees mucky from dirt and sweat, everyone laughing, TJ and Lawrence both reached to help Daddy up. Their smiles dropped off their faces. Daddy took both hands and stood. TJ walked toward the back of the house while Lawrence sat on the front stoop.

Mama tossed her purse and hat onto a chair in the living room. "You children run off and clean up. Hurry, Frances, I'll need your help with dinner."

Daddy led Pastor Myers to two raggedy chairs on the front stoop. Mama brought them jars of new tea, still twirling from where she'd mixed in sugar.

I don't know where Lawrence went, but TJ and I ran down to the spring, plunged in, and came out as clean as two farm boys could be without lye soap and burlap rags.

"What was all that?" I said as we slid on clean clothes, cold water dripping onto my feet.

"You know how Daddy gets when he wants to make up. Mean old bastard don't stay mad too long. He came back whistling the 'Battle Hymn.' We'd all come back about the same time looking for a biscuit or something. He starts picking around, flicking water, tugging on hair. You know, be nice time. None of us want to upset Mama. It ain't over, but we can sure put it on hold."

It had always been the same with Daddy, whose anger leaped up in a blaze, then cooled down quickly.

By the time Mama had finished cooking, the tin roof on the house and the hot stove had heated the shack into a baker's oven. We gathered on the front lawn, our plates dangling from laps, sitting on stoops and the elders sitting in the bare pine chairs. The Mason jars of tea sweated onto the boards darkening them in dirty circles. Pastor Myers looked like he wanted to ask about TJ's face, but he never did. I wondered if he thought Daddy had hit him. Instead, he and Daddy talked about farming. We learned that the pastor was from New Rochelle on Long Island Sound not far from New York, out where the city crept closer every year but had not yet grown, so farmland still filled the landscape. They talked about acres and trees and critters. We all laughed and joked and talked all day, never TJ and Lawrence straight to each other, but everything else seemed fine. At one point, Daddy said he wished he could keep his boys from tussling with others in town. That's when the pastor stopped peeking at TJ and seemed to accept the cuts and bruises.

When Lawrence started talking about corn to Pastor Myers, TJ wandered off, Irene played with her blocks, Frances took to sweeping the dirt yard, Mama washed plates, and Daddy dozed in his chair. I took up a cornhusk broom and swept the long planks. Lawrence said, "There ain't just the corn you city folk know of—not just popcorn and sweet corn. Nope. There's dent corn for slop and flint corn that's red and yellow, sometimes black and blue. Flour corn for flour and pod corn you can't eat. Yes, sir, mister pastor, there's a heap to know about corn." Lawrence told the pastor about corn until Pastor Myers' eyes seemed to stare off, the way mine must have when I listened to most sermons.

At some point, after I'd drifted off pretending to be a spy in Berlin, Lawrence had gone off with Pastor Myers to look up close at the corn stalks. Lawrence pointed at the tassel and the silk. He held up two fingers, so I knew he was saying that a miracle stalk might come off with two ears, but most grow one, and those that grow none we hoe down so it don't pull any water from the others stalks that might just grow something. Pastor Myers crossed his arms and nodded.

By the time Mama said, "Lawrence, leave the good pastor be, will you? You've gnawed at his ear for an hour," Lawrence had laid out on the ground the different types of corn, their husks pulled back showing off the kernels.

"Oh, an hour? Look where the time has gone. I've got to go to Palmer Field." Pastor Myers hobbled his way toward Mama. "Sister Quick, that was the most delectable ham I've ever tasted. Thank you so much for dinner."

"Always my pleasure, pastor."

Daddy woke up. "Why don't you take Jimmy with you?"

I wasn't sure I'd heard Daddy right. I wondered why

he was being so nice, what he'd been drinking or what news he had that kept his good mood up.

"Glad to have his company," Pastor Myers said. He looked across the field as if looking at his own land, distant, way out toward the far off trees.

"Really, daddy?" I said.

"Sure. Why not? You always listening to the news about war."

I thanked Daddy, kissed Mama, and ran off toward the Army car before Mama could protest.

Pastor Myers turned back toward Daddy, who brushed biscuit crumbs off his lap. "Mr. Quick, sir?"

"Luther, Pastor," Daddy said.

"Alright then. Luther, sir, how many acres you say this is?"

"Hundred and sixty, half mile by half mile. One hundred forty four football fields, so I'm told," Daddy said, looking out across the swaying corn.

"You farm them all?"

"Heck, no, pastor. We have to rotate 'em. Got beans and peanuts, corn and cotton. I tried tobacco, but ain't no good at it. Shame, too—makes good money."

"That's quite a bit of land to farm."

"Well, you know, don't you? It ain't easy, but we manage."

Mama and Daddy made their way down to the car, Mama wiping her hands on her aprons. "Okay then. Mrs. Quick, thank you so much for that lovely meal."

Frances came out of the house with a basket full of biscuits and ham slices. She trotted down to the car. "Here you go, pastor."

"And there's plenty more where that came from," Mama said. "You come back anytime."

"Anytime I'm invited."

"Invitation always open, son . . . pastor," Daddy said.

Pastor Myers motioned for me to get into the car.

As I opened the door, Daddy said to the pastor, "Why you ask about the acres again there, pastor?"

"Well . . .," Pastor Myers looked to me, then out across the fields, ". . . ain't nothing."

"Alright, then," Daddy extended his hand.

When the Pastor took it, he said, "Just that, well, I don't know anything about a football field, but I was attached to an artillery unit—cannons, for some time in North Africa. Them boys could drop a shell in every acre of a country, if they wanted. I'd say, looking across this fine piece of land you got here, you're short about twenty five percent . . . about forty acres. Course, I could be wrong. I never fired one of those big guns."

Daddy's smile flattened out. He glanced over the top of the car, toward town, toward the Old Man's house. "Huh, you don't say?"

15

*B*efore the war came to town, Palmer Army Airfield had just been Palmer's old plantation. It lay opposite Bennettsville from where our little piece of land sat. I'd heard from Matthew and others about a POW camp there full of Nazis. I'd never been there, though Matthew had said I could come out anytime I wanted so long as I told him before.

On the ground and in the air planes old and new, large and small, blue, gray, green, and yellow. P-36's, Thunderbolts, Corsairs, and Mustangs buzzed and rose and dived like mosquitoes about a summer fire. Olive drab Taylor and Piper Grasshoppers, their engines whining, little props a blur, coughed smoke while men in brown coveralls took wrenches and a boot or two to the planes. An old bi-wing came to a hurky-jerky stop, tilting up onto one wheel, the pilot climbing down tossing his leather headgear to the ground. An officer grabbed him by the collar and yelled, his jaw wide, though I couldn't hear anything above the humming and thrumming of the engines. Gangs of men, in uniforms I'd never seen in town, black, gray, POW painted across work shirts, loaded and unloaded C-47s, fat Commandos, four-engine Constellations, and long-nosed Loadstars.

An MP guarded the front gate next to a wood sign with "Palmer Field United States Army Airfield" painted white on it. He saluted Pastor Myers, and said, "Good afternoon, Captain."

Pastor Myers stopped outside a long building, the white paint neat and clean, only two steps up to black doors that stood open. Inside, fans attached to the ceiling spun at a blurring speed like the props along the airfield. A black sign with white removable letters read, "Protestant Services 4:00. Captain Myers."

The chapel sat along a fence just opposite a line of planes that first looked ramshackle and falling apart, but then I saw that men in brown coveralls worked on them with wrenches and blowtorches and a hammer here and there. A few had missing wings, flat tires, even bullet holes down the length, one particular shot dead centered on the white star.

"I don't see a problem with you walking around if you want. You said you know some of the MPs. If anyone stops you, tell them you're with me or ask to talk to your MP friends, but I think you'll be just fine. Getting in is the hard part. Stay out of the way and don't go onto the airfield."

During our drive, Pastor Myers spoke more of Africa, but he stayed away from the land mine and the killing. He talked about the mist that forms above the desert sand just as the sun sets. He told me about places right in the middle of nowhere, mountains as far away as Heaven, and the ocean a two-day drive to their backs, where trees, sometimes flowers, and a pond of water would suddenly be. "Oasis," he said. I listened, he seemed happy to talk, and though I didn't learn much about the war, I kept thinking how I'd like to go to those places with a camera and take pictures of them. Maybe pictures that would get into *National Geographic*.

Waiting inside the chapel door, several privates and a sergeant came to attention as Captain Myers entered. Wide and tall fans stood on metal poles and spun so fast and so loud that they rocked on their stands.

I looked up the length of a wide dirt drive at buildings, all in green, except for the chapel, each long and narrow, wide spaces between them. They reminded me of soldiers standing for inspections, each alike except for their name tag above each door. Commissary, Hospital, Supply,

HQ, NCO Quarters, Officer's Quarters. I walked and read, but no one entered or left these buildings while on the tarmac and metal runways beyond, the planes came and went, men worked and pulled and cursed. Other buildings read WAC, Red Cross, Civil Defense, Civil Air Patrol, Liaison, Mess. I stopped at this last building. While some of the other signs made sense and some didn't, this word I knew but didn't know why it would be on a building, especially an Army one, when everything seemed not a mess at all. At the back of the building, Negro soldiers leaned against the wall. One sat with a tall metal pot between his legs, peeling potatoes. Another smoked on a long cigarette, then flicked the ashes into the potato pot.

Just beyond the Mess building, that I figured must be where the Negro soldiers lived since they sat around out in back, a wide strip of land separated the green buildings from a fence. Standing up out of the ground like a forest without leaves, rough-cut wooden posts ringed another camp. A guardhouse stood outside gates, tall pine-logged watchtowers in each corner, and another gate beyond the first. A sign read "United States Army: Fort Jackson Auxiliary Prisoner of War Camp." Inside the first fence, a second fence, this one topped in bobbed wire, twirling about like a snake, going through the links, some of the barbs new and shining, others rusted red and brown.

Every few feet along the fence, signs proclaimed: "WARNING: STAY BACK: POW CAMP"

Along the narrow strip between camps, dust rose before a meandering crowd of those people, the POWs in brown work shirts and trousers. From the other direction, a crowd came in black and gray uniforms, buttons glinting and sparkling on some, and like the bobbed wire, ready to fall apart on others.

Nazis.

I felt my stomach pull, ready to flip or flop or leap from me. My ass squeezed a bit. I expected to find evil walking along the South Carolina red soil, an evil that I could only imagine looked like my idea of the devil, or perhaps a bit like Frankenstein or Dracula, maybe the Wolf Man.

Each Nazi carried a pink card in one hand and a

duffle in the other. When the first Nazi got to where I leaned against the fence, led by a mix of Negro soldiers, veteran soldiers, and white MPs, most of the Nazis looked old, a few very young boys, scruffy stubble, dirty clothes, smelling from their labor.

"Jimmy, that you?" The second MP to pass said. "What the futz you doing out here? Matthew tell you to come over?"

I looked at him and blinked a few times recognizing Frankie's voice before his face.

"Pastor Myers brought me while he does his sermon."

"The Chaplain brought you? Hey, you wait here while I get all these goons lined up and into chow, then we'll talk. I'd leave them all out there to drink the rains and eat passing roaches, but the War Department says the Geneva Convention says we've got to feed them. Can you believe that? Huh, bet our boys over there aren't getting the kind of food these fellas get. They even let them have their own Nazi cooks to make up crap like kraut and wiener-this and schnitzel-that. Can you believe it? Anyway, wait here, I got to get them all up here first."

The Nazis stopped before the guardhouse. Two MPs came out, their rifles slung. No one but me seemed afraid of these people. A few of the Nazis looked young, only a little older than me, but not by much. The brown shirted POWs went through the gates first, while the ones in black and gray formed up as what must have been Nazi officers and sergeants yelled orders to them in German. Though I'd seen red and white and black Swastikas on the arms of Nazis on war posters and Newsreels, none of these men wore one. Gray stripes, colored bars on their chests, eagles, skulls, crossbones. They talked in gibberish, to each other. I laughed out loud, thinking how the skulls and crossbones reminded me of pirate stories.

A Nazi officer with a tall hat turned toward me. "What do you laugh at, little boy?" he said.

I sucked in a passing gnat.

This officer knew how to speak English! He was much taller than me. I leaned back onto the fence post harder, hoping that it would give way and I could fall away from his still blue eyes. I shook my head.

He stepped toward me, and I pushed away harder.

Leaning down, he took my chin and turned it first one way, then the other. He squatted to look into my eyes. He smelled of soap, he didn't have stubble, his cut hair looked fresh, his teeth gleamed, his breath exhaled the smell of bacon. "What are you?" he said.

I wanted to push away.

His men all looked over, their gibberish quiet. I heard someone say in English, "What's going on?"

I looked each way, my eyes straining not to look at the officer. I saw Frankie way down the line of men running toward me. German officers motioned for their men to remain in ranks. MPs ran up behind Frankie pulling long sticks from belt hoops, pushing POW officers.

One MP yelled, "Get your men in ranks."

I looked the other way, knowing I could run, but the line of brown shirted POWs bent around waiting to enter the camp, a wall of Nazis, an MP pushing through them unslinging his rifle. The veteran soldiers had all unslung their rifles, a few pulling back on the bolts.

"You are not the Irish or English. Certainly not German."

I ground my teeth together. He turned my head.

"Your nose," he said. "You are not a Jew."

Frankie ran hard, his arms pumping out, his rifle down by his side. "Get your fucking hands off him!"

The Nazi turned my head again. I tightened my neck so that it wouldn't go any further.

"Ahh, I know," the Nazi officer said. "You are an Indian, no? Yes, I think you are an Indian. But not just an Indian like Sitting Bull or Geronimo. You have something more in you." He pulled my head around to look at him. He narrowed his eyes and grinned so wide that I could see deep along his rows of teeth. "Do you know that if you were in my country, you'd be put in a *Konzentrationslager*? Hmm? Perhaps you'd be killed."

In a flashing moment, his thumb bent back and lay across his wrist and his other fingers splayed back as Frankie brought the end of his heavy M1 rifle down on the officer's hand. Another MP whacked the Nazi over the head with his baton. Out the open mouth of the black-suited officer came a "Pop," that seemed to replace a scream. His broken and battered hand, unnatural and evil, lay in unnatural angles.

"Holy shit, Jimmy boy, you okay?" Frankie said.

A veteran soldier grabbed the Nazi officer around his neck and pulled him to his feet. Bones in the officer's hand stuck out white against a gush of blood. Once standing, the officer regained the air in his lungs and screamed, high and loud, like the whine of a falling plane. The POWs had turned their faces away, their officers yelling at them in their gibber-jab language. MPs pushed and pulled on the POWs rushing them toward the gates, leaving a heavy cloud of South Carolina soil sparkling in the late afternoon sun.

MPs drove up in Jeeps and Plymouths, on foot, Harleys, and bicycles. Pastor Myers led a pack of men from the chapel, the entire base looking away from the planes, their eyes on me.

Frankie said again, "You okay?"

I nodded, feeling my insides quivering.

Pastor Myers said, "What happened? Jimmy, they hurt you?" His eyes darted about, looking at the last of the POWs rushing into the compound, what seemed like hundreds of Army soldiers pushing them, a few batons falling on slow backs. Nazi officers pleaded with their men to move quicker. A boxy ambulance arrived, the driver and another man passing the Nazi officer, bleeding and moaning, to come to me.

"Hey, kid, you okay? What them bastards do, huh?" the driver said. His red cross on white armband slipped down to his elbow.

I hunched my shoulders, and realized I'd been standing there, the whole world looking at me, but I hadn't said a word. "I'm okay."

The MPs and veteran soldiers closed the gates to the POW camp. A man with dust streaking down his sweating face pushed through the growing crowd of soldiers. Eagles soared on his shoulders, silver and shining, a colonel. Out of breath, he panted and huffed. "What's going on here? What the ever living hell is going on here?" he said.

Frankie stood up from checking my face and mumbled, "Nazi bastards." He saluted the colonel. "Prisoner got a hold of this civilian, sir."

"You okay, son?" the colonel said.

"Yes, sir," I said. The colonel looked big like Daddy, wide like Lawrence, tough like a rat caught in the barn by a cat, but I wasn't afraid. All these people had turned out, stopping their training, putting down their tools, pausing their war efforts, because of me, and I was beginning to think I'd be in some heap of trouble for causing such a commotion. Even the airfield went quieter, the pilots and crewmen coming through the gates to see the crowd.

"Alright, sergeant, get those prisoners locked down. No chow for them tonight. Do a sweep through their little domiciles," the colonel said. "Glad you're okay." He patted me on the head, turned, the wall of GIs parting like corn before a twister. Passing the bleeding Nazi, still being held about the neck by a hefty veteran soldier, the colonel said, "Corpsman, give this man some treatment then lock him in solitary." The colonel stepped into a Jeep that spun its mud-caked tires and pulled off.

A wall of soldiers mumbled and walked away. Frankie shouted orders to MPs. All of the ones who had come running unslung their rifles and formed ranks. The POWs moved away from the gate. They mumbled to each other, some ran for their barracks. Others pulled on cigarettes, flinging them to the ground then moving away from the fence.

"What did he do to you?" Pastor Myers said.

"Talked to me," I said.

"What that bastard say, kiddo?" Frankie said.

A guard in one of the towers whistled, then shouted, "Hey, hey!" and pointed to a scuffle between brown shirted POWs and black shirted POWs.

"I got to go, Jimmy boy. Hope you're okay," Frankie said. He turned and ran for the gate.

"I'm okay."

I felt sorry for the Nazi officer—at least about his hand spread back across his wrist. He scared me enough that I'm pretty sure some piss had leaked out from me. I didn't like that he said he'd kill me if I was in his country, and just for being an Indian, Cherokee I wanted to tell him. I felt the heat of his hand still on my chin. I rubbed at it.

Pastor Myers took me back to his Plymouth, where I sat on the bumper sipping on a Coke a sergeant brought me.

He spoke to his congregation gathered on the steps of the long, white chapel. As we left, I waved to Matthew standing guard at the front gate. As we passed, he shouted, "You okay?"

I nodded and waved out the window. "I'm okay!"

16

*P*astor Myers asked me, "Are you okay, Jimmy?"

I nodded the first time, then said too quickly, too harshly the second time, "Yeah." He didn't ask again during the drive home. I looked out the window watching the corn rows rush by, looking up them, thinking how they flickered like the pictures at the movie house.

The Nazi officer scared me, but not so much because he was a German—anyone grabbing me like that would have nearly made me mess my pants. What he said was as strange to me as that dark alley where TJ came out bloody. Like inspecting a cow, or more like when I saw Daddy picking out another mule after Lawrence let Stitty run off, he turned my head as if he wanted to check my teeth or like when the doctor says, "Stick out your tongue." I didn't think of nothing while he done it, till I realized he was making fun of me. He surprised me, too, that he spoke English, though I didn't understand all the words he said.

"Captain Myers? How did he know about me being an Indian?"

"Is that what he asked you?"

"Well, no. He didn't ask me. He told me."

"Huh."

"He somehow knew I wasn't all Cherokee, either. Grandpa was Irish and a Confederate. Grandma was the Cherokee."

"I don't know, exactly, Jimmy. There are rumors, though. Bad ones. About the Krauts killing off people." Pastor Myers stopped talking and the silence inside the car felt stiff and solid.

After a few moments, I asked, "Like soldiers?"

"No, not just soldiers. Civilians, too. Lots of them."

"Why? I thought killing civilians was against the Geneva Convention."

"Good lord, son, you sure do know your stuff. Well, they kill them mainly because they aren't German, or Nazi especially. You ain't a Nazi, right?"

"Right. Never."

"Then, that's what he meant. Anyone not a Nazi isn't good enough for them."

"Can we just talk about New York?" I said.

"Sure, my friend. Sure." That's what Pastor Myers did. He laughed about his family, telling me how much he missed them. Then he told me that people do go to the top of the Empire State Building and to the crown and torch in the Statue of Liberty. He told me that after the war they would let the lights of Broadway glow again at night and that everyone should go there some day to see such a sight. Before long, I'd put the Nazi in my back pocket and asked the pastor how much a train ride to New York would cost.

As the pastor pulled up to our house, the rusted roof orange in the lowering sun, heat dancing off it, I saw everyone out in the yard gathered around Daddy, but this time there wasn't any horseplay.

"Pastor Myers?" I said.

He stopped the car at the edge of our yard, then turned and looked at me.

I watched TJ walk along the edge of the corn rows heel to toe as if he were walking across a narrow limb strung across a creek. He wavered his arms as if about to fall over, his tongue stuck out, concentrating—counting, I thought.

"I'd appreciate it a lot if you didn't tell no one about what happened."

Pastor Myers nodded. "I don't know if you know this, but when you tell your preacher something, it's supposed to stay just between the two of you." He put his hand on my shoulder. "You want to say anything?'

Daddy had a piece of old rope pulled out, Irene

holding one end, he the other.

"No, sir. They knew about that Nazi they might not let me go no where." I sneezed twice, real quick behind each other.

He nodded, patted my shoulder, and worked his way out of the Army car. "God bless you, my son."

I didn't know preachers had to keep quiet. That made little sense at all because when Brother Frankel came to dinner he would tell us all about other folk around Bennettsville.

As we walked up closer without a head turned from anyone, I saw that Lawrence had a two-dollar bill stretched between his hands, laying it along the rope, then picking it up in a way that copied TJ's toe-to-heel walk.

Frances counted each time Lawrence moved the Jefferson. ". . . Two, seven feet. One, two, eight feet . . ." she said.

Mama held up her hand as Pastor Myers removed his hat.

". . . One, two, nine feet. One, two, ten feet," Frances said, closing all her fingers into fists.

Lawrence took the rope just at the end of the bill. A piece of the old hemp braid dangled down another eight or so inches.

"Evening, Pastor," Mama said.

Imitating Grandpa, I asked, "What in tarnation is going on here, Mama?"

"Seems your Daddy's got it in his mind to go on and measure the fields from one end to the other. Foolishness, I told him, but he went digging in that tool shed till he found that old piece of rope." Mama wiped her hands on her apron and shook her head.

"Oh, my, Sister Quick, I think this is my fault," the pastor said, rubbing his forehead.

"And how might it be, Pastor Myers, that you're the cause of my husband being about as willy in the head as a rabid coon?"

"Well, I just mentioned that the farm might not be a hundred and sixty acres."

Mama looked up to the pastor. Daddy wouldn't rest until he had the fields measured, one way or another.

"Pastor, how on God's green earth would you know that?"

Daddy said to Frances, "Count it again, I want it to be right." He laid down the rope and showed Irene how to sit it down and pull it tight. "He was part of the artillery."

"Artillery?" Mama said.

"Cannons," I said.

"I know what artillery is." Her tone hard hurt. She and Daddy must have argued about his foolishness. I figured she'd lost the discussion as usual.

"Yes, ma'am," Pastor Myers said. "I didn't do the shooting, but it's kind of hard to spend months in the field with a unit and not learn what they do."

"And you figure this here field of ours ain't no hundred and sixty acres?"

"Well," the pastor looked along the roads in each direction. "Well, Mr. Quick told me that your land is bordered down there by Hickory Grove Road." He pointed into the distance. "Here by Wilder, which goes off at an angle down to Hamlet," he said, turning and pointing. "And, of course, bordered by the front road where my car is parked."

"Uh, huh," Daddy said, nodding.

"One hundred and sixty acres should be about a half mile by a half mile, but I'd say it ain't quite like that. But Mr. Quick, sir, it'll take you a long time to measure using that rope."

"Reckon we'd better get started then. We've already measured TJ's foot. Like an Army truck—nearly twelve inches. He'll double check what we're measuring."

Then no one had anything to say. Daddy looked at Mama who looked at Pastor Myers who nodded, unbuttoned his cuffs, and rolled up his sleeves.

"What were you doing with the money?" the pastor said.

Frances counted off, "One, two, ten feet. Daddy, we've done it five times. It's close enough."

Daddy said, "I've heard tell that a two-dollar bill is six inches long. Had to have something to measure with."

Pastor Myers nodded. Mama brought out tea and honey. I sneezed and coughed a few times feeling a little dizzy. I followed the crowd down to the edge where the road met the corn.

TJ heel-to-toed out ahead of us. Twice he passed back, huffing to himself, having lost count. He picked up a branch and pulled out a rusted pocketknife Uncle George gave him for Christmas three years before. There were too many of us to have any good use with that rope. First, Frances and the pastor held it and Daddy counted. Daddy lost count, we started over, no one back talking Daddy though we had it in our minds what the count was. Mama and me held the rope. Mama and Irene went off to the house. Daddy and the pastor held the rope. Lawrence wandered up and down the corn, pulling bad ears, bending over dead stalks, yanking up weeds. We measured the length of the piece of Patterson land we called our own.

"Two hundred times that ten foot rope," Daddy said.

"Two thousand," Frances said.

Daddy looked at her as if she'd suddenly said, "How do you do?" only in French.

Pastor Myers nodded his head, "Two thousand is right."

Frances had always been smarter than she wanted people to let on.

Daddy looked back up the field, where TJ stood a thousand feet behind us, stopping to put a notch in his branch, his tongue still stuck out.

"I don't think I know just how long a mile is, there pastor," Daddy said.

We all looked up to Pastor Myers. I knew as well as anyone how to plant corn, pull cotton, rotate crops, even keep the farm books, but it never entered my mind even once to know the size of the fields we planted.

"Well, just over five thousand feet is a mile, so half should be at least two thousand, five hundred," Pastor Myers said.

"We're five hundred feet short just on this one side," I said.

"I heard the man, boy. I ain't been through the schooling you've had, but I can figure we're five hundred feet short." Daddy dropped the rope and walked off up the side we hadn't measured yet.

Crickets chirped and coons scampered down the dusty

road. Not full dark, the sky had turned purple, streaking clouds running from the light.

"Maybe we made a mistake," Pastor Myers said.

"Ain't no mistake," Frances said. "Your word is as good as a whole harvest, pastor. If you hadn't of said it before we done it, that would have been one thing. Measuring was just checking to be sure."

Daddy came back, down a row of corn, pulling on a tall weed that we'd somehow missed.

"Let's get a moving. Got the rest of the field to measure," Daddy said.

We all waited a moment before Frances picked up the rope. "Come on, Jimmy boy."

"Daddy, it's near dark. We ain't going to finish before sun up. We've taken two hours to count one part. We got three sides to go," I said.

He scratched his stubble.

"Jimmy's right," Frances said. "We'll figure it out."

"I feel just terrible, Mr. Quick," Pastor Myers said.

Daddy's eyebrows went up, his forehead folded deep, dirty rivers of sweat seeping down his face. "Terrible? You did the right thing. I would have never guessed. All these years wondering how we never made ends meet. How our share never worked out in the old man's books. Patterson charging us a full share for only part. Damn him."

We stood, silent, an owl screeching by, then a flutter of bats.

"We don't have to measure all four sides," Pastor Myers said.

"To know how short of land we are, we do," Daddy said.

"Well, isn't it square, maybe a rectangle?" Pastor Myers said.

Daddy nodded. "Almost. Bit of an angle there." He pointed back toward the house and Wilder Road.

"Then we just need to measure two sides. I can figure out how much land there is from two sides and take away a little for the angle."

"Still, it's pretty dark. Just a few minutes till there ain't no light at all," Frances said.

"I can measure the rest with my car," Pastor Myers said. He turned and began hobbling toward our shack.

"Pastor, let me get it," I said. He stopped and turned back toward me, then looked toward the car again. "It'll take you too long. I can drive."

"You can drive?" Daddy said, straightening up.

Pastor Myers tossed me the keys, and I ran off as fast as I could as if I ran to get a general's Jeep.

When I got back with the car, TJ had caught up. Daddy said, "If it ain't a mile long, how can you count it? Those little numbers inside only measure a whole mile at a time."

Pastor Myers pulled off his watch. "You're right, Mr. Quick. We can time it." He handed Daddy the watch.

"You're just full of surprises," Daddy said.

"Frances, can you run off and stand right at the edge of where your land ends and the next one begins?" Pastor Myers said. "Mr. Quick, you can ride with me and time it."

"It'd be better if Jimmy did that," Daddy said.

Pastor Myers handed me the watch.

Lawrence stood just inside the field in the gap between two rows of corn. He gnawed on an ear of corn, pulling a little brown sack with salt from his pocket, sprinkling it on the corn, eating some more.

"TJ, you mind standing at this end of the field, right at the edge?"

"Yeah," TJ said, meaning he'd be glad to do it. "I kept losing count with my feet, sorry."

"We'll get it done now," Pastor Myers said.

"I still don't understand how you'll do this," Daddy said.

"I'm going to back that Plymouth up way down Hickory Grove Road here and hit the accelerator like I was running from a Nazi battalion." Pastor Myers looked at me, then back to Daddy. "I'll get it up to sixty . . . not much traffic on that road is there?"

"Traffic? Be lucky if a car's ever been on that road. You might squash a coon or two, but ain't never been a farmer minded that too much."

"Okay. I'll get the car up to sixty and Jimmy'll count off the seconds. Thirty seconds is a half a mile. Simple."

"Simple, huh? Well, you go right on ahead there, pastor," Daddy said.

When Pastor Myers had settled in behind the wheel and he put his stick onto the pedal, he took the watch from me and wound it. He held it to his ear and smiled. "You know how to use the second hand on that watch, don't you?" He handed the watch back to me.

"Which one's the second hand?"

"You can't tell time, can you?"

"I can," I said. "Just ain't never heard no one call them 'second hand' before."

"See the one that moves? That's the second hand. See, it clicks over to each little hash mark? That's a second. Each big number is five seconds."

"I get it," I said. "So, if it goes from twelve to two, it's ten seconds."

"Right. So here we go."

Pastor Myers waved to Daddy. Lawrence tossed his cob into the rows, wiped his hands on his overalls, and then his mouth with the back of his hand. He walked over and stood next to Daddy, saying something.

As we turned onto Hickory, I saw Frances way down the road waving a kerchief. TJ stood nearly in an irrigation ditch to be right at the corner. He slipped, one foot landing in the water. Then he straddled the ditch.

I waved and we turned.

We did pass a dozen coons, trailing each other here and there like ducklings. Pastor Myers turned on the headlamps. The light shone little with the black tape across them. Trees overhung the road, thick and heavy, drowning whatever twilight remained. It took him a few times pulling forward and backing up to turn that long car around on the narrow road. When he did, I couldn't see TJ, Daddy, Lawrence, nor Frances. I thought he'd drive by so quickly, I'd never have a chance to start counting.

"Now, as soon as the car comes up next to TJ, you start counting. When the car comes up next to Frances, you stop counting. Got it?"

"What part of the car?"

"Doesn't matter. The bumper. Your door. Just start counting."

"Okay," I said.

He gunned the engine. It coughed a few times, spitting out some more of the weak war-time gas, but then it

120

growled like a big cat and the rocking and pitching stopped.

"Here we go," Pastor Myers said.

He jammed the stick down onto the pedal, let go of the break, stuck in the clutch, put it in gear, and away we went. A blur of trees passed, coons dashing into the brush.

"The watch. Pay attention to the watch," he said.

I looked down, realized I couldn't see TJ like that, nor the watch face. Leaning forward, I put the watch out before me so that it rested on the dashboard. We cleared from beneath the trees, the watch face glowed orange from the very faintest of sky light. TJ waved his hat out ahead, lit up just a bit by the headlights, more by streaks of distant sunset red.

It didn't matter, bumper or my door, we went by so fast, it was likely the trunk when I started counting. "One, two, three, four, five . . .," I realized then that a second felt like a long time. I wanted to count faster than the seconds ticked by.

Frances waved her kerchief, orange and glowing. We zipped by, again, the bumper likely the point when I stopped, ". . . nineteen, twenty, twenty-one."

"Whew!" Pastor Myers said, down shifting, letting off the gas, the car drifting.

"Twenty-one!" I shouted. "Twenty-one seconds!"

Pastor Myers didn't bother trying to turn the car around. He drove down to Wilder, connected to Hamlet, then back home, past the shack to where the drive had started.

Mama stood there with an oil lantern, the day all gone, not even a distant glimmer. The moon stood large and strawberry-colored behind the hedgerow trees.

"Wow! That was great," Frances said, running up as we got out of the car.

"Nearly blew me over when it went by," TJ said, happy and smiling.

"Twenty-one seconds!" I said.

"What does that mean, pastor?" Daddy said.

"Let me figure it out here." He took TJ's branch and drew figures in the sand at the edge of the road. I looked at it upside down. He had "21" drawn out and longer numbers. I knew he was doing all the math he could, adding, multiplying, dividing. When it looked like he'd finished, he scratched it out and did it again.

When he looked up, Daddy's face lowered from its grin, the edges of his mouth hanging low.

"I'm afraid it's even shorter than this side. I get just over one thousand, eight hundred feet," Pastor Myers said.

"Supposed to be over two thousand, five hundred feet," Frances said.

"Yeah," TJ said.

Lawrence walked off, back up a row of corn.

Mama put her arm around Daddy's waist.

"So, we're quite short of our acres, ain't we?" Daddy said.

"Yes, sir," Pastor Myers said.

"What you going to do, Daddy?" I said.

"Looks like I'll be visiting Old Man Patterson tomorrow."

I felt what seemed like hot water rush through my heart. Confronting Old Man Patterson wasn't often a good thing to do for the sharecroppers. It didn't happen often, but when it did, they sometimes found their credit lost at the general store, a higher charge for equipment, sometimes their leases ended. We'd heard a few times where a man would walk off to see the Old Man and come back with a wagon to cart off his belongings.

17

*A*fter Pastor Myers said his goodbyes and welcomed me again to come see him at the hospital anytime I wanted, Daddy pushed us off to bed. I heard Lawrence click on the radio, Mama pour some tea, Daddy say something, and the three of them settle into the living room.

I pushed myself off the floor, the room hotter above me. I didn't care if TJ saw me. I lowered myself out the window coming an inch from falling on a opossum that hissed at me, then it scampered under the house. I kept my head low as I passed the windows and crawled below the panes in the front door, then stopped outside the living room window next to the radio's windmill. Sweat dripped from my elbows and off my ears, and for just a moment I felt as if I might topple over. Leaning against the wall for a moment, I heard the opossum scampering about under the house. After a few moments, I felt better.

Through the open windows, the thin curtains billowing in the evening breeze, I heard Mama and Daddy's voices. I expected Daddy to be ranting about the missing acres, but it looked like this would be a fuming anger instead of a yelling one.

I could just hear the announcer say over the radio, "This is London." Then the breeze turned the gentle-turning fins on the windmill into a flapping a kin to the chickens being chased by a fox. I didn't hear anything else until the front door opened and slammed shut.

Following the opossum, I scurried beneath the house. Daddy's pant legs and bare feet stood just before me at the edge of the house. They were thick in hair and dirt. I wondered if Mama let him go to bed like that. He picked up a twig and put it into the spokes of the windmill, then went back inside.

"Nobsey, be sure I pull that twig out before going to bed so the battery don't die," Daddy said.

Without the windmill flapping, the night quieted making room for the sound of crickets. An owl screeched through the trees. Whatever the reporter said came to a close without me hearing the story.

Then, the announcer said in his deep, unshaken voice, "We now replay for you today's draft number call. Remember, if your number is called you are to report to your nearest induction station within 24 hours." Static came across, then the needle dropping onto the record.

Another voice started. "The oak plank from Independence Hall is being lowered into the mixing bowl. The judge is now mixing the capsules," the voice said. A sound like hail striking the tin roof came through the radio.

Mama said something that I couldn't hear.

Lawrence shushed her.

"Don't shush me, boy," Mama said.

"Mama, please," Lawrence said.

The record playing over the radio hissed and popped, then a man said, "Quiet please. Quiet. Mr. Jeffries, please rotate the chamber."

A rattling sound started and a rustle as hundreds of small somethings seemed to crash around.

"Now, Mr. Andrews, will you please draw the first capsule?"

The screech of a small door or gate. The rustle of a hand reaching through a pile of what sounded like eggshells.

"Number one five eight," a man said.

"Number one five eight," another repeated. "Continue, please."

Eggshells again.

"Number seven zero one three," the man said.

"Number seven zero one three."

This went on for a few numbers. The lottery sometimes went on and on, so I turned to go back to bed.

Then Mama said, "Why are we listening to this?"

"Mama, please," Lawrence said.

"Lawrence?" Mama said. "What's going on?"

"Boy, there a reason we're hearing this mess?" Daddy said, his chair squeaking as he stood.

"Number one five seven two," the announcer said.

Then there was that horrible click that always promised to wake everyone up when someone shut off the radio.

"Lawrence?" Mama said.

I heard him get to his feet and shuffle across the boards, all of them squeaking and moaning, the sound of his steps coming from beneath, echoing out from where I'd cleaned, chasing the Nazi bastards away.

He went into our room.

I crawled as fast as I could back to the bedroom window, throwing up a cloud of dust behind me. There was no chance I'd get through the window and into bed, so I just stayed outside. A heavy sneeze built up deep inside my lungs. I covered my mouth, but it didn't help. Putting both hands up to my face, I let out a hail of air and snot. I waited for the stomping of feet as Daddy came charging from the house, but nothing happened—not a sound from above.

Beneath the bed, each of us had two things where we kept the stuff that we called ours. I had two old carpet bags. Where they came from, I don't know. TJ had his stuff in two Pepsi crates, no lids, but covered in old burlap moth eaten and haggard. Lawrence kept his in an egg crate and an old potato sack. I could hear the sound of Lawrence's crate as he pulled it out, grit rubbing against wood.

"Yeah. Huh?" TJ said, rolling over.

"Nothing," Lawrence said. "Go back to sleep."

Lawrence pulled something out, sat it on the floor, then flipped through a few papers before going back out to Daddy and Mama.

I scampered back around the house, not caring this time if my head poked above the edge of the window or darkened the door's panes.

"Lawrence, son, you ain't never registered for the

draft. You don't have to," Mama said, her voice pleading.

"Boy, you supposed to work on the farm," Daddy said. "You're essential."

Lawrence unfolded what sounded like a few pieces of paper.

"No, Lord. No," Mama said.

"Boy, they say you're essential to the war right here," Daddy said.

"I'll have to go," Lawrence said.

"You ain't even registered," Mama said.

"Mama, that's what that piece of paper is. I went to town and registered," Lawrence said.

"You're essential right here!" Daddy said.

"Number one five seven two is my number. I'll have to go," Lawrence said.

"You ain't even registered," Mama said.

Then I knew where Lawrence had been when he disappeared those days after the alley. First, registration, which sometimes took all day to walk to town, wait in line, walk back. Then tests, so Matthew and the other GI's told me. I'd seen the men waiting outside the "Uncle Sam Wants You" office in town. Tests to see if a man could read a little, write a little. Tests on the eyes and ears. Tests on the heart and lungs. Check the feet to see if they're flat.

"I'll have to go," Lawrence said, then I heard him moving toward the front door. He walked out the front door and down the dirt path toward the road, the moon before him, large and white, kind of honey in color.

"Luther," Mama said. Her voice creaked, then hitched before a great cry escaped her.

I walked in through the front door, but Mama and Daddy didn't say anything. They didn't even look at me as they whispered to each other. I sat down at the table with them. Then Frances came out, easing the door shut, peeking back at Irene.

Frances looked at Mama, who patted at her tears with a kerchief. "Something happened?"

Daddy looked at me. "The draft," I said.

"But you're too old, Daddy. They can't take you," Frances said.

"Lawrence, not Daddy," I said.

Frances covered her mouth, gasped a little, then put

her hand on Mama's shoulder. Mama patted her hand.

Daddy got up and went into the backyard. A hound tucked his tail and meandered around him.

Mama prayed and Frances found the hidden coffee in a paper sack at the back of the cupboard. She made a bubbling pot of it and poured everyone some. I loved the smell of coffee waking me, the bitter taste making me wince.

"Sugar, Mama?" Frances said.

Mama hesitated. "What am I thinking?" she said. She got up.

"I'll get it," Frances said.

Mama ignored her, went to the cupboard, pulled down an Arm & Hammer baking soda tin, and sat it on the table.

Daddy came in, the floorboards creaking. Frances handed him a chipped coffee cup. He shoveled in sugar like moving a pile of manure.

"Lordy, Luther, they're going to take my boy," Mama said. A moan escaped her this time.

I covered my eyes. I felt proud of Lawrence, but I could feel a dark place somewhere below my heart. I could picture the table empty of the big man. I'd seen the preacher and officers early on bringing bad news to mothers, but then that stopped when too many of the men died and Western Union boys began delivering the messages on yellow pieces of paper.

"He's essential right here. I'm going down there and tell them that myself. They can't take a farmer like that. Who will feed the army if they take all of us? Hmm? Tell me that?" Daddy said. He stuck his finger into his coffee and stirred it about.

"Ain't the Old Man on the draft board? Huh, Daddy? Can't we talk with him?"

"Yeah, that's right, Luther. Go talk with him. You play cards with the man, don't you?"

Daddy looked as if he might protest about him playing cards, but we all knew he did. He waved it all away. "Yes. Maybe."

Lawrence came in through the front door.

"Lawrence?" Frances said, going to him and hugging him.

"What have you done, boy?" Daddy said.

"They can take me, Daddy. I'm eighteen since March twenty-first. I signed myself up."

Mama went to him and looked as if she wanted to whack him across the head, but instead she put her arms around his waist. He patted her head and kissed the top of it.

"It's a war, Lawrence. Don't you understand? You can get killed there," Mama said.

"Mama, I could get killed by a rattler out in the fields."

"Ain't no one getting killed," Daddy said. "You ain't going off to the war. We'll hide you somewhere. Hell, they don't know nothing about these fields. You'll stay with the McCormicks. Or, I'll send you off to Baltimore to George."

"Yeah, Uncle George," Frances said, stepping forward, her eyes wide and teary. "You can hide there."

"I ain't hiding. I'm going."

"We'll send you to Baltimore. They sure won't know you're there. You'll stay with George," Daddy said.

"Yes. Yes, you can stay with George," Mama said, dropping her grip on Lawrence.

"I signed up, and I'm going."

"Nobsey, I'll need to go to the mill to make a call."

"I'm going! I signed up, they need me, I can do it, and I'm going!" Lawrence shouted, lifting his head toward the ceiling.

Mama seemed to lose all the strength in her legs. She went down to her knees so that they thumped on the floor. "Oh, Lawrence. No. No," she said, weeping again.

Lawrence bent down next to her and said with a soft voice, "Sorry for yelling, Mama. It won't be right away. They'll send a letter when it's time."

A tone of doubt covered Lawrence's words. Like the man on the radio said, those called were to report right away. Somehow, Lawrence knew the rules. Since many of the country folk might not have radios or even talk with others all that much, a letter would also come by messenger out to the farms.

Dizzy and weak for a moment, I leaned against the kitchen wall, the rafters seeming to swing back and forth. I went out by the radio and lay on the rug letting the yellow light from the dial spill over me.

I woke up well into the morning to the smell of bacon. Mama stood at the stove, stirring grits, staring out the window toward the pigsty.

Lawrence yelled at the hogs as he slopped them, "Here pig. Here piggy, piggy, piggy."

TJ came in with a pail of milk, Ham relieved for the morning. Irene sat in a chair watching me. I felt hot and sticky, though a light fog filled the morning air. My heart pounded heavily, my mouth tasting like I'd sucked on a cotton bulb all night.

In the backyard, Frances clucked, tossing corn out to the chickens.

I tried to get up, but felt like my muscles had all decided to quit, taking a day off from work.

Out the front door, I heard what must have been our cart and mule come to a stop, the hemp guide ropes snapping, Daddy saying, "Whoa." Then, the brake lever pulling tight.

He came through the door, covered in dust, having already made a long trip by wagon to someplace or another. I tried again to get up, but couldn't find the energy.

Mama turned from the stove.

"Old Man Patterson ain't nowhere to be found," Daddy said. "Mrs. Patterson said he went off to Charlotte and won't be back for a week or more."

"Give you time to think about what to say to him."

"I ain't got to think about it, Nobsey. He either cuts our tithe back or gives me more acres. There's part of the Breedon's ain't being used at all."

"Luther, that's quite a bit away from here."

"Sometimes a man's got to move to get done what needs doing."

18

We didn't get sick too often because we couldn't afford the doctor, which is why he sometimes came to dinner and went home with a basket of fried chicken and buttermilk biscuits, fat back, bacon, peach preserves, cabbage, and a watermelon in the summer and a pumpkin in the fall and Mama's love and appreciation the rest of the year. If we couldn't help but get sick, no one could lie in bed all day without doing at least the chores, much less the field work. "Better be sicker than if Satan had a hold of your foot dragging you down to Hell," Daddy would say.

I first felt as if all the air had been let out of my head. My reflection in Mama's little face mirror in Daddy's bedroom hardly looked like me, more like a pale rat.

"Something you got from them dern Nazis," Mama's voice said, floating through a fog of water and mist.

"I'm sure it weren't the Nazis. How'd you find out about them?"

"Mama has her ways." She made me sip chicken broth, then plopped two *National Geographic* magazines onto my bed. "Came for you while you were out."

"How long was I out?"

"Four days. Pretty feverish, too. If it ain't something from them Nazis, then Lord help us it ain't tuberculosis. The Great War, so many of them soldier died from it. This war, too, I suppose."

I was laid up for three more days. I don't know if it

was the flu, a cold, TB, or some German mixture of hell on God's earth. I could hardly breathe, hardly stand, hardly talk at times when my throat felt as if it burned like a desert. I didn't fall asleep easy, but then didn't wake easy either. I felt weak and hot and cold and my skin looked pale and red and dry and sweaty. I would wake to see the sun rising, then again setting, but sometimes not knowing which. I'd hear Big Ben toll one o'clock, then toll one o'clock the next hour. Frances would feed me something and I'd go to sleep, waking up to find her still feeding me or feeding me again.

While in that bed, I dreamed of New York, Baltimore, and Washington, but my mind mixed things up. I saw the Statue of Liberty sitting next to the Washington Monument. The Capitol Building crowded out the ships at anchor pictured in a photograph Uncle George sent from Baltimore's harbor. People passed in and out of the room and once I thought Uncle George had leaned over the bed and asked, "Where do you want to go next?" I was certain it was him—his dark hair cut short and his skin glowing. I struggled to pull myself out of the deepness because I thought I'd missed our yearly trip with him, though Myrtle Beach had passed and it would be Christmas or next summer before I'd see him again.

I heard TJ and Lawrence whispering, hard, gritted, angry, but I wasn't sure if they were in the tiny room or just on the other side of the door, and while I worked it around in my mind, I thought they might also be outside, just beyond the bedroom's planks.

One minute hot and kicking off the blankets, then the other cold and shivering. Daddy brought me water either late at night or early in the morning when the moon had beat out the sun. His hands felt bumpy, uneven, coarse as he dragged them across my arm or cheek, then patted my head, leaning down to kiss me, his tough whiskers sharp against my cheek and lips. Daddy kissed me. He kissed me.

Frances spooned chicken soup into my mouth and rubbed my neck until I swallowed it. It tasted too salty, too hot, and too tiring to eat, but I didn't resist—I just threw it up a few moments after the dry biscuits went down.

I woke one time to see the door open. From out back

the hogs squealed and there came the sound of metal clapping against metal as if Daddy was working on the plow. Irene dabbed my forehead with a cool cloth. She stood back from me, leaning in, ready to run like a mouse scampering from hole to crack.

My thinking seemed to work fine at times, like when I noticed that some of the boards inside the house did not fully cover the spaces of the planks making up the outside wall. I saw a spot of sunlight glowing on my blanket. It warmed the quilted cover. I wanted to rise from my sweat and cover the hole because I realized that it must be that space between the boards where the wasps that sometimes nested in the corner of our room must enter—though that was silly because the windows and doors were open most of the time to let the breeze run through the hot box of wood and tin roof, which not only let in the wasps, but the boweevils, cotton worms, lady bugs, caterpillars, ants, and bees.

Brown and gray field mice scampered about. I thought one nibbled on a string dangling from the patchwork quilt, then started talking to me: "That just ain't right, Amos, that just ain't right," he said, his whiskers twitching.

For what seemed like a whole day, I saw Nazi soldiers, their swastikas bright red, their tanks and trucks loud and crashing, pass by the bedroom window. I shivered a very long time. I wondered if everyone had hid, if Daddy, Lawrence, and TJ fought the Nazi bastards with pitchforks, axes, and hoes. Then the Nazi planes rolled by the windows, slow, their props spinning, still crashing. The dogs barking, Daddy cursing, "Them worthless mutts. Kill that coon TJ," and another crash from the kitchen.

Mama stayed with me. I awoke and she was there. I dozed with her holding my hand. I would crawl out of what seemed like a deep well, dark, and then breathe in heavy, rattling, wet. I heard the doctor come and go with the sun behind him glaring through the window and I wondered where TJ and Lawrence had laid their bedrolls. My heart felt bad because the doctor had come and I knew that would be another bill we couldn't pay.

I woke up feeling my head beating, thinking about the Nazi invasion of South Carolina. Mama looked out the window across the fields. It must have rained—the panes still wet, the sky streaked twilight orange red blue purple. I could only see Mama as a shadow, her hair pulled back. She sang both the verse and chorus, "Our father, *our father*, who art in heaven, *who art in heaven*, hollowed be thy name . . . ." She sang softer than how the congregation sang it.

I gulped in air. The rattle in my breath and chest felt like a few pebbles tumbling about a stream. Mama didn't turn. She prayed, out loud, in a soft voice.

"Dear Lord above," she said, then she was quiet and staring.

I didn't move. I felt weak and drowsy and thinking of throwing up again, but that thought passed.

"If I could, Lord, I'd build you a church right yonder on the other side of that mud road." It wasn't a prayer. She was talking with God. "It wouldn't have to be too big, but it sure would be close." I feared the power of God would come through her and she'd start talking in tongues like some did down at the church, but I didn't know how to lay hands on, or even why I would.

My head crept down, then shot up as I felt a crash in my dreams, but as I pulled my head up I saw that the light looked the same and Mama hadn't moved. It was quiet. I wondered where everyone else went. Then I heard through the plank walls someone stirring something in the kitchen and I smelled hoecakes cooking in fat. My stomach whined.

"Lord, Lord. I'll come to see you every week for as long as I can, but these legs of mine are getting old and I don't know how long I'll be able to take those eight miles on Sundays. Maybe when this here war ends we can get that old Model T working again, but this here craziness seems far from over. Yes, Lord, if I could I'd build you a church right yonder. I ain't being selfish, Lord, though it sounds like I am, but I ain't the only one who'd gain from a church right yonder." Her finger tapped the glass as she pointed. "Maybe these youngins of mine might see the light and wander over there when the hymns start and tambourine shakes and the preacher says 'Praise the Lord.' And there's others, too. Some of them don't go and some of them can't go, Lord, so a church right there would do many of us good."

133

I imagined a little church just across the narrow dirt road from our house. It would be like the beginning of a village, and before long there would be a general store and a gas station and a drug store—a town called "Mama."

Mama took a breath and put her hand up to the window. I'd never heard Mama say so many words at a time. "Lord, I know eight miles ain't nothing against what You've done for us and You walked all those many miles in Your time and here I am complaining about eight miles but I know that You won't mind if I have to stay home because there are times when the storm's too tough. You know Lord that there's times when the wind's too strong and the farm needs fixing. And Lord I thank you for them, but sometimes the youngins ain't right and I stay and pray while I cook or clean. Sometimes there's sewing or mending to be done and You never seem to mind. Those eight miles do me good, Lord. It's my eight miles, yes, Lord, my eight miles of time when I can think for myself and talk with You and imagine what Heaven is like, but here it is I missed that chance again and I'm hoping for a church across the road someday, dear Lord."

Sunday. I'd taken ill the past Monday—near about a week I'd been there.

Then Mama went into whispering, her head bent as if looking at the window ledge. It wasn't just talking. I imagined Mama on the pulpit giving that same speech to people dressed in overalls and flour-sack dresses. Many of them would be barefoot. Most of the women wouldn't have hats suitable for church and the men would leave theirs outside on their wagons or mules or propped up against the side of the white clapboard worship house. They'd have hand fans made of paper or leaves or a thin piece of wood that would wave back and forth falling into beat with Mama's delivery so that every hard word and pound on the pulpit was met with a longer swipe rushing air by, swaying the hair of others. There would be thick wooden pews instead of bending benches. When the sermon ended, Mama would stand on the front porch of the church next to rocking chairs and some hanging benches so that all day, every day it could still feel like a good place to talk about all the things she read in her Bible. Mama would have regular Sunday church dinners because she knew that many around them parts didn't eat regular. She'd have sassafras or mint tea, and after the war there'd be real lemonade made with real sugar. I imagined all of these things for Mama.

As if she were finishing a letter, Mama raised her head and said, "Amen. Love, Novaline."

The back door of the house squeaked open and then slammed shut.

When she turned from the window, my eyes were closed but I looked at the twilight's orange glow on the back of my eyelids. That gleam turned dark as Mama bent over me, her cold and damp hand laid against my forehead, her chapped lips kissing my cheek, then she shuffled away, the door latch clicked up, and she whisper-yelled, "Sshhh. Jimmy's trying to sleep." She went into the kitchen, pulling the door shut behind her.

19

When I came up out of my sickness, it seemed as if I'd fallen into that deep well out on the old plantation and had to climb a long ladder. As I climbed, I could see light way above me. I knew when I neared the top of the well because I understood again what went on about our little piece of land.

I heard Daddy and the cart go before sunup and comeback as the rooster crowed. "Damn him," Daddy said a few mornings. On the morning I felt well enough to be getting up I heard Daddy out in the front yard talking to Mama. "He's been gone more than a week now."

"You think he's just hiding from you?"

"Him, hide? He's no reason to hide from me. Hell, Nobsey, he's got both oars and all I have is a leaky boat. Nope, he's gone off for a while. Irks me every second to think I'm getting charged at the store for hundred-sixty acres, at the scales for hundred-sixty acres, and every month for hundred-sixty acres. Damn him."

"I heard tell that a lawyer might help. That big courthouse in town must have a lawyer we could get," Mama said.

"Nobsey. For Christ's sake, you know how much a lawyer'll cost? I'd be better off getting short changed by the Old Man."

They walked off, leaving me to find my way out of that bed. I flipped back the quilted cover that my two grandmas had made together. There were patches of denim, burlap, flour sack, curtain. A piece of lace looked as if it fell apart and was then patched with linen. My favorite spots had yellow places folded into triangles and stitched with heavy black thread.

I sat up, my head feeling as if it were rocking about. I smelled the rankness of my old sweat, snot, and mess that hadn't been cleaned up. The thin cotton sheet looked stained in long, beige streaks where sweat dried. The pillowcase was dark where my greasy hair pressed in. With the window open, cool morning air made me shiver, but it felt good for the tiny shakes to move me, waking my insides.

I leaned against the sill, remembering how I climbed down to listen to the radio, but instead, heard about the draft. Then, I sat up straight thinking Lawrence had gone off to war. "Oh, Lawrence." My chest and arms felt heavy. I'd laid in bed so long I must have missed my brother going off to war. I thought I might never see him again.

Coming through the morning mist a bit down Wilder Road, TJ walked toward the house. I'd been in bed for what seemed like years. In that time, TJ had not stopped his meandering ways at all. With the sun burning off the coolness, TJ didn't pause a second, but walked right into the yard and up the front stoop.

I opened the bedroom door in time to see TJ pick up a chunk of cornbread off the counter, kiss Mama, and walk out the back door as if he'd just gotten out of bed.

Mama watched him go, turning to see where he came from.

Then I saw Lawrence out back slopping the pigs. I pulled on my shirt and ran through the house.

"Whoa, there, Jimmy boy," Mama said.

When I stopped on the back stoop, I thought I might fall over from being dizzy, but it passed.

"Lawrence." I said.

Lawrence stopped tossing the husks long enough to stare at TJ, who gave him no never mind at all, but walked straight toward the barn.

"Lawrence!" I called louder.

He turned toward me and waved. "Jimmy, you're

up!"

Daddy came out of the barn just as TJ entered, the two passing without word. Then Daddy turned as if he might say something, but TJ had disappeared deep inside the darkness of the barn. Ham mooed loudly, like a ship's horn.

Two days later, I felt like a shiny new penny except the back of my head and neck, down to my shoulders, felt stiff and hard as if I'd been lifting heavy stuff above my head. I figured I'd laid on my head for more than a week, so it deserved to be a little sore at me.

Daddy had taken to going to the Old Man's house later and later each day. Before too long, Daddy would leave close to midday. Other than the chores, not too much happened on our little farm.

Daddy stopped the cart and mule before the house and got down to get something from inside.

When he came up to the stoop, I said, "Can I go with you, Daddy?"

"Ain't no pretty business I got with the Old Man if I ever find him."

"Well, can I go see Pastor Myers?"

"At the hospital?"

"Yes, sir."

"You go there and get sick again, what we going to do?"

"Well, not much else is happening around here." I should have been out in the fields with Frances, Lawrence, and TJ hoeing or harvesting the summer crop, but Mama said it wasn't time yet. From what I could tell, the harvest wasn't jumping off the stalks, the cart coming back just full enough each day.

"Well, I don't think they're all that sick, Daddy. Mostly wounded, the soldiers and all."

Daddy rubbed the thick whiskers on his chin. "Tell your Mama."

I tore off to find her.

I stood before the red brick hospital watching the soldiers enter and leave, their brown uniforms, buttons glinting in the sun, polished shoes mirroring the summer leaves of the chestnut tree in the front lawn. Some wore green uniforms, often tattered. Some men used crutches and others rolled about in wheel chairs with white-dressed nurses, Red Cross patches on their sleeves, talking, assisting, giving.

I read the Historical Society's sign, a Union Jack and Stars-and-Bars at angles across the top, telling of the hospital's use by Confederates that were then driven out so that the Yankees could occupy the building. The hospital's white trim, cracked and flaking, still showed a few musket shot holes and dents. Someone had replaced a few windowpanes with wood. Other panes had jagged cracks creeping from corner to corner. Above the front door, to the right of the center window, a pock mark, a dimple, pink and splintered and shallow where a musket ball, Union or Confederate, remained.

I stood there for an hour; half the time Daddy gave me to wander the town. He had gone to search for Old Man Patterson who he'd heard had been busy at the courthouse for days. Daddy would also talk with other farmers, and register at the courthouse for the fall's harvest so that the government would pay for the crop. Wiping the brim of my hat with my kerchief a dozen times in that hour, I wanted to enter the hospital, but it seemed wrong to bother the Pastor away from his important work.

We hadn't talked much about the war itself, so I wanted to know what he knew. When I thought of the war, I thought mostly about Europe, the landing at Sicily, the drive up the Italian boot. Africa was more rare. Few soldiers came to Bennettsville from Africa. Like the war against the Japs where, I supposed, the soldiers who came back for recovery or surgery or whatever they did in these hospitals went to California or Hawaii, I figured that soldiers coming back from Africa must have gone to other places—New York, Boston, Baltimore, somewhere north.

I stood chewing on a blade of grass, the edge rubbing against my cheek, until I'd sucked the bitter juice from the grass and left nothing but a husk. The Nazi officer came to mind. He'd been whacked hard enough to break apart his hand. Perhaps he'd been brought here, his hand bandaged.

I imagined him getting away and tugging at my chin. I stood while the morning grew away from its crimson light into blue, clouds lifting high, towers of white. The image of the dead sailor at Myrtle Beach, his arms ebbing and waning with the waves, made me wonder if there would be someone inside who looked as bad as he had, but still managed to live. I stood, afraid to cross into the building, where darkness waited just beyond the square of light laid out on the floor in the shape of the door. Mama's warning about the soldiers from World War I crept back into me. I didn't want to be sick again the way I just was. I feared I'd never crawl out of such a deep well again. I stood, looking down the corridor to another entry at the end where people walked down steps, their hats and heads the last thing I saw, into what must have been a backyard. I stood hoping, wanting someone to say, "Come in. It's okay for you to walk the halls, to look around, to find the pastor, to talk." I stood on the first step, then sat on the little wall that flanked each side.

A nurse brushed past me, her white-starched cotton skirt rubbing against my hand, stiff, the scent of fresh and clean. A soldier in a gray undershirt, gray loose pants, on crutches, came to the door, lowered one crutch onto the landing, then the other, swung his leg out over the jamb. He didn't have another leg to swing. Khaki bandages wound around the stub, up the calf, ending in the crotch. He smiled at me before repeating his motions down a ramp that led into the front yard.

I stopped in the doorway, the morning heating my back, the fans twirling in the ceiling cooling my front. The square of light ended, the dark beyond brighter than I'd expected. A breeze rushed down the hallway from entry to exit, the air passing my face, pulling the sweat off, chilling. Like the blades on airplanes, half a dozen fans whirled about the ceiling, one wobbling ready to crash to the floor. Behind me a gaggle of nurses, soldiers, those I thought must be doctors, stuff hanging from their necks, pens in pockets, walked toward me, the hospital. I could stand there and get run over or walk in and get out of their way.

"Never get in the way of a working man," Grandpa used to say.

Just inside the front door, I moved aside to let the

dozen or so pass me. As the nurses went by, their cotton skirts swishing, I removed my hat and watched the sweat drip onto the wood floor. So much cooler inside. It smelled clean at first, but a stench akin to horse pee filled the air, too. Perhaps medicine, or something they cleaned with. Papers, scrawled and typed, covered a corkboard. A poster hung from the wall—a dirty Hun, his eyes glowing, his helmet low on his head, big and angry, looking down on two little people, little lines coming from their mouths indicating that they were telling secrets, said, "Silence is Bliss." I didn't know what "Bliss" meant, it sounded German, but I understood "Silence."

"Loose lips sink ships," I said, my voice echoing in the entranceway.

Doors lined the hallway. Above them, little lights, white on top and red below. Some lit, some not. Near the end of the hall, a red one blinked on and off. Nurses peeked in that doorway from the hall. Soldiers gathered behind them, looking over their shoulders, under the armpits, around them into the room. A show, a game, someone telling a story. Just inside, on my left, the first door, closed, a sign written on paper and tacked to the dark wood, read "Pastor A. Myers." Putting my ear up to the cool panels, I heard nothing inside. Light seeped from beneath the door. I watched it for shadows, but none crossed it.

Pastor Myers had said, "I'm always there," but I guessed "always" didn't really mean every second of the day. I thought I should leave, to come another day to ask him about Africa, but whatever was going on down the hall, in that room, where everyone looked in, gawking, "Don't stare," Mama would say, but they stared, without movement, frozen like a Norman Rockwell picture on the front of a *Saturday Evening Post*, but the colors all wrong, the colors too dark to be on the cover of a magazine, that place pulled me toward it.

A man, gray mixed with his brown hair, his face young, sat in a wheelchair, his feet flat on the ground, his beige uniform stained in front with darkness, like ink, his hands covered his face, he didn't seem to move, nor breathe, nor live, he just sat there.

Silence came from the group. No one laughed, no one

cried. No loud voices, but people whispered. Muffled voices behind some of the closed doors and more coming from down the hall, at the gathering. Passing opened doors, soldiers, one eye covered, both eyes covered, arms, legs, chests, stomachs, necks, feet, hands bandaged, some missing from the elbow down, from the shoulder down, from the knee down, from the waist down, some both, some one, some none, some staring, some rocking, some covering their ears, one walking in a circle, one rubbing his eyes, rubbing his eyes, rubbing his eyes, I wondered if he would rub them out, they'd fall to the floor or he'd push them back into his head, he rubbed them so hard. Nurses bent over these missing, bandaged, covering people—whispering to them and they whispering back. Doctors listening with those things about their necks stuck into their ears pressed against chests and backs. Whispering, whispering. I wondered how they lost their arms, legs, eyes, their entire lower half. When men died in the movies they fell over, a final breath to wish their mother or wife goodbye, then they were gone off to Heaven. Never had a man lost an arm.

On benches, families sat, mothers in old hats that looked bought before the war when the style was different, when the style was to wear hats because people had them and the war didn't need them, old mothers, mothers who looked too young to be mothers sat with husbands, old and young, not from the farms, but from cities and towns where they must have driven here because they weren't farmers and I knew then that the hospital shared like a good little hospital should and these people were from Charlotte and Memphis and Richmond and Baltimore and Atlanta come to see their sons sitting beside them on the benches. I knew there should be laughing, joking, crying, hugging, slapping of backs, patting of faces, hand shakes, kisses, embracing, because these boys had come from Europe, from the fighting, and these parents had come to see their children, young and old, and they should be taking them home, walking out that door, down to the parked cars in the streets, where the fathers must have borrowed gas ration coupons for the fuel to drive all the way out to Bennettsville because Bennettsville was far from everything, or so it seemed to my farmer's mind where far was the other side of the fields and farther was the Pee Dee river and farthest was everything else.

Instead, silence.

When I got to the gathering, I could taste the horse piss stench. I felt spit build up in my mouth and I wanted to run to the back door and throw that taste from me, but I stopped at the gathering. Beneath the arm of a nurse who leaned into the opening, her hand pressed against the jamb to hold her steady, I looked into the room, and knew before I did it that there was no puppet show nor joking nor important card game happening. I knew that I'd see something horrible.

A boy, young, laid on a gurney, blonde hair that seemed white, his head tilted back, his body sagging. A nurse, her white uniform red, wrapped bandages about his wrists, his hands, his lower arm. The bandages red, blood flowing out from beneath them, running down the boy's arm, down his long fingers, down to the tips, then dripping down onto the floor. The floor, pale green tiles, slick with blood, a thin layer, just enough to slide on. A man, a doctor, pushed on the boy's chest, another man then lifted and lowered the boy's un-bandaged arm, the doctor pushed again, the other doctor lifted and lowered, push, lift, lower, push, lift, lower. The boy's stomach expanded with each push. His muscles jiggled and rocked and swayed with each push. The boy's skin the color of old ashes that it was my chore to clean from the wood burning stove in the kitchen. *Stop*, I thought. *Stop pushing on that boy.* Whatever wound he'd received, in the wrist, or hand, or arm from those Nazi bastards had killed him, I'd seen death before, the hogs boiled and hair pulled off, the chickens' necks wrung limp before chopping, the cow beyond milk years fat on its side in the barn, the coons shredded by the hounds, the rabbits torn by the cats, the sailor's limp hands banging against the breakers as crabs pulled and a boar tugged at his innards. This boy's face was without human color, the tone of the body, uncaring to live, not wanting to be part of this place anymore, I'd seen this before. *Leave the dead alone.* I wanted to shout this, but I felt like I wasn't supposed to be seeing this—what must be an adult game. I had no business being there, not just in the hospital, but there, at the doorway like the others looking in. Some must have wanted the boy to live, the man in the wheelchair, his uniform dark with ink that I then knew was blood, the mothers and fathers and sons silent on the benches, but others just watching what must have been yet another death in this place. This place. I knew he was dead. I knew he was gone and if he had a soul as Mama believed, it had left from his body from this room from this place. I knew, but I wondered why they didn't.

I turned to leave, to run, to scramble, to flee, smelling the sweat of the gathering. Pastor Myers walked toward me down the hallway, wobbling on his bad leg, his heels squeaking on the tiles.

He passed me, his face focused on the gathering. I kept walking not wanting to look back not wanting to talk, not now, seeing the boy like a pile of meat that we might eat come winter but he was a boy that would be buried and the messenger on his motorbike would ride to the boy's house with a yellow telegram from Western Union.

"Jimmy," Pastor Myers said.

I turned. He'd stopped, leaning against the wall, his bad leg raised from the ground, his leather case, black, counterbalanced him.

"Yes, sir," I said.

"Wait for me in my office."

I just stood there. I didn't want to wait because I didn't want to be here in this place that was so quiet. Quieter than the cemetery and the spring when it snows that one time each winter. Quieter than the night when everyone sleeps, no one snores, too hot for the crickets to chirp. Quieter than the silence that descends on the hogs just before we begin the slaughter as if they know, can understand what's about to happen to them.

Pastor Myers wobbled off toward the gathering. When he got there, he pulled a Bible from his dark leather case, the nurses and soldiers parted, then filled in the space he'd made as he entered.

20

*T*he dark wood door to the pastor's office made no sound as I opened it. Light colored the room in yellows and grays and whites, dust floating through the rays, a green metal desk with a green metal chair with green padding, another chair with green padding but gray metal and empty gray metal bookshelves—the greens like the uniforms the soldiers wore, a washed out forest, olive drab they called it. On the desk sat seven bibles, stacked one atop the other, another book covered in silver etchings, another book bound in leather, a red ribbon dangling from the spine over the edge of the desk. Other books, a yellow note pad.

On the windowsill behind his desk, the panes raised a foot and supported by a stray piece of lumber, two black-and-white chickadees alternated, *chick-a-dee-dee-dee, chick-a-dee-dee-dee,* between picking and pecking at a pile of seeds and berries. Their tune covered the silence, the quietness, the whispering. Light wavered through the chestnut tree's leaves, which swished like the nurses' dresses.

I decided to stay, to speak with the pastor, but my time was almost gone and I would have to meet Daddy beneath the Confederate Soldier memorial next to the courthouse. I knew I'd be waiting for him because the line was always long and Daddy would be there longer than two hours, closer to three, so I had time, a little time to wait for the Pastor.

His office needed cleaning. It smelled less of the horse piss stench, but more of being old, mold building up in a dark corner, a thousand bodies, sweat leaving stains on walls and the memory of the body behind.

On a ledge behind the desk running across the bottom of the window the pastor had stacked pictures an inch high, each pile held down with pebbles. A rock sat on a green patch with the number "1," red and woven, the only symbol. I brushed my hand across the rocks, wanting to pick them up, but remembering Mama's command not to touch other people's stuff when I visited their homes. Brushing my hand across something wasn't touching. A black rock sharp and jagged, a brown pebble rusted on the bottom smooth on top, a red stone shiny and smooth, a blue crystal rough cut with craters and dimples, a large sea shell.

Outside the window, I saw the Historical Society's plaque where I'd stood waiting and wanting to come in to this spot. A WAC leaned against the sign. A soldier—a lieutenant—stood before her, laughing, smoking, giving his cigarette to her for a few seconds, then taking it back.

Beneath the four stones, the top picture, fresh, still unscratched, showed a group of ten soldiers, hugging each other, mugging for the camera, smiling—their teeth showing, one's tongue sticking out, rifles, pistols, Tommy guns, shotguns raised. Behind them lay flatness and sand. In the distance a rise, perhaps a mountain. The soldier on the end, the cross on his collar plain to see, stood the pastor, a Colt 45 still gripped in his hand hanging at his side.

"Thou shall not kill."

I turned quickly toward the door. My body shivered at the sound of his voice, unexpected, though I knew he'd return. The chickadees flew away.

He closed the door. As I moved around one side of the desk, he moved around the other. He sat his briefcase on the desk, dust puffing up into air. Unlike the quiet door, the green-padded chair squeaked and moaned as he sat and leaned back. I'd never seen a chair that leaned back without the legs leaving the ground. He put his hands on top of his head and closed his eyes.

I sat in the gray chair with green padding. I wanted to rise and leave. I imagine myself storming out, slamming

146

the door behind me, but I knew I wouldn't. I sat and smiled as if I understood everything that going on in the hospital. The blood, the doctors pumping and pushing, the people gathered at the end of the hall.

He leaned there and I could hear his watch ticking. When he moved, the chair squeaked. He rubbed his forehead, leaned forward, and cracked all of his knuckles with one intertwined stretch of fingers.

"Did you see what was happening down the hall?"

I nodded. "Fella looked dead."

"Yeah. He's dead all right."

"What were they doing to him, pushing and all like that?"

"Looks pretty strange, huh? Some say that they can contract the heart from the outside and breathe for a person."

I didn't know what he meant. "Kind of scary."

"It is. It is. I think that if he wanted so bad to die, they should just let him."

I tilted my head to one side and repeated in my head what he said, wondering if I heard it right. "Why would he want to die?"

"Hmm. Well, they told him they'd have to take off his leg. They were going to do it this afternoon."

I'd seen his arm bleeding and tried to imagine what his arm had to do with his leg. "But his arm . . . ."

"Yes. Well, he decided that he'd keep his leg but give his life. He committed suicide."

Suicide—a word that I'd heard as a child when grandma talked about those who couldn't face the Depression. They *committed suicide*. I didn't understand the word *committed*, but the *suicide* equaled death, so then I knew what the pastor meant by "Thou shall not kill."

"Why would someone kill himself?"

"He was sad, Jimmy. So very, very sad. He'd seen his friends die in Italy."

"Not Normandy?"

"Oh, still too soon to have fellas back from that unless they're in the convoys. Might find a sailor or two about who have been there, but I doubt it. No, he was from Italy. I don't know exactly what happened, but they should have

worked on his leg over there. Too late when he got back
here. Gangrene and all."

"He can live without his leg. Right?"

"Yes, he can, but some people just don't want to. It's
many things put together, I think. What they call shell
shock, some of these men say they just re-run something in
their minds, like a friend dying right next to them or the
bombs going off for hours and hours. It gets in them and
just stays there. It's not too unusual for a few men to
commit suicide."

"Thou shall not kill," I said. "Not even yourself."

Pastor Myers raised his eyebrows. "Yes. Yes. I
didn't mean him, but that's true. He did kill himself." He
spun around and pulled the picture out from beneath the
rocks in one quick motion so that the patch and pebbles slid
only a little while several seeds tumbled to the floor. He
looked at the picture, then turned it over. "I meant me."

"You?"

He laid the picture flat on the desk and pushed it
toward me. I leaned forward. He tapped his image several
times. "You saw the picture. Thou shall not kill."

I wasn't sure why he'd repeated this. I'd heard Mama
say it about the Bible and church, so I figured he knew what
she knew. "I haven't killed anyone."

Pastor Myers smiled. "No, not you. The Fifth
Commandment."

I shook my head.

He looked at me while I thought about meeting Daddy
beneath the Confederate memorial, milking Ham this
afternoon, why the beige-uniformed sailors had stripes and
ranks so hard to understand, the people walking down
Market Street, the Colt 45 in the pastor's hand in the
picture.

"You don't know what I'm talking about, do you?"

"Well, I ain't killed no one."

He nodded and smiled. "I didn't think you had." He
picked up the picture again. "What do you think?"

I hunched my shoulders.

"You were looking at it, weren't you?"

I nodded.

"The Battle at Kasserine Pass. Do you know where
that is?"

"Africa," I said.

"Very good. North Africa. Tunisia. I was in the Big Red One." He turned the picture around, his eyes seemed to move from person to person in the picture. "The Germans pushed hard there. A few thousand GIs were captured. We had our backs against the wall. Fight or die. Just after that picture . . .," he turned the photo toward me and pointed to a man kneeling before him, "This guy, Sammy the Cutter, stepped on that landmine I told you about. It killed him and tore my leg apart."

I took the image from the picture and built a scene in my head. Rommel's tanks rushing toward the Americans. Hard fighting. Don't shoot till you see the whites of their eyes.

"What were you thinking about when you were looking at this picture?"

I hunched my shoulders, but then it came to me. "I've wondered all along how a pastor can be a soldier too. It doesn't seem to fit together too good. Mama said that the Bible says thou shall not kill."

"Ah. Well. That can be a tough commandment. Of course the soldiers upon the fields need God in their lives. There are times when they are afraid and need comfort. There are baptisms done. There are men who need the last rites given to them. There is Sunday school." He patted the stack of Bibles on his desk. "We even deliver occasional sermons and prayers in other faiths—Judaism, Catholic."

I had no idea what he meant. Most of it sounded like church or school when the pastor or teacher spoke. I had no idea what they meant either, but I think I could learn it if I wanted because I picked up on things that interested me, like the soldiers and the war.

"What about being a soldier?"

"Well, since we go where the combat is, the Army puts us in uniforms and gives us honorary rank—"

"—You're a captain." I'd studied the ranks from a newspaper article I found in Breedon's Drug Store one night. I took it home and studied it. Before the MP at Palmer Field had called him "Captain Myers" I knew that two silver bars meant captain.

"We don't really train as soldiers, but we're out there

with the men." He tapped the picture, now lying flat on the desk. "This was a tough battle. An exception."

Out his window, across the lawn, down to the courthouse, I saw the Confederate Soldier standing high above the square, the bronze dark and black from this distance. Daddy wasn't there yet.

"The Panzers drove literally over our heads, right through our fox holes. When they ended up behind, in front, and among us, we all had to fight. They'd given me a gun, showed me how to fire it. I remember the sergeant who trained me said, 'You'll probably never need this, Father, unless you get overrun.' He was right. I had to fight alongside everyone else. I had to pray for myself, for once, not to die in battle." Pastor Myers pulled a black and smooth stone from a drawer. He rolled it around his hands, his eyes unblinking, just watching it and seeming to just feel its weight.

A sparrow landed on the windowsill, picked up a berry, flew away. I waited.

He held the black stone in his fingers as if he'd just picked a cherry from a tree, inspecting it, deciding if he wanted to eat it. "See this? Black onyx from Egypt. I've picked up stones along the way—turquoise, quartz. I even found Fool's Gold in California." He picked up the large shell and held it to his ear.

"Want to hear the ocean?"

My mouth sat open for another second or two before I stood up and took the shell from his hands.

"Just put it up to your ear. You'll hear it."

The shell's edges were thin, but the center felt heavy and thick, pink and smooth inside, rough and bumpy, sort of like a crown with spikes outside. I put it to my ear and heard it, the ocean rushing, swishing inside.

"It's a conch shell. I picked it up in Miami where they taught me how to shoot that pistol. Hear it?"

I nodded, wanting everything in Bennettsville to be quiet so I could hear.

"They say it holds the sound of the ocean for years," Pastor Myers said.

I pulled the conch shell away from my head and looked down into its curling body. Then I switched ears, and heard it again, a swishing sound like when we slept on the sand at Myrtle Beach.

Pastor Myers sat with his hand supporting his chin until I'd heard enough times the water rushing. I handed it back and he returned it to the window ledge and picked up his black onyx.

"Did you have to kill someone?" I asked.

He looked up from the black onyx. He looked at me, then back to the stone, then at me again. I'd shown my ass, as Mama would have said. I shouldn't have asked, but it just popped out. In the picture, he held a gun. He rubbed his chin, then looked away, as if watching the dust float through the light shining through the window.

"Yes. I did."

Someone crying passed in the hall, out the front door, down the steps. Outside, she wailed. Through the open window I heard a man say, "Oh, oh God dear. Dear, dear. I love you. Oh, God." Then he shushed her a few times, trying to convince her everything was all right. They walked away across the lawn where she, a mother, her hat tilted to one side about ready to fall off, fell to her knees. The WAC leaning against the Historical Society's sign came to the couple. The soldier with the cigarette followed her.

Pastor Myers stood up, opened his case, pulled out his Bible, black leather, the edges brown, a crease down the middle, the page ends wrinkled as if they'd sat in a thunderstorm or floated down a stream. "The boy's parents."

"What about 'Thou shall not kill.' Isn't that a sin?" As soon as I said it, I knew my ass was showing again. I rolled the brim of my hat, feeling the felt crack, smelling the mustiness of the old, dry sweat creep from it. "I'm sorry—"

"—No need, no need. This is a fine time for an education." He weighed the black onyx, then slipped it into his pants pocket. "Well, Jimmy, you sure get right in there, don't you?"

I stood to leave. From the window I could see the courthouse and the edge of Marlboro Drug and Café on Marlboro and Market Streets. I felt bad asking. I'd sat and listened to the soldiers, but rarely had a chance to speak. Never before did I have the nerve to ask, but I wanted to know, if they'd killed people.

Pastor Myers looked out the window at the grieving mother, a nurse and the WAC supporting her, the mother's hat in her husband's hand, the soldier with the cigarette walked behind them as they went toward a car, but made it only as far as a bench along the sidewalk.

At the door to the office, a hand on my shoulder and a hand on the doorknob, the pastor said, "Sometimes, Jimmy, I think the Fifth Commandment should read, 'Thou shall not kill or be killed.' I've discovered there are times when it is necessary, it is them or you, it is a sin that must be prayed for." He leaned toward me and whispered, "Sometimes, a person has to kill just to survive."

I stepped out into the summer heat, the trees rustling, their leaves dark green. Pastor Myers wobbled behind me. I stopped to help him down the steps, but he managed them without me. I looked at the lady wailing and felt sorry that her son had died, committed suicide, killed by the Nazis, just not over there. Pastor Myers went to them and I went toward where Daddy should be waiting at the Confederate Soldier wondering just how sad Daddy was, feeling guilty that I'd had the idea to put an axe into his head. Praying he wasn't as sad as the soldier at the end of the hall.

21

Western Union brought the draft notices to the poor young
men and new fathers of Bennettsville's fields. Throughout
the war years, above the rustling summer corn, we saw
across the fields the rooster tails thrown up by the
motorcycles and heard their grumbling engines miles before
the riders came into view. Some of the folk out there in the
fields volunteered rather than wait for the lottery to pick
them. Joining up gave a man a chance to choose Army,
Navy, or Marines rather than letting some man with thick
glasses behind a desk in Washington do it.

A few people out in those cotton and corn fields
didn't exist—at least as far as the draft board knew. They
had been born in the tin shacks and tiny homes beside
swaying corn, chickens clucking, the father in the field and
the mother pushing life into the world. No one had written
a birth at the courthouse or in the church's records. Maybe
they'd put it inside the cover of the one Bible kept on a table
near a chair, if they had one. They had no driver's license.
Too young to marry, never in trouble with the law, and not
often religious, records of life on the farms were sometimes
just words passed among folks.

Not for us. Mama and Daddy believed in Roosevelt's
New Deal as surely as they trusted that summer would be
hot and water was wet. Mama saw fit to register all of us,
so that even before we had learned to scrub our own teeth

with cotton wood twigs we had a Social Security number.

Lawrence stood on the front stoop, his thumbs tucked into pockets of his overalls. He looked across the land, the wind making his hair twitch.

"All right. Day light's a burning," Lawrence said.

Frances put down the rag she had and looked at Mama.

"Daddy ain't here, Lawrence," Frances said.

"Don't matter none," Lawrence said. He turned from the stoop, marched to the table, picked up the Mason jar, and downed the remainder of his tea.

"What's the sense in it?" I said.

"Just because Daddy is all fired up about Old Man Patterson don't mean there ain't corn and cotton to be picked, weeds to be pulled, and potatoes to be watered" Lawrence said. He put his hat on, then grabbed it by the crown and slid it around until it must have fit right. He kissed Mama on the cheek and went out the front door.

TJ looked at me and hunched his shoulders.

I shoved another piece of fat back into my mouth, kissed Mama, put on my cornhusk hat, and followed Lawrence. I heard TJ and Frances running to catch up.

I shuffled along tossing up a plume of dust behind me.

"Lawrence," I said. He kept walking toward the corn we'd planted earliest, not far from the house this year. When I caught up to him, he glanced down at me, winked, then seemed to walk faster. "Lawrence, when you think they'll send for you?"

"Don't reckon I know," he said.

I looked back toward the house to see Frances almost caught up with us. TJ walked fast, but not fast enough to catch up. Mama came out the door with a bushel basket in her arms and Irene clinging to her apron.

"Mama's coming out," I said.

Lawrence looked back toward the house, but kept walking.

"You scared?" I said to my big brother, looking up into the shadows beneath his brim.

He walked several more paces. "Nah. Ain't nothing to be scairt of."

"War don't sound too fun."

154

"Ain't supposed to be fun. Hell, they say it'll be over before Christmas."

"They say that every year."

"Well, one year it'll have to be true." He picked up his pace, faster than I could keep up.

After we'd been in the field for an hour or so, Mama turned and looked up the long row of corn.

"Lord." Mama set the basket of fried pickles and okra, fat back and biscuits, tea and honey onto a pile of husks.

"What is it, Mama?" I said.

She held up her hand and turned her head as if listening to a distant secret.

TJ kept pulling at the stalks, rustling the plants.

Lawrence said, "Quiet, boy." He raised his hand toward TJ. Lawrence listened, then walked up to the road.

Then I heard it. It sounded like one of the many airplanes that passed overhead, but it seemed low to the ground and coming quickly.

Frances, just crossing the dirt path with Irene, each carrying a pail of water, stopped, pulled her head to one side like a dog, and lowered the bucket to the ground. "Oh," she said, the air rushing from her as if a mule had kicked her.

Above, a hawk screeched and circled, then dived and plucked a sparrow from the sky. The sound of a mechanical engine clattering and clunking through its gears came closer.

From within the stalks we couldn't see the dirt blown up by the motorcycle. Mama hobbled to the end of the row running as best she could. I followed. Frances stood in the middle of the road, her mouth open, her head still cocked. Mama stopped there. Frances nodded toward the house.

"What is it?" Irene said. Her water bucket fell over and the hungry road sucked up the water, drying in the daytime heat.

Mama had once scurried like a rat getting us all under the house when a tornado came. She had sprinted another time when TJ fell from a tree and broke his arm. Our wayward mule passed by the shack one day with Mama close on its heels. Those were the only times I could recollect Mama running anywhere until the sound of that motorcycle filled the morning sky.

Mama ran off toward the house as if her feet had never hurt her in her life. Frances ran close behind Mama putting her feet in Mama's prints. I ran as hard as I could, but couldn't catch them. I glanced back once to see Lawrence way behind, walking away from us. TJ ran toward the house as hard as he could, Irene trying to keep up.

When I rounded the last corn block where the road stretched straight to the house, I could see beyond the rusted roof, down Wilder toward Hamlet, where the dirt paths stretched on to the McCormick's, the Johnson's, the Murphy's, the Breeder's, the Copper's, and the Sweat's, the dusty plume rising high above the shrubs, hedgerows, stalks, and trees. It moved at the speed of a twister. Dirt devils sprung up behind it in the rising summer heat.

"No, Lord. No." Mama raced on and met the messenger as he stopped before our ramshackle home and turned off the engine to his motorcycle. "Not my boy. No, oh no." Mama's cry covered the sound of the cicadas and the lowing cow, and the crows perched in the chestnut trees at the edge of the cotton field.

Red grit covered the Western Union boy's olive green uniform. Only where the strap of the sack carrying the papers crossed his chest was there a clean spot. The yellow band around his hat looked nearly brown. His face was dark with dirt, his goggles caked in crimson. The yellow shoulder patch with "WU" had a streak of dry mud across it. I could taste the grit of the dirt his bike had thrown into the air.

"Ma'am?" His eyes did not shine, nor did he grin. His feet barely touched the ground holding up the Harley.

I'd seen him driving about the county with the little pieces of paper that ordered torn hearts and lost harvests and restless mothers and angry daddies and sons and brothers and fathers and nephews and uncles to leave the red soil and go out and be, for once, where before the thought had never crossed their minds, patriotic. He had been the only one, so I thought that there was no way, after he'd seen so many mothers cry and yell and collapse, for him to smile or be anything other than polite.

Then Mama, her two daughters holding her about the

waist and shoulders, went to her knees and then sat down on the road as the coated boy removed a yellow envelope from his satchel. "Lawrence Quick."

Mama wailed.

"Is Lawrence Quick here?" the boy said. Smeared rouge crossed his cheeks as sweat created trails along his face.

Frances sat on the ground next to Mama and the two seemed to try to drown the boy's words in their wailing. TJ stood at the edge of the road, his back turned to the show, kicking his foot back and forth, back and forth. Irene stood next to Frances.

I'm quite sure I didn't blink. I'd studied and listened and learned all that I could about the war, but I never once thought that my own brother might be one of the men going to fight. I thought of the hospital and the men there with missing legs and arms and hands. I could smell the clean of the wards that was really only that stench that reminded me so much of the farm, that I knew must be covering up the rotting and the dead and I knew that I should cry or scream, but I just watched and listened as the boy asked again, "Is Lawrence here?"

"Aye." Lawrence had walked up the road and just come around the corn block.

"No. No Lawrence," Mama said, trying to stand. Frances held her down.

"Lawrence Quick?"

"I'm . . . That's me."

"The War Department—"

"—I know."

Lawrence took the yellow envelope from the boy's hand. He looked at Mama, then across the fields. The letter shook in his hands. His feet twitched. He stepped toward the corn rows as if he might drop the letter and run off through the high stalks. Slow at first, he shook his head, then a bit faster, but unstopping—a hundred, two hundred shakes. I knew what each one meant because there had only ever been one thing for Lawrence. *No, I'm not leaving. No, I can't leave. No, there is nothing for me outside of this place. No, I know nothing but here. No. No.* No each shake of his head must have meant.

A rattle, a whoop, and the clop of the mule's hoofs

brought Daddy around the corner, the cart left off somewhere between the farm and town. "Jesus Christ." Daddy bounded from the mule and nearly knocked the boy over as the messenger mounted his motorcycle. "Jesus Christ, are you sure it's for us? Are you sure?" Daddy grabbed the green sleeve of the messenger.

More dirt cascaded off the boy as he nodded his head.

TJ had sat to the ground, still facing away.

A buzzard circled above. A field mouse scampered from one side of the road to the other. Building clouds in the west prepared for an afternoon sprinkling.

Irene cried, not understanding everything happening, but knowing that it was something bad.

Without another word, the letter carrier nodded, his eyes sad, me wondering how he could do such a hard job. He turned the motorcycle, roared off toward Hamlet Road, kicking up a long train of dirt that settled on us like a light snow. Daddy pulled Mama to her feet, hugged her, and then the two of them encircled Lawrence, whispering to him and kissing him. Daddy's massive hand patted Lawrence's shoulders and back in a light tap that sent clouds of red grains into the air.

Mama took the small savings that she had managed to gather from eggs or from what Frances might give her. We had money from the pecans we sold in town and from the honey we'd sell to Breedon for his lunch counter. With it, she bought Lawrence a new shirt. We'd never had most of the things they said Lawrence could take with him, so Frances went to town with Mama and spent her own money buying Lawrence a wooden-handled toothbrush and a metal comb, some chewing gum, paper, envelopes, and stamps, though Lawrence could barely read or write. We didn't have enough money on such short notice to get him a new pair of trousers, so he went in the only ones he had. They came up above the ankle and stretched tight across his hips.

I would have given up our Saturday trips to town just to be sure Lawrence got all the stuff he needed, but we hadn't thought much about what we knew might come some day. It came quickly, between our ice cream or movie trips. I found a small empty tin in the tool shed and filled it with the red dirt of our farm and the dry kernels of several types of corn, something for him to remember the farm by.

I wanted to ask him what had happened in the alley that night with TJ. I wanted to tell Lawrence that I would miss him. I wanted to say to him that I thought it was important and right and best that I had him as my second father—my father of the fields.

I felt happy to know he was going because there would be one less person to call me "Boy" and treat me as if I were just another plank making up the wall of our shack. I felt happy that there would be more room in the bed and I could sleep next to TJ instead of on the cold and hot and dirty and dusty floor. I feared him leaving as much as I feared him staying.

The next morning, while I milked Ham, Lawrence came down, tapped me on my shoulder, and nodded at the cow. I moved over to let him do it one last time. It had been years since he'd done it in earnest. His first two pulls made Ham kick. Then Lawrence found his rhythm and the milk sloshed and rang off the side of the pail. I put my hand on his shoulder. He looked up at me. A trail of milk darkened the floor. "I'll miss you," I said. He nodded and then leaned his forehead against Ham's side.

Mama hugged Lawrence for what seemed like a full hour. We all stood before the house watching the two of them, the red morning sun promising humidity like walking through a swamp. Mama cried, Lawrence whispered to her, they laughed. They walked down the road, Lawrence pointing to the cotton, Mama slapping him on his wide arm. When they meandered back to the front stoop, Irene slept against Frances' side, TJ and I leaned against the house, watching, blades of long grass slipping between our teeth. Mama and Lawrence hugged again until Daddy wrapped his long arms around both of their shoulders and coaxed the two apart.

"Oh, Lawrence, my love," Frances said. "Take me with you. Of all the gin joints in all the deserts of Africa, why did you have to walk into this one?"

"Frankly, my dear, I don't give a damn," Lawrence said.

"Listen to that mouth," Mama said. "Already talking

like a sailor."

Frances kissed Lawrence over and over until the two of them laughed so hard they started snorting like pigs, which made them laugh harder. We all laughed for a few minutes.

"Soldier, Mama? I'm going into the Army, not the Navy," Lawrence said. He picked Irene up, sat her on his shoulder, and walked off into the yard away from us all to talk to her privately.

"All I know is you ain't going to be here, Army or Navy." Mama turned away, walking down to the wagon.

TJ and I lay out in the back of the wagon, the boards and rusted metal covered in fresh straw. Daddy and Lawrence rode up front. Lawrence waved to Mama, Frances, and Irene until we turned the corner onto Hamlet. Mama near about collapsed into Frances' arms, but Lawrence couldn't see that—he'd already turned his head.

22

*T*own bustled like when the circus used to come. I'd never been there so early on a Monday morning. The times when I'd come to town with Daddy—to the post office or hospital—it was usually after supper when the Carolina sun pressed down on the land like a sack of stone slung across a young boy's shoulder. Army trucks and buses lined Main Street and wagons and Model-T's, a few buckboards, a horse or two, dozens of mules, and people—lots of them, filled the streets and sidewalks.

A line of boys and men came out of the recruit station door, went down the corner toward Main, bent at the JC Penney's, and ended by Sanitary Cafeteria.

Whistles blew as MPs directed the loading of baggage into the Army deuce-and-a-halfs. Boys, who'd just learned how to rotate crops and keep the farm books, and who'd yet mastered a hog slaughter, and, perhaps, had just been given charge of weighing out the cotton, lined up near the buses.

Mama sent breakfast with us. The bacon, salty and dry, went down hard, while the biscuits, dry and salty, went down harder. We finished what we had as the edges of town grew into ever taller and wider buildings. "Looks like we're late," Lawrence said.

In the alley behind Breedon's Drug Daddy searched for a space to tie up the mule. "Ain't late. They're all early."

TJ pulled his pocket watch out from his overalls. "Yeah, ain't but seven thirty."

"Maybe they won't take you if you're late," I said, knowing that wasn't even close to truth, but I didn't want Lawrence to go and I knew no one else did either.

"Best get in line there, son." Daddy inclined his heard toward Sanitary Cafe. "You boys can wait with us or mill about, but don't miss it when he gets on the bus."

TJ and I looked at each other. It didn't feel right to meander about town while Lawrence waited in line. There seemed to be much to say, stories to recall, things that still had to be done with my oldest brother. Somewhere in my brain, like a movie playing overtop of another movie, I saw what the line meant. At first, the Army sent staff cars around with a couple of officers, a priest, and a lady from the Red Cross to tell mothers and daughters that their men wouldn't be coming home, but the war became a glutton and swallowed so many that the very same boy who sped about the country on his motorcycle ordering boys to duty would also deliver messages that read something like, "The War Department regrets to inform you that . . . ."

"We'll stay with you," TJ said to Lawrence.

"It's okay boys. I need to talk with Daddy." Daddy put his arm across Lawrence's broad shoulders and walked down the alley toward the lines of men. "Why don't you go up the line to see who else got their numbers called?"

"We'll see you at the bus." I pulled on TJ's sleeve and went up Main as Daddy and Lawrence went down it. Many of the people I knew and Daddy would know better. Mr. Hill, Mr. Meleney, Mrs. Novak's oldest boy. There were Caddeos, Bodes, and Smiths. The red-headed Reed boys stood there, while the Clemens brothers looked as if they'd come without their daddy or mama. The lottery seemed as if it had long arms reaching into the town, out into the fields, pulling in whatever it could grab hold of.

Not more than a second after we rounded the corner where Main enters the town square next to the Confederate Soldier Memorial, did TJ say, "I'll see you at the bus." He stepped away, but I pulled his suspenders and he stopped.

"Where you going?" I sounded more like Irene.

TJ looked at me, then toward the crowd of soldiers

loading the trucks. "Just to talk with some friends."

"Why don't you ever let me meet them?"

"You wouldn't like them." TJ slid my hand from his straps and walked away.

I watched him go, trying to tell who he went to talk with.

I wandered back to the corner and saw Daddy and Lawrence way down at the end of the line laughing about something. A few others came up behind them.

TJ went around a line of trucks, almost out of sight, but I could make out his worn shoes and frayed coverall legs among the ironed uniform pants and new boots beneath the body of the drab trucks. I crossed the street and hid behind the Confederate Soldier's Memorial where I could just make out the side of TJ's head between the body of a truck and its tarp-covered rear.

I could see down the line just far enough to know that Daddy and Lawrence wouldn't come to that corner any time soon.

I looked about wondering if anyone paid the least bit of attention to me. No one did. MPs directed traffic, soldiers loaded trucks, officers stood below the "Uncle Sam Wants You!" sign looking at papers that the men standing in line had, then checking papers on clipboards, nodding, pointing inside.

I felt invisible, like a spy in Paris. It was up to me to uncover what happened when two Nazi generals met. They had secret maps, I decided, and I had to eavesdrop so that I could report what I'd learned to the French Underground.

I picked up a paper left on the bench beneath the war memorial. Casual, like a Sunday morning along the Champs Elysees, I strolled toward the line of trucks and leaned against the hot bumper.

TJ said, "When can we meet again?"

"You want me to get my ass beat by your brother?" Then I knew it was the soldier from the drug store and the alley. I wondered if he still had a bump where our heads must have collided. Lawrence had done the beating. "Go away. I'll get in big trouble."

"For what? For talking with someone?" TJ said.

"Yes, TJ, for talking with you. Geez. Some of the

guys already suspect. Hell, I think they know."

He rustled pages as he flipped through papers on his clipboard.

The soldier said in English, "Saturday, at the movies?"

"With my brother going off, we might not be in town." TJ's voice traded places with the other Nazi general.

Someone passed by. "Hello." When they seemed to be alone again, he said, "Then when? What?"

"Damn it. I want to see you, Tony." A plane passed overhead on the landing path to Palmer Field. "Come out to the farm. I'll meet you during lunch."

"The farm? That's a bit crazy. What about your father?"

"I don't know. I don't know. We'll work it out."

"You work it out and let me know Saturday—"

"—But, Saturday—"

"I know. If you come to town on Saturday, we'll meet. You'll find me. You've always managed to get away before."

"Yeah. But in the alley I got my ass beat."

"Same brother who's going away today?"

"Oh. Yeah."

"Saturday night?"

"Okay. If not—"

"—Then next Saturday night." The soldier flipped some more pages. "I have to go."

"Yeah."

Tony—not three-letters, as Matthew had called him. Though TJ wanted Tony to come out to the farm, I knew that it would be more like TJ sneaking off on Saturday night regardless if Daddy let us come to town.

Walking back toward Sanitary Café, I said hello to Fred off the Matthew's farm and George from down the Alexander's.

Then I passed a boy in the line without a grown man laughing with him or shouldering him or carrying his bag. He stood alone, his face looking in toward the buildings and windows. He looked too young to be standing in that line. Like me, he should have been wandering about, thinking about the world, but instead, he stood there stiff like an oak.

I knew him, but couldn't quite remember from where. I crossed the street and sat on the McCall Block store window ledge, behind the awning in the shade. The farmers in front and behind paid him no attention. I thought that I might have been mistaken. He could have been older. Maybe I'd seen him at the drug store, the Marlboro theater, in town someplace. He might be one of the kids who hung out at Breedon's Drug.

He carried a small, leather case—unscuffed. His shoes looked clean, maybe new, his pants ironed like the soldiers' uniforms, also new. His button-down shirt had a crease along the arm. He wore an undershirt that showed just a bit of Clorox white above the top button. His hat sat back on his head revealing eyes unlike everyone else standing in that line. His eyes stared unmoving, unliving, unseeing, but looking at a world no one in that line could see—the war before him or some battle he was leaving, so I thought.

No one came to stand with him. He sneezed so hard his hat near about toppled off his head. Mike Hooper, whose family lived in town, but went to Brother Frankel's church out in the cotton fields. Older than me, maybe TJ's age. Allergic to something, I knew if I'd see him closer his eyes would be puffy and watering. I wondered if the Army would take him, but realized if he'd make it past on age he'd get by on allergies for sure.

I wondered why it never came to me to join up. I could follow Mike. Perhaps I could cross Main Street, say "Hi" to Mike, stand next to him as the line moved forward. He'd want to know what I'm doing and I could say, "Going with you." We'd be buddies going off to war. Some day, someone like Hemingway would write about us being heroes.

"James."

I felt myself starring at him. I saw myself reflected in the window beside him, across the street, as cars passed between us, and the crowd grew larger and noisier and people came and went from the cafeterias and the drug store and the five-and-dime, which opened early to serve them. I couldn't blink as part of my mind wandered with the boy to

Brussels and Amsterdam and Rome.

"Jimmy!" Lawrence called to me. The line had moved up a dozen places or so and Daddy and Lawrence laughed about something. "Jimmy." Lawrence motioned for me to join them.

I hugged Lawrence before he got onto the bus.

Mike sat there, against the window, leaning so that his head pressed against the glass, his eyes closed.

TJ just said, "Goodbye." Daddy stood at a short distance and shook his hand—his hugging having been done back on the farm. No country women had come to town with the boys, but town women cried quietly, white kerchiefs dabbing at their eyes and noses.

Pastor Myers stood at the door to the bus handing out small New Testaments bound in green.

"Mr. Quick? Lawrence? I didn't know you'd been called up," he said.

"Yes, sir, I have," Lawrence said.

Pastor Myers took him by the elbow and looked as if he wanted to pull him aside, but Lawrence stood firm. Pastor Myers shook Lawrence's hand. "Alright then, son. May God go with you. The Army will take good care of you." He held out a book, Lawrence took it and tucked it into the pocket on his new shirt.

"Marines," Lawrence said. "I thought it would be the Army, but they put me in the Marines. Going to some island."

When Lawrence got on the bus, Daddy shook Pastor Myers' hand.

"He doesn't have to go. You know that, don't you?" Pastor Myers said.

"Was his decision to go," Daddy said. "Marines are pretty tough."

Pastor Myers nodded. "You let me know if there's anything I can do. I grew up on a farm, as you know."

We waited and waived until the bus pulled away, went down the hill at the edge of town, and out of sight.

On the ride back to the farm, Daddy faced home without a glance toward town. TJ hung his legs off the rear of the wagon, and I stretched out on the straw.

"TJ?" I whispered. He ignored me or didn't hear me. "TJ?"

He turned and looked at me, then back toward town, his legs swinging.

"Who's that you were talking to?" He pretended not to hear me. "TJ?"

He hunched his shoulders, but otherwise didn't respond.

"TJ?" My whisper was louder. "You're getting pretty dumb. What if Daddy would have caught you?"

"What you two whispering about back there?" Daddy spit and then drank water from a jug.

"Nothing, Daddy," I said. TJ said nothing.

"Huh?" Daddy turned, expecting an answer from both of us.

"Nothing, Daddy," we both said.

TJ laid back on the rocking wagon and shut his eyes. I hunkered down onto the hay pretending to hide from the Nazis as the French Underground sneaked me out of Paris, but instead, I decided to follow TJ the next time he sneaked off.

23

*S*aturday came without discussion of going to town. Mama could just about get herself out of bed and do little else. She moped about, her feet scuffling across the sandy boards, the same way she'd done since Lawrence left. I found her looking out across the fields toward town, tapping her foot to some tune no one else could hear.

Daddy wasn't much better. He gave each of us a share of Lawrence's chores, not taking any for himself, but it didn't much matter because he filled his day looking at his books, measuring the land, and riding off to find the Old Man.

No one said a thing to me. Daddy was doing what he'd taken to do. TJ stayed in bed past breakfast, then got up and spread chicken feed. Frances sat on the front stoop, her knuckles tucked up under her chin. Irene played with her wood blocks on the rug before the Zenith.

After milking Ham and eating a hasty breakfast of just oatmeal, I hitched the old nag to the wagon and wheeled it out to the corn, hoping to catch as many ears as I could before they turned bad.

I picked the corn as fast as I could, every third or fourth ear rotten. The bad ears went into burlap sacks, the good ones into the back of the wagon. An hour or so into my pulling, I'd finished a row, one of thousands, and had just turned down the next row when I heard the dry crunch of stalks being pushed aside.

"Jimmy, boy, where are you?" Frances said.

"About another ten rows over, Fran."

She pushed through, a few stalks collapsing to the ground. She carried supper in a basket, biscuits and dried beef—still no cooking going on in that house. Then behind her came snapping, the sound of someone pushing over the rotten or used up stalks.

"Daddy and TJ's coming to help," Frances said.

"Things are falling apart." I pulled my cornhusk hat off and wiped my brow. "Daddy's heart ain't into this place no more."

"Nope. I suppose it ain't."

"What you think we're going to do? We're about to lose at least half the corn crop."

"I don't know, Jimmy." Frances sat the basket down and picked up a burlap sack. "Pick corn, I suppose."

Daddy and TJ bent over the stalks, stepping on them to crush and snap the trunks. They said nothing. TJ went right to pulling the ears like a cat chasing a white-tailed rat. He'd done half a row in the time it took me to do a dozen plants. Daddy glared at a stalk the entire time it took TJ to finish a row, then he pulled, slower than I'd ever seen Daddy work before. Slow, like the way a ditch can fill up with only a trickle feeding it. By sundown, after a full day in the fields, we finished little and I felt sorry that something had dug its way into Daddy's spirit.

I went to bed next to TJ, happy to get off the floor and sleep like a man might sleep. I considered taking up snoring, but decided it was too much work. Our little house out amongst the corn fell quiet and empty. Crickets cheep cheeped and coons out in the fields chirped and cooed to each other. One of the hounds sleeping beneath the house bumped up against the floorboards, rushing to chase after whatever roamed in the dark.

TJ got out of bed, not trying to hide his noise. He put on his nice shirt and trousers, and slid out the window. When he stepped down onto the ground, he peered back through the opening and saw me looking right at him. He turned and walked away.

I'd left my shoes tied and kept on my overalls so I wouldn't be too far behind TJ when he left. My knee caught the edge of the sill as I dropped down to the swept-dirt yard. "Damn it." I could feel a tickling trickle of blood seep down my leg, but the scrape hadn't been bad enough to tear the thick denim.

The three quarters moonlight came and went as clouds pushed about above. Fireflies winked on and off across the fields. In the distance, heat lightning flickered.

TJ's long legs and quick stride took him well out ahead of me. He walked fast. I ran to catch up, lowering my overall straps, near about losing my britches, but managing to pull on a shirt with one hand while keeping the bottoms up with the other.

I huffed loudly, my feet scuffling along the dirt path. When I got close enough to hear TJ's shoes kicking rocks here and there, I slowed and looked for places where I'd hide if he turned around. The moon lay hidden deep behind clouds, barely a silver glow coming around the edges. Overhead trees cast deep shadows like being in molasses. In the gaps between trees, the bare sliver of luster from the moon lighted up the gap in a silver shine. In places, the darkness was full and heavy, while other spots glowed and glimmered.

TJ's back and stride reminded me of Daddy's and Lawrence's—long and steady. As he passed in and out of the shadows, I realized he'd gotten taller over the summer.

I figured he'd be out trying to meet Tony in town, which they'd planned when Lawrence left. Besides the saloon and the drug store where I know the two had met before, I couldn't imagine another place they could find each other.

As TJ passed the McCormick's field he seemed to pick up his pace. I had to run every few yards just to keep up. Alongside the Hollander pig farm, the stench forced us both to cross the road and cover our noses and mouths with our hats. He passed the old pumping station, the railroad crossing, the Wicket's farm, and a red brick house surrounded by a Victory Garden where a jumble of corn, peppers, beans, tomatoes, watermelons, squash, and a dozen other plants pushed against each other. A light burned behind the front door glass of the red brick house. Hanging in the window was their service flag with three blue stars— three boys in the Service.

I became a British assassin, I told myself in my finest Churchill accent, following a Nazi general trying to kill President Roosevelt. I hunched down, walked slower, not wanting to be detected, but TJ kept up his pace and I almost lost sight of him, so I resigned my duties.

We crossed into a long, thick row of magnolia overhanging the path. The darkness deeper, even cooler, thicker. As TJ emerged back into the light, he stopped at where Hamlet and Cheraw Road meet. Within a pace, I stopped beneath the thickest magnolia, its red seeds scattered and squished along the road, stinking of rot.

He turned. I crept back into the shadow of the magnolia. He stood out in the open, his face glowing in the moon, then disappearing into shadow as another cloud passed, then back to glowing. He seemed to look toward me, but I don't think he saw me. The water tower, tall and rusted, stood off the road a few paces, its metal legs like an alien from outer space. Its long shadow ended deep into a field of beans.

Then I heard what must have made TJ turn. Someone walked behind us as fast as we'd been walking toward town.

TJ pulled the head off a weed dangling along the side of the road and put it into his mouth.

I turned to see who might be coming up fast behind. For just a blink, I feared it might be Daddy.

Feet crunched on gravel. A rock skipped past me. Somewhere behind me a person approached, then they passed me in the shadow, a piece of material brushing up against my arm, a smell of farm and something fried, covered up with lye soap and the rubbings from a yellow sweet clover that smelled like new mown hay.

"Frances?" I said.

She took another step, leaving the shadow, and turning. "Jimmy?"

"You following us?"

She turned and looked about her, then stepped back into the shadow where she searched the darkness, her hand outstretched.

"What you doing here?" she said. "Of course I'm following you. I just want to know what you're doing here? Why did I have to follow you?"

"Frances, you near about run into the back of me. You didn't know I was even here."

"Well, what you doing standing in the middle of the darkness like this?"

"Watching TJ looking at me, and probably you."

"TJ? Where's he?"

"Come on." I grabbed her by her print frock sleeve and ran off toward town.

The next I saw TJ, he'd slowed his stride as he rounded the corner off Hamlet into town just where the Catholic church stood tall and reaching into the night air.

I stopped walking and Frances took two or three more steps. "You ain't following us, then what you doing?" She turned back toward me. A car passed. From The Gulf I could hear music playing, but not the tune, just the beat.

"You been sneaking around, too, ain't you?" I said.

Frances stood there and looked between town and me. She seemed to look up at the water tower. "Yeah. I have."

"You've been coming in to see Matthew?"

Her face sagged, her head bent down a little, as if I were Daddy or Lawrence giving her hell for doing something. It felt nice to have that power for once.

"Seems to me there's a whole bunch of sneaking going on around the Quick farm these days," I said.

She raised her head and pulled her shoulders back.

"Sure is. What you following TJ for?"

"Finally had enough of his sneaking. I want to know what he's doing."

"Told you before, he's got himself a girl."

We walked into town, turning the corner at the Catholic church, our pace slower. I figured I'd lost TJ by then, but might still find him if I just took my time and thought about it.

"I don't think it's a girl," I said, recalling TJ and the Army boy talking by the truck. "Where you meeting Matthew?"

"Down the dance hall on Marlboro."

"You're too old to have to sneak about. Daddy should

just let you."

"We could've made a regular trip to town tonight, but it didn't seem right to even talk about it with Mama acting all low and heavy. Matthew would have come and got me down on the road, but he didn't know we weren't coming to town anyway."

We stood at the town square at the corner of Market and Marlboro where The Gulf met Bennettsville proper. I could see down the street to the hospital where Pastor Myers' office glowed brightly.

Frances hugged me, kissed my forehead, and turned up Marlboro where crowds of town folk, sailors, WACS, soldiers, and a few Marines walked. She turned back toward me, "You ain't going to tell Daddy, are you?"

"Frances, if I tell it means I was out sneaking about, too. I'd have to tell him about TJ, too." I stepped toward her. "It's okay for you to see Matthew. You're old enough."

She smiled, waved, and skipped a few paces, then walked as quickly as she could to meet the crowd spilling out of Breedon's Drug Store heading for the dance hall.

After three carloads of GIs turned the corner onto Marlboro, a group of them whistling and calling to Frances, I cut across the street and walked through the town square toward Breedon's. A soldier, Robbie his friends called him, who I'd spoken with a few times about Italy, sat with a town girl on a bench. They held hands and leaned in close, whispering and laughing. I passed another couple kissing, their hands moving through each other's hair. People stood about the square, smoking and talking.

From the Confederate Soldier Memorial I could see into Breedon's. Mr. Breedon wiped the counter as Mrs. Breedon swept the floor preparing for when the movie would let out. Three kids sat in one of the booths sipping on a milk shake. Heading up Marlboro, the dance crowd whooped and hollered, Frances running to catch up.

Then I saw through Breedon's tall windows TJ and the soldier coming out of the bathroom in the back. They both stopped with a surprised look on their faces, as if they didn't know that the crowd had received its silent signal to go dance. Mr. Breedon looked up from his counter and nodded. The soldier smiled and put his hand on TJ's back, pushing him toward the door. I thought for a second that I'd run over to them. I raised my hand getting ready to call, but when they came out the door of the drug store, they turned away and ran up Main Street.

I ran after them, keeping to the other side of Main. They stopped half way up the block and leaned up against a building, beneath an awning, disappearing into the dark. I thought I heard one of them laugh, not TJ.

I waited in the doorway of the Ford dealer, its windows boarded over, a sign reading, "Be back after the war." Then I moved to the narrow alley next to Sanitary Café. The place stunk of fried onions. A flock of flies lingered around the windows and doorway.

I couldn't see into TJ's shadow. They walked out of the darkness toward Marlboro Theater, their shoulders close, almost touching. I waited until they'd crossed Main between cars passing, then I ran up the block and peeked around the corner. I thought they might be going to sneak in the Coloreds Only entrance and watch half the movie, but they walked past the alley, then past the ticket booth, then past the building, and rounded the other corner.

I ran again as fast as I could, my feet slapping the sidewalk. I bumped into a town man. "Sorry," I said over my shoulder. Peeking around the next corner, the windows of the hospital were dim. Market Street sat black and nearly empty. I couldn't see anyone. The shadows had shadows. They'd made a long passage around the block heading back toward the town square, the water tower, The Gulf, and The Rendezvous Saloon.

At the square, the glow from Breedon's lit up the dark park. People walked toward The Gulf where the light got sucked up again and the buildings made a black cutout of the stars above. A shooting star darted by.

I ran across the square to the edge of The Gulf. A Negro man sat on a stoop, his face glowing maroon as he sucked in on a cigarette. He seemed to be standing guard. I expected him to stop me, to ask for my papers the way I'd seen the Nazis do in the movies.

He drew in long on his cigarette and blew the smoke out. "Evening."

I stopped. "Yes, sir. Evening."

He didn't say anything else, but closed his eyes and

leaned his head back against the door.

People seemed to stand everywhere in The Gulf. They grouped in alleys and doorways. Laughter came from inside the houses, the windows and doors wide open. One place played music real loud and I saw just Negro folk coming and going through the doorway.

Then I saw up ahead The Rendezvous Saloon. Its red-pink light filled the street in the shape of squares. Still leaning against the window, the air raid warden slept, a glass of beer on his belly locked between his hands.

I passed a house where I saw through an open window an old Negro lady in a rocking chair. Her glasses hung low as she stitched something with long thread.

I leaned up against a building across the street from the saloon. Inside, crowds jammed The Rendezvous. People in uniforms and civilian clothes pressed their backs against the glass window. People stood on the steps, down onto the sidewalk. Perry Como's voice mingled with glasses knocking together and a low rumble--the grumble of dozens of voices.

Men walked into and out of the alley. I stepped toward the alley, then backed up and pressed myself against the wall behind me. I couldn't go up that alley looking for TJ again, if that's where he went. Darkness spread across The Gulf so heavily he could be standing just across the street and I wouldn't know. I sat on a stoop opposite the alley.

"Hey, fuck?" a man said.

I leaped up and turned around. "Oh, I'm sorry." In the darkness of the doorway, I could just make out two bodies behind a dark coat. The man lit a cigarette, the match glowing bright. Robbie and his pretty girl glared out from the red bloom.

They stepped forward, their faces glowing red from the saloon's light. The pretty girl patted Robbie's chest. I thought I'd seen her around town carrying her schoolbooks from the high school. I knew I'd seen her on Saturday nights in the drug store with a different soldier each week.

"Jimmy, that you?" he said.

"Yeah. Robbie? I just saw you up in the square."

"No privacy there, Jimmy boy. Know what I mean?"

He chuckled. "Sorry. Didn't mean to yell. I thought you might be some freak wanting to get a close-up view. You know Jane?"

"We've seen each other about," Jane said.

I looked back toward The Rendezvous, not wanting to lose TJ, if that's where he went.

Then I saw him. He stepped down out of the bar with a glass of beer in his hand. "Holy shit," I said. There were a dozen things TJ could have been sneaking around for that summer. I hadn't believed he wanted to drink beer, but the proof stood before me just across the street.

Tony squeezed between the people standing on the saloon's steps and stood next to TJ on the sidewalk. TJ leaned in and whispered something to him. Tony nodded and they walked toward the alley. As they passed into the darkness where the pink light glowed through heavy smoke and tiny lights flickered from the ends of burning tobacco, the soldier put his arm across TJ's shoulder.

The move wasn't much. Daddy had done that to us. The picture in Pastor Myers' office showed the same arms around each other's shoulders. At the county fair, to run a three-legged race, we always put our arms across the other guy's shoulders the same way. But this time looked different.

I stepped down off the sidewalk, looking both ways for cars. Then, I felt myself being dragged back onto the sidewalk.

"What you doing?" Robbie let go of my collar.

I thought I shouldn't say because I didn't know. Spying? "I'm looking for my brother."

"Lose him, did you?" Robbie said.

"Well, I guess so." I looked toward The Rendezvous and felt the back of my neck tingle as I thought about how the alley still reminded me of what the entrance to Hell must be like—smoky, red, things creeping in dark corners. I remembered TJ coming out of there bloody and the boy knocking me to the ground.

Robbie said, "You aren't thinking of going in there, are you?"

I shook my head. Robbie and Jane smelled of smoke and beer.

"Good. Isn't a great place for you to be going."

I turned away from the saloon to look at Robbie. Jane straightened the ribbon in her hair. She put her hands behind her and seemed to wrestle with her bra. Her white bobbie sox were pushed down, showing her ankle.

"You know," Robbie said, "the scuttlebutt says that place is for three-letter men and very loose dames, if you catch my drift."

I caught his drift. Though I'd heard Matthew call TJ's friend a three-letter-man, I'd had no idea what it meant until I saw that arm go across TJ's shoulder.

Jane blew air out her nose. "You're all wet. The Rendezvous is just a Negro bar. GIs like it cause its got cheap beer, and the women like it cause they just cheep. Ain't nothing funny happening there."

"I'm all wet? Broad, you're so wet water's coming out your ears."

Jane stepped away from us.

"You don't know, do you?" Robbie said to me.

"I know."

"He's from the country, Robbie," Jane said, as if her status in Bennettsville amounted to a grand place in New York.

"Dummy up, will you? Jimmy's a friend of mine. I'm trying to educate him here."

Jane stepped away from Robbie and crossed her arms.

"You know—the girls are cheesecakes, flappers, floozies. And the guys are three-letter-men."

"I get it. Fag," I said.

"You got it. F-A-G. Fags. Sissies. They go for each other instead of for girls. That place is very verboten, but the MPs don't care so long as there isn't any trouble. Get it?"

I got it. I sat down on the stoop, my eyes as wide as they could be. I knew then what had been in the dark shadows. I knew then why the darkness up that alley seemed to move. I knew why Lawrence had gotten angry enough to beat his brother and why TJ snuck around but didn't much smell of smoke or beer. I knew then how TJ could be sure he wouldn't get a girl pregnant.

Jane walked into the darkness, back toward the square. Robbie patted me on my back. "I'll see you around,

Jimmy. Be careful of that place." He turned and I heard him say, "Don't get in a lather, girly girl."

I looked at The Rendezvous and up the dark alley. I could see the ends of cigarettes glowing in the deep darkness of that entrance to Hell. I struck my leg with my fist. "Stupid. Stupid. Jesus Christ. Stupid. How did I not know? God, TJ. Good God." All of it jumped clearly into my head, obvious at that point. TJ and the soldier being quiet and away from everyone. Tony saying he'd get into trouble, that some guys suspected. The sneaking off.

I understood then why I'd started the summer knowing everything about TJ, but didn't seem to know him at all as the summer grew long. Pulling myself off the stoop, I walked toward Hamlet Road and the water tower that peered over the rooftops down into town. I never looked back toward The Rendezvous Saloon.

24

*T*J and I stood in an irrigation ditch up to our knees in still water that had drawn mosquitoes and critters looking for a good place to drink. When we came out that morning, just as the sun turned the sky to ash, a pack of deer, the buck's antlers wider than I am tall, had their heads down just up stream where the water trickled through.

Since Saturday, TJ whistled a tune beneath his breath, the pitches of a song coming through, but the tune known only to him. Frances skipped and jogged and danced about. Daddy stopped riding into town to find Old Man Patterson, having been told the landowner had gone off to Washington with a delegation of other owners to speak with the War Department. Mama's legs weren't swollen as badly on that Sunday. She pulled herself from bed, moaning, and trudged off to church. When she came back, she sang the Lord's Prayer, not caring who heard. Even Irene giggled more, I guess because the others felt better.

I felt worse. I didn't much care about the farm, but the way I figured it, I'd rather be cheated on 160 acres than have nothing, even if Old Man Patterson took bread right out of our mouths. Frances sneaking off to find Matthew wouldn't be good if Daddy found out. In some ways I wished I didn't know, but I spent some time wondering how long she'd been walking to town down the long dark roads.

Worst was knowing about TJ. I thought about the time we'd been down the old plantation playing about the slave quarters. Still a child, two or three years earlier, Daddy hadn't quite made the farm work so hard on me. TJ and I played war—me often the Indians, him the cowboys. Other times, he'd be a Jap and me a Marine. This one time, I sneaked about his enemy camp. Quiet. I even surprised that ancient cat that slept around the old plantation. I heard the enemy moving about inside a shack. I leaped through the door with my dogwood-branch gun. There, on the floor beneath a window on the old bed frame, wood slats but no sort of mattress, just a blanket, were two boys I'd seen about town. Their britches lay in a bunch on the floor and their hands pulled on each other's things. They didn't hear me. They didn't stop and I watched for a second not sure what to do. Then TJ leaped through a window yelling, "Got you! Got you!"

Those two boys curled up like opossums trying to protect their privates. Then one of the naked boys jumped up and grabbed his pants. "What the hell?" he said.

TJ ran toward me, I turned, and we both fell out the door. Picking ourselves up, we ran away laughing. A few yards off, we turned around to see deep in the shadow of the shack someone peering out, a streak of light falling across his face from a hole in the roof.

Standing in the ditch tugging on a heavy black willow branch, I wondered if seeing those two fellas gave TJ the idea to like other boys. To be a sissy. A three-letter-man.

Since Saturday, I slept in the living room, Daddy not much caring what happened about the farm. I tried to turn on the radio, but the yellow light didn't glow, the dial just clicked. I went out to check the radio's windmill and found the stick Daddy jammed into the spindle the night Lawrence's number came up. The battery on the Zenith had died. I slept on the rug, telling Mama my room felt too hot. I let TJ have the bed alone, to come and go, to not be close enough to bother me.

I'd heard rumors and tales of people out on these farms doing things to their kin. Ain't never happened in our house, but it didn't feel right to stay in that room with TJ.

I felt my feet sinking into the sludge at the bottom of the ditch. We'd cleared most of the blockage and the water had seeped down a bit, but a willow branch held up the rest of the show. Slime and mosquitoes covered my legs. I'd heard tales from guys with buddies in the Pacific who'd found their bodies covered in leeches after wading through water.

"I hope there ain't no leeches," I said. We really hadn't spoken in days.

Frances and Daddy pulled corn in the field next to us. The two moved like machines, peeling off the ears faster than most people can chew gum. Irene walked behind Frances, sitting in the dirt, playing with weeds, watching ladybugs crawl across her hand.

"Pull," TJ said.

We heaved and the branch let go. TJ stumbled back and plopped onto his ass into the muck so that water made a dark line across his chest.

The water drained away quickly, turning into channels that took it throughout the field, along the edges of the roads, down toward the house. TJ held out a hand covered in a thick layer of goop. I laughed at him.

When he stood up, he threw his straw hat onto the dry ground and looked toward Wilder Road.

Out of the rising sun, with a telltale trail of dust rising in the morning breeze, the sun winking and twinkling off those grains of sand, a man walked toward us.

Not yet above the distant trees, the sun had dried the earth. Whoever walked our way passed through shimmering mirages that wavered like water on a pond. The silky air parted, then filled with dust, and collapsed behind him. He looked tall and broad. He walked quickly, his pace hard, hitting his heals into the ground.

"Yeah. Someone's coming," TJ raised his chine toward Wilder Road.

"I seen him." I climbed out of the hole that stunk of manure and decaying leaves. TJ slid back into the muck a few times before grabbing hold of some weeds for leverage.

Ditch water evaporated from my legs, leaving behind a film of black and red sandy earth. I shaded my eyes with my hand and looked at the approaching man still distant, nothing but silhouette and dust cloud. "Coming at us fast."

"Look at that rooster tail. Would've thought a motorcycle was buzzing this way." TJ scraped mud from his legs, arms, and back. He pulled the brim of his hat low shading his eyes. "Should I yell for Daddy?"

"Man ain't got a right to walk up a road?"

"Yeah. But there ain't nothing up here but us and the farms."

"Jesus, TJ, you're in charge now. Lawrence ain't here."

TJ looked toward the house and then up the corn rows as if measuring the quickest way to Daddy. He turned toward the approaching man and walked to the middle of the road. "Yeah. Guess we'll just see what he wants."

I stood next to my brother, crossed my arms across my bare chest, slapped at a mosquito, and set my jaw as if to say, "This here's our town."

I wanted to say something to TJ. To ask him what he was doing in the alley. I still hoped he just wanted to drink beer, but I didn't believe it. The image of the soldier, Tony, not three letters, putting his arm across TJ's shoulder kept slipping to the front of my mind no matter how hard I wanted to push it to the back.

We waited as the man grew. When he reached the edge of our fields he came out of the shadows of the overhanging trees and the high morning sun cast him in silhouette. He looked tall and dressed in light clothing. His shoulders and chest and waist stood wide. His long arms and thick shoulders slumped forward so that his knuckles seemed to hang too low. His pace kept quick and straight, but he occasionally stumbled or slid.

"Damn," TJ said.

"Damn," I said. The man was big—at least the size of Daddy, perhaps bigger. His steps seemed angry, his motion unstoppable. I uncrossed my arms. Glancing up a corn row, I could see Frances and Irene pulling off ears and beyond them, perhaps another field or county away, Daddy changing from a full sack to an empty one.

"He's a big one," I said.

"He's Lawrence." TJ picked up his hat and slapped the dust from it.

Lawrence's hair, never too long before, had gone down to the nubs. Light brown pants replaced his overalls. An undershirt, stained rouge with dust, peeked above the top button of his matching shirt. A red film of sand coated his skin, dry and light in color in some places, but dark and matted elsewhere. Sweat created little rivers and body mud down his arms.

"Lawrence," TJ said.

I ran up to him. "Lawrence?"

He stumbled at a dip in the road and walked past us. I thought he mumbled, "Boys," but it could have been the distant shout of Daddy, or a branch knocking against a trunk. He stunk of exertion as if he'd worked in the fields all day and had not yet dipped into the spring or washed at the well.

"Lawrence!" Frances called from up the corn row.

Daddy dropped his burlap sack and ran past Frances and Irene.

TJ and I didn't move for a second or two. I thought maybe I'd imagined Lawrence, the mirage brought on by the heat or maybe the mosquito bites swelling on my arms.

When we turned toward the house, Lawrence had already made it to the gate. He didn't pause, but pushed it open, it flipped back, slapping against its post. The open front door let whatever slight breeze might come to blow through the house, cooling the heat from the cook stove.

I ran toward the house and heard TJ behind me. Daddy crossed through the rows and burst onto the road next to us.

Irene grunted somewhere behind me as Frances must have yanked her off her feet during a full trot.

"Lawrence? It's Lawrence?" Daddy said.

We didn't answer.

"Lawrence," Mama shouted from inside the house, something heavy crashed to the floor. "Luther!" Mama screamed. "Luther!"

Daddy ran faster, leaping the low fence.

As we came through the door, Mama stood in the kitchen, an iron skillet on the floor, the smell of frying fatback filling the house. In one hand she held a pan of biscuits. The other arm she had wrapped around Lawrence, who seemed to have let most of his weight collapse onto Mama. He sobbed heavily, his big arms encircling her waist.

Daddy paused at the door. Then, as Lawrence sunk to

his knees, Daddy rushed forward and grabbed his big son about the waist.

"Lawrence, boy, you okay? Lawrence."

Frances nearly dropped Irene on the front stoop and pushed past me and TJ.

"Lawrence, honey," she said.

When Lawrence's weight came off Mama, she reached to her lower back and tossed the pan of biscuits onto the stove. She held onto the sink as if she were about to throw up into it, her eyes closed tight, one hand rubbing her spine.

"Mama." I went to her, putting my hand on her back. She flinched. "You okay? What's wrong?"

She nodded. "Get . . .," she said, then stopped, wincing and squeezing her hands against the edge of the counter. ". . . Get him some water."

I ran out to the well and pumped as hard and fast as I could. My shoulder ached. I didn't have the bucket sitting right, so it fell over, the water spilling onto the ground. I righted it, filled it again, and ran back to the house.

Mama stood upright again. Daddy had dragged Lawrence to Mama's chair at the kitchen table. Frances mopped Lawrence's head with the hem of her dress.

I dipped the water up to Lawrence, but most of it spilled out and onto his shirt, turning the dried dirt there into more mud. I poured the water into a Mason jar. Mama came over and held it up to his lips. He drank.

"What are you doing here?" Mama said.

"What happened, boy?" Daddy had his hands on Lawrence's shoulders.

TJ came in holding Irene's hand. The two sat on the living room floor.

After a few sips, Lawrence sat forward and took the glass. His lips were blistered, his face sunburned. He drank the whole jar down. With each swallow, his face winced. I filled it and he drank another half.

He sat his elbows on the table and put his head into his hand, wincing at the burn. Then he cried.

"What happened, honey?" Frances patted and rubbed his back.

"Give him a second, there," Mama said.

"I ain't rushing him," Frances said.

"I said, leave him be," Mama said.

We all sat quietly, listening to Lawrence go through his crying. Heavy at first, it turned to mild moans, then a slight wail. He cried and wiped his dirty face onto kerchiefs Mama brought him. He blew his nose, but hid his eyes, covering them while he cried.

Irene got up and sat on Daddy's chair next to the radio with her mouth open, her eyes unblinking, looking at the table.

It took a few minutes, but then Lawrence tried to talk. "I . . .." He grabbed his throat, his face squeezing in pain. It must have been sore if his face and lips showed any indication of what his whole body must feel like. Then he cried some more.

Irene lowered herself from the chair and went into the kitchen, TJ following her. "Why's Larry back?"

"I don't know, honey pie." TJ came into the kitchen and pulled a biscuit from the pan to give to her.

"Well, maybe the war's over," I said. Frances looked at me and shook her head.

"Don't you think you'd better turn on the radio to find out?" TJ threw his thumb toward the living room.

I put my finger to my lips to quiet him.

"Why you shushing me?" TJ said.

"Will you two stop it?" Daddy said. "Why don't you turn on the radio?"

"It ain't working." I didn't look at him.

"Ain't working?"

Saying that he'd not removed the stick would make Daddy look stupid, but he asked me. "I found a twig in the spokes of the windmill, so the battery's dead. Maybe the wind blew it in there."

Daddy rubbed his chin. "You take the twig out?"

"Yes, sir. Maybe it'll charge it back up."

One of the hounds got up off the back stoop and came in. I petted him behind his ears, down along his spine. His tail wagged, then he turned and ran outside.

Lawrence sat there shaking his head and wiping snot. It was calm. Everyone seemed bewildered, no one knowing where to look, what to do.

Daddy said, "So, boy, what's happened?"

"Don't know what to say, Daddy."

"How about the truth?"

"I ain't going to lie to you. I just don't know how to put it."

Mama patted Lawrence's arm. "Take it slow."

Lawrence nodded. "Well, I don't know a lick why I was there."

"Marines said you supposed to go, boy," Daddy said. "You signed up."

"I know, Daddy. I don't know. There wasn't nothing there I understood. Men yelling at us. Pushing us. They fed me good, but I didn't know what the stuff was." Lawrence rubbed his hand across his head. "They cut off all my hair." He tugged on his dirty uniform shirt. "They took my clothes and gave me this."

"Well, what'd you expect?" Daddy spread his hands. "You've seen the soldiers here. They all look like that."

Lawrence stared at his Mason jar.

"I don't know, Daddy. I'm sorry. I was lying there with a hundred other fellas and I heard half of them laughing and joking and half of them crying and sniffling and I just didn't know why I was there. I wished I would've talked with Jimmy more about the war."

Lawrence looked up at me and grimaced.

"It might sound dumb, but I never really paid any attention to what everything meant. I just knew when I was lying there and they were playing some sad music that told us to go to bed and they turned those lights off that I had no better place to be than here on the farm. Those boys all seemed to know so much about everything and I just know how to farm."

Daddy wiped his mouth with his sleeve as if he'd just finished a plate of food. My stomach rumbled hard. I'd been out to the ditch since before breakfast. I ate a biscuit.

"So you just up and walked away?" Daddy said.

Lawrence shrugged.

"Ain't nobody stop you?"

"I didn't see no one."

"Honey, did you tell them you were leaving?" Mama said.

"I didn't see no one," Lawrence said.

"Don't you think they'll come and get you back?" Daddy said.

"I don't think so. You should've seen all of them. There's thousands of people there marching and running and jumping up and down and yelling. I ain't never seen so many." Lawrence sipped more water. "I don't think they'll miss me."

"Won't miss you?" Daddy shook his head as if a bug had landed in his ear. "How you figure that?"

"There's just so many people, Daddy. What do I matter any?" Lawrence raised his head. "I don't want to go back." He cried more, but the tears ended quickly.

"I told you that you didn't have to go before you left," Daddy said. "Don't you think you should have thought more about this then?"

"I know. I know. I thought about it. I thought all that time I went off wandering." Lawrence looked up at TJ, who turned away. A yellow spot remained where one of the alley bruises still healed. "I thought I wanted to get away from this place," Lawrence said. "They made me a Marine. I signed up for the Army, hoping to get in the Air Corps, but they made me a Marine. Sent me to Parris Island. I ain't never met such a bunch of mean people before as that place."

"Ain't that their job?" Daddy said. "They're mean to get you ready for the enemy."

"They ain't just mean, Daddy, they ain't human. Yelling, screaming, pushing, shoving. Starving some boys. Slapping boys. Making grown men feel like animals. They made me stand in the rain all night because I turned one way when they told me to turn another. I stood there not knowing why I was there. I knew I didn't have to be. I needed to be here helping with the crop. Couple boys told me they'd cut off an arm to be the eldest son of a farmer so they didn't have to go. I should have stayed, Daddy. Can't I stay?"

He put his head back into his hands. Mama patted his back.

"So you left?" Daddy said. "They just let you leave?"

Lawrence shook his head. "I ain't supposed to have gone, but I did. Don't make me go back, Daddy. I don't want to go."

"It's okay," Mama said. "It's okay. You ain't got to

187

go. They said you're essential to the war effort right here. You ain't got to go."

Daddy slammed his hand down onto the table. We all jumped. He stood. "The hell you ain't going."

"Daddy!" Frances stood.

"You signed the papers. You wanted to get away. Well, you're going. If I've got to hog tie you and haul you there in the wagon, you're going. This is a war, son. This ain't life on the farm. Hell, I've been a tough old bird in your life, but those men yelling at you are trying to make you strong. If you don't see that, you're dumber than I thought."

"Luther, the boy has walked all the way from the other side of the state. You think he would do that if it wasn't necessary?"

"I don't care if he walked all the way from Hell itself. You're getting yourself cleaned up and fed. Then you can sleep here tonight, but in the morning I'm taking you down to town myself and making sure you get on another bus to Parris Island."

"You were the first one to say we could hide him," I reminded Daddy.

"Shut up, boy," Daddy barked.

"Luther. Listen to me. This boy of ours ain't going nowhere he don't want to go."

Daddy pushed over a chair and rushed toward her. Frances stepped back. I leaned away expecting something to explode—flesh, blood, wood, air.

Lawrence bounded from his chair and blocked Daddy's way. Daddy had been moving so fast he bounced off of Lawrence, stumbling back half a step. Daddy looked down to Lawrence's feet then back up to his eyes.

They stood face to face. Big Ben ticked off seconds, the big hand clicking over to the next minute. Daddy raised his hand, Lawrence leaned back, then Daddy wiped his hair back onto the top of his head.

"You're going, boy," Daddy said. He turned and walked out the front door, and turned just outside the gate, down the long road that bordered our cotton fields.

"How'd you get away?" I sat down next to Lawrence as he retook Mama's seat.

"I joined in a squad of men marching across Archer

Creek Bridge off of Parris Island. No one seemed to notice me, so when they turned one way, I kept walking straight."

"You walked the whole way?" Frances said.

"God, no. I caught a ride a few times, then hopped a train that took me all the way to Florence. That's about where I started doing most of the walking, late yesterday."

"That's near about forty-five miles," Mama said.

"Yes, ma'am." Lawrence rested in Mama's seat, leaning against one hand while Mama held the other. "Got anything cooked up, Mama? I'm so hungry." Lawrence tried to get up, but his knees seemed to tremble a bit.

Mama pulled herself away from holding onto Lawrence's hand. Frances brought over some fat back and the rest of the biscuits. Mama and Frances cooked up hoecakes, succotash, bacon, cornbread, and squash. Lawrence ate fast, juice dribbling down his face, sopping up white gravy with dry biscuits.

Daddy came back. Mama wiped her hands. Lawrence put down his fork and put his hands on the table looking like he might pounce. Daddy went into the bedroom and came back with his farm books. Frances sat a plate of food at Daddy's spot, but he pushed it to the center of the table and opened up the books.

"Son, you know Old Man Patterson's been cheating us all the years I've worked this piece of land." He unfolded a long, wide, hand-drawn map.

"Yes, sir."

TJ leaned forward to look and I walked around behind Daddy. The map looked like our farm, our house a square, the fields lined out. In the center of blocks dark eraser marks nearly ate through the paper, "Corn 1934" crossed out, followed by "Beans 1935" crossed out, followed by "Empty 1936" crossed out. Daddy's plan for rotating the crops. Once the war years hit, all the blocks said either "Cotton 1942" or "Corn 1942." Then, just the years changed, a few fields came and went switching between cotton and corn and wheat. I thought of the times when corn came right up to our bedroom window, and other times when cotton did the same.

"I got to thinking that the Army, or the Marines, whichever one took you, might not be such a bad idea. At least you wouldn't have to be a farmer," Daddy said.

"I like farming. It's all I know." Lawrence leaned toward the books.

"Then I thought how you could . . . well," Daddy said, rubbing his temples. "Things don't always work out too well. War and all. I've been a lazy man this summer."

"You ain't never lazy, Daddy," Frances said.

"This summer, I have been. Near a third of the corn gone bad. We got most of the cotton up, but that corn is going to put us behind. Sun up tomorrow we're all going out and picking fast as we can."

Lawrence looked up from the map.

Mama came over to the table and put her hands on Lawrence's shoulders. "All of us, Luther?"

Daddy nodded, then picked up a piece of bacon and ate it.

"What about the Marines?" Lawrence said.

Daddy looked out the door, where off beyond Bennetsville, toward the ocean, dark thunderclouds made a deep line in the sky—near black out there and blue inland. "The way I figure it, if they come for you, boy, you're going."

Lawrence clasped his hands together as if he was about to pray, but then he rubbed them like grinding a mud pie.

"You're going," Daddy said, looking at Lawrence. "Understand?"

Lawrence said, "Yes, sir."

"Until then, far as I'm concerned, you're essential right here."

When we finished eating, Daddy, TJ, Lawrence, and I went out and put the boars in with the sows. Daddy thought we'd make up some of the lost corn with piglets feeding off slop from the rotting corn.

A distant, low rumble of thunder made my ears tingle, my hair shimmer.

25

I had read in my *National Geographic* about how the storms that touched our farm came from the other side of the country, sometimes the other side of the world. Snow, rain, thunder, lightning. Each one felt and breathed like something that lived. I sometimes wondered what a rainstorm might think about or how snow felt about falling.

Heavy rains started as the sun set. Those clouds out over the ocean seemed to turn and rush in like an army invading. I sat on the front stoop, Irene pulling on my collar before she roamed off to play inside. The lightning went sideways for what must have been miles before turning down toward the land. Though distant, rumbles of thunder like the Western Union motorcycles or the planes landing at Palmer Field, growling, humming, booming, rolled about the countryside. Rain fell in a line, starting way off, blowing across the fields, flooding the low ground. I watched as the ditch TJ and I had just unplugged filled with leaves and twigs and clogged again. Lightning jumped out of the black clouds, through purple ones that attacked the edges of our land. It struck down sending dirt up, the thunder so hard and loud that my chest pressed in, my teeth clamped shut. I covered my ears. The cats disappeared into the darkness beneath the house. The dogs howled and shivered. I stood up with the door wide open letting the house cool as the temperature dropped. Water blew into the house, leaving puddles near the front.

"I'll wipe it up," I yelled to Mama.

Rain fell from the sky as if it had a point to prove. More lightning tore up trees while thunder shook our home. During moments of calm I heard Ham bellowing from the barn. The boars and sows squealed loud, painful sounds, as if they detected us about to slaughter them.

As the water fell on the sheet metal roof it sounded much like the beach with rushing and waning. Rain roared across the metal, then back. In places where the sheet metal joined or had rusted through, drips fell into the house. Mama and Frances rushed about with buckets and pans so that a whole band of pings and twangs started. The sound of running water made me want to pee, but I held it back. From beneath the house, through the spaces and cracks in the old wood planks, cool air pushed up from the wind.

Daddy sat with Lawrence going over more of the books. "If I'd done the math better I'd have known why we were always coming up short or just barely enough."

Irene stayed close to Frances, no matter where Fran went or what she did. "'Renie, honey, go sit in the living room," Frances said. Irene went, but came back with the next clap and flash from the sky.

TJ knelt before our bedroom window looking out at the storm. A twig propped up the window a few inches. His hair blew from one side to the other. Water crept across the sill and dripped onto the floor.

I sat on the bed and watched him for a minute or two. I felt as if I had about caught a rat in a corner, only the rat didn't know it yet. TJ seemed to be staring off toward town.

"Wishing you was in town?" I said.

TJ looked back toward me. Water seeped down his face as if he cried. He wiped it away with his shirtsleeve. "Yeah, I suppose I am."

"Me, too. I miss talking and listening. Just one week away and it feels like I've never been there. Sometimes, I feel real anxious when I don't get a chance to see a movie. Know what I mean?"

TJ sat with his back against the wall, water dripping onto his shoulder. "I know you followed me to town Saturday night."

I thought I should deny it, but a person knows what a

person knows. "Sure."

"Frances was right behind you. Besides, you can pretend to be a spy all you want, don't make it so."

"Seems like you don't much care who knows you're sneaking around."

"Yeah. Well, don't seem like Daddy knows."

"If Daddy wants to, he knows."

TJ looked out toward the kitchen.

"I thought I lost you the other night." He'd lowered his voice. "Did you find me in town?"

What had I really seen? If I hadn't been told what that alley meant, it would have always been just two fellas walking into an alley. The arm across the shoulder came to mind again. "I saw you."

TJ pushed his head back against the wall hard. He closed his eyes tight. "Damn it."

Air came up through the floorboards cooling my bare feet.

"What did you see?" he said, looking at me, but past, over my shoulder.

I twiddled my thumbs for a second or two. "I saw you going into the alley by The Rendezvous."

He put his forehead into his hands. "God damn it." He was too loud. If the storm hadn't been bellowing outside, Daddy would have heard his cursing.

I went over and eased the door closed leaving just a crack. Then, I went to TJ's side and knelt there on the floor.

He cried. "Oh, God. You know?"

I nodded. "I know."

He stopped crying, sudden and short, wiping his eyes. "That why you been sleeping out by the radio?"

I wanted to lie to him. I'd already made up a lie in case he ever asked. That with Daddy not caring too much about the place, I'd taken to listening to the radio every night after everyone went to bed. I'd already said it was dead. "Yeah. That's why."

"No sense in that. I ain't never going to bother you none."

"I know."

"Then why'd you sleep out there?"

I shrugged, then leaned against the bed.

Wind howled through the window knocking the little stick away. The window slammed down followed by the bedroom door. We both started, me clear to my feet, TJ letting out a slight "yelp."

"Come on out here, boys," Daddy called above the growing wind.

"Yes, sir," we both said.

We stood up. TJ punched me in my shoulder. I rubbed it, then punched him in his.

"You ain't going to say nothing, are you?" he said.

"Nope. Course not. But you seem set on telling on yourself."

"Yeah. Don't mean to, but it's just coming along that way."

"Boys!" Daddy yelled.

Mama had turned down all the lanterns to save on the kerosene. Around the kitchen, on the radio, sitting on windowsills, tallow and beeswax candles glowed. Most of the candles looked short, caked in their own drippings. A few fresh ones put off light high and grand. On the table, a stubby one with a long wick jounced each time someone touched the rickety slab of old oak. Mama had scattered pecans and peanuts about the table, set out jars of tea and coffee, cut watermelon and left it on the counter for anyone who wanted it.

"Whose turn is it to start the stories?" Mama dumped two pans of water into the yard.

"I did last time," Lawrence said.

"Oh, then it's my turn." Frances said, happy and then giggling. Each time a storm trapped us inside, we took to story telling and walnut eating and tea drinking to pass the time.

Last time, Lawrence had told the tale of a white dog who wandered about the countryside telling those about to die whether they might go to Heaven or Hell. My story had been about Nazis off of U-boats pretending to be Americans wandering into towns and buying up supplies. TJ told a story where a man as mean as a rabid dog had died, but when they burned up his body, the heart wouldn't burn because it had turned solid as a rock.

"Okay, now, shush everyone," Frances said.

Lawrence cracked two pecans in his hands. Frances

194

slapped him.

When the whooshing and washing of the rain, a clap or two of thunder, and the moaning of the wind were the only sounds, Frances said, "They say if you stare into a flame long enough, you can see things."

Irene looked at the flame for a moment and then scrunched closer to Frances. "What kind of things?"

"Be quiet, honey, and I'll tell you," Frances said.

"No voodoo in my house," Mama said.

"Ain't no voodoo, Mama. The truth." Frances extended her arms and moved them about slowly. "They say you can see things. The future, the past, secrets in men's souls."

"Not in women's?" Lawrence laughed. Daddy joined him.

Frances shushed them. "The future, the past, secrets. Secrets." Her voiced wavered like in a scary movie.

We all stared into the flame. Down deep, near the wick blue and white glowed and flickered. Red, orange, and yellow near the top shimmered. It wavered, tossing long shadows that moved this way and that across the walls and ceiling. We stared deeply. Long. Something appeared in there. The blue like water, down deep near the wick. The blue like water.

"Secrets. Future. Past." Frances' voice went lower, almost a hum. "I see Uncle George heading south."

I looked up at Daddy. His face lay deep in shadow, unmoving. He looked at the flame, then leaned forward. "I see a man dead down by the spring."

"You just want to string up Old Man Patterson," Mama said.

"Maybe, but that's what I see."

"I see a train," Irene said. "It's going around and around."

Everyone sat quietly, looking deep into the fire. I saw the water, then a boat.

"All I see is a big-assed Marine yelling at me," Lawrence said. Everyone giggled.

"Come on now." Frances scowled at Lawrence.

"Well, all I see is the flame a flickering," Mama said.

"Look deeper, Mama," Frances said.

"I am looking deep. Maybe it's the burning bush."

"I see water," I said.

"Water?" Lawrence sipped some tea.

"The blue, down there by the wick. Water. Like the ocean."

We all went quiet again, looking deeply. I felt tired. Lightning lit up the windows.

"What you seeing, TJ?" Frances said.

His wide eyes reflected the flame moving back and forth across the dark, shining center. "I thought I saw a dead man down by the spring, but that's just Daddy talking." He went quiet for a second. He blinked, then said, "I see tall buildings."

Lawrence split open a long peanut. Everyone breathed deeply as if waking from a long nap.

"No more of this. Too much like witchcraft for my liking." Mama got up and dumped two buckets of water out the door.

One of the sheet metal plates that made up the roof shook loose from its nail and banged against another plate.

"Damn it," Daddy said.

The plate banged harder, lifting off the rafter, water pouring in.

"TJ, go down to the shed and bring back the ladder, a hammer, and some nails."

"Luther, the boy can't go out in this here mess."

"Either we fix it or that whole roof will come off. Wind will get up under those plates and toss them off like leaves from a tree."

TJ stood at the back door, measuring the rain as it fell like the waves on the beach. At times it came very heavy, other times it eased a bit. He ran off, slipped in the mud, but then disappeared into the darkness. A flash of lightning showed him by the tool-shed door.

Mama stood at the sink watching TJ through the window. Daddy leaned forward in his chair and looked through the open doorway.

"You ain't going on the roof to fix that tonight, are you, Luther?"

"No. We'll have to try to fix it from in here."

Irene lay down on the rug in the living room. I went and sat beside her, rubbing her back. Then I stretched out there and rested my head on the floor, feeling that cool air coming up from below. Another flash of lightning and I could see down there, below the house. The dogs hunkered down together, shivering and whining. The cats formed a circle near the dogs, their eyes glowing.

Then the rain stopped. A gust of cold air rushed through the open doorway. Something heavy banged into the roof and rolled down the sheet metal. I jumped up and followed the rolling sound. It fell off the roof and landed on the back stoop. An ice ball the size of my fist lay there white and melting.

"Oh! Dear, Lord," Mama said.

Daddy jumped up and stepped onto the back stoop. "TJ. Get back in here. Forget the ladder."

The hail seemed to fall all at once. The pounding on the roof sounded like all the fireworks at a carnival going off at one time. It banged and pounded. The ice balls were so heavy, they dented the hard metal. After the bang, the ice scraped and rolled then plopped as it came off the roof and landed in the ground.

Lawrence grabbed a wooden Coke crate. Shielding his head with it, he ran into the backyard. Daddy picked up a skillet and did the same. The hail pounded on Lawrence's shield and thunked onto Daddy's. They went into the blackness lit by flickering sky and the passing of white balls into and out of the candlelight.

I picked up Daddy's chair and turned it upside down over my head.

"No, you ain't." Mama grabbed my collar and held tight.

"They might need help."

The hail roared and rushed. Irene covered her ears and screamed. Frances went to her and picked her up.

Mama let go. As I stepped onto the stoop sliding about on the melting chunks, the hail pressed down on me and the chair. Daddy and Lawrence came out of the darkness dragging TJ between them.

A gash across TJ's forehead bled. Lawrence's and Daddy's knuckles bled, too. For a moment I thought they had both taken to beating him, but then I realized the sharp edges of the ice, falling from the sky like a bullet, ripped into their skin.

Daddy skidded across the stoop and then dumped TJ into a chair. He wrapped his hand in his blue kerchief. Frances and Mama dabbed at TJ's head and Lawrence's fingers.

"Watch that blood. Don't let it drip on the floor," Mama said.

"Shut up about the blood already. The boy's hurt, Nobsey."

A rush of wind came just before a loud creak and crash. "The hog house," Daddy said. The hogs squealed louder, their whine socking through the hammering hail. "God almighty."

He stood in the doorway looking out, just a shadow when the lightning flickered, glowing from around his body. In those flashes of light, the hail seemed huge and unreal. Boulders or goose eggs dropping from the sky.

Lawrence got up and found his Coke crate, dented and broken. "I'll try to rustle them into the barn."

Daddy stopped him at the door, holding Lawrence's two shoulders.

I'd never heard such squeals as the hogs calling through the hail, like a train whistle at times, then long and hurting, dozens of different tones, then a few, then just one as the hail pounded into them, crushing skin and bones. I figured a big one to the head is what killed most of them.

Another whoosh and crash brought down the tool shed and hen house. Chickens flapped out into the twinkling light, their squawks quickly smashed by the falling ice.

Above the kitchen, the sheet metal roof collapsed as a hailstone the size of an apple crashed into it.

Irene screeched.

Hail bounced off the floorboards, denting and scraping the wood. Mason jars drying on the counter shattered. The kitchen window exploded as hail sailed through it.

I pulled the washtub from beside the sink.

"Jimmy." Mama held out her hand as if I was about to drown and she wanted to pull me to safety.

A chunk of ice hit the edge of the tub and dented it. The crash and dinging of the hail as it filled the metal basin got so loud that everyone covered their ears.

Then it stopped. A final piece of ice knocked the chimney off the cook stove. It rolled down the roof and landed in the front yard.

"Lord, above, thank you," Mama said.

"What are you thanking him for?" Daddy said.

"For bringing us through that."

"If he was going to do anything, why didn't he prevent it?" Daddy stepped out into the backyard, followed by his sons. Lawrence brought a lantern. TJ lit it.

We slid our way down to the hog pen. The gate was a shambles of splinters and wire. Two hogs lay piled atop each other, dead and beaten, their heads bashed in, the flesh on their backs beaten and torn. The rest died inside the falling structure.

"Jesus," Lawrence said.

TJ held the lantern up, checking every corner of the sty. "Only two of them here. Must be a dozen or more missing or inside that pile of wood.

"Maybe a few pushed that gate over to get out." Daddy took the lantern and bent low to the ground. "Tracks are washed away."

Lawrence walked across the yard. "Hens ain't much better. Killed most of them." His voice seeped through the darkness.

Daddy said to me, "Boy, check on Ham and the mules. That old barn should have held up better."

Lightning flickered. I counted to five before the thunder rolled in.

26

At dawn, the sun grew big and blood red into the blue morning sky. All signs of black storm clouds had passed, but they'd left humid and thick air, promising more rain before long.

"Ain't a good crop left in any of the fields," Daddy said, kicking his mud-caked boots against the stoop. "Most of it's been beaten down to nothing." He clumped into the kitchen bringing mud with him. Mama brought a bucket and scrub brush over, knelt down on her knees, and scrubbed away the mud.

We boys stood in the kitchen barefoot, the legs of our overalls rolled up to our knees, our chests bare.

Daddy looked up at Lawrence. "Take them out to the north field and start picking anything that survived, boy." He went back onto the stoop. As he looked out across the fields in each direction, he rubbed his hands across his gray stubble.

Lawrence turned to TJ and me. Then he stepped toward Daddy. "Pick what? There's nothing left."

"We can sell off the ears as slop. Lot of hogs need feeding in this county. Lawrence, get on. Don't be wasting time around here. Nobsey, pack them their breakfast. Got to get up what we can use for feed before it rots into the ground."

Mama already had biscuits, ham, cornbread, and bacon waiting for us in two buckets. Frances picked up one and I the other. Lawrence and TJ slung piles of burlap sacks across their shoulders.

"Lawrence," Daddy said, "I'll be out later to help. I'm going to look for them hogs. Fill those sacks till I bring the wagon around. Save all the corn you can."

Water overflowed the ditches turning the front yard into a lake. What wasn't covered in water had been beaten into hills and runnels. Where corn stood tall the day before, flat land clear to the trees that bordered the fields stretched today. In a few spots entire rows stood while every row around it was beaten into corn pulp. Water flowed along the corn rows like tiny rivers.

In places, we sank to our knees in mud, while other parts of the road had cracked and split from the summer heat. A chestnut tree along the side of the road moaned in the breeze.

"Watch that tree, it's coming over." TJ pointed to the tree as it leaned toward the road.

Another gust and the tree tilted, lowering itself onto its side, not quite falling as the roots pulled up out of the ground, but sort of just giving up.

"There ain't going to be much out here to save," Frances said.

"What does he expect us to do? Every farm around will be out pulling up corn for slop. Who we going to sell beaten and rotten corn to? I've never heard of such a thing." Lawrence picked up his pace, his heels digging in wherever dry and cracked dirt crisscrossed the road.

When Frances and Lawrence got way ahead of us, TJ turned to me. I could feel him looking at me, then away, then back. I thought he might want to talk more about the alley, so I made up my mind to say that I didn't want to talk about it.

"Think we can go to town tonight?" he asked.

I looked at TJ and shook my head. "Why? So you can leave us again? Go off into the darkness? You're crazy."

"Yeah. No." TJ said after a few strides. "I just want to go to town."

I left him talking, running to catch up with Frances and Lawrence. *The White Cliffs of Dover* had started playing at the Marlboro. By missing a real trip the week before, I felt as if there might not be a world outside the farm. I couldn't get past the image of TJ and the other guy going into the alley. I just didn't understand what he saw in another boy. I wanted to get to town, too, but we had to pick the corn, the hogs missing or dead, the chickens killed. I wondered if the soldier Robbie thought that I had a reason, a reason like TJ had, to go into that alley. I worried that Robbie might tell Matthew and Frankie that I was a three-letter-man.

Up ahead, mirages that looked like the swaying trees pranced about the road. I kept my eyes on the shimmering heat wondering if we'd ever get to it, but knowing that the closer we came the further away it would be.

We marched on until we came to a dry intersection of two roads without names. Lawrence paused and waited for all of us to catch up.

"Come on, TJ." Lawrence kicked mud off his feet on a fence post along the edge of the road.

Hawks and crows circled the south field diving to feed on what must have been mice and coons chased out of their holes or drowned.

Locust in the trees buzzed. A bee zipped past me.

Irene ran to catch up, her hands in the air stretching for Frances to pick her up. "Frannie," Irene said.

Frances stopped and turned on Irene. Irene ran into Frances' legs. "Renie, you're just going to have to learn to walk on your own. I'm tired of carrying you around all the time."

"Leave that child be," Lawrence said.

"You mind your business and I'll mind mine. Irene is my responsibility and it's high time she learned to walk on her own. Don't none of you be picking her up."

Lawrence opened his mouth a few time, as if he wanted to yell back at Frances. I smiled at how bold she'd become, but hid it with my hands.

When TJ caught up, Lawrence headed off again without saying anything. Lawrence far out ahead, I said to Frances, "What was that all about?"

"Irene's got to learn to walk on her own."

"That ain't why you were yelling."

"She wants to get to town just like the rest of us," TJ said.

202

"I don't know what you're talking about, boy," Frances said.

"Frances, he knows we were behind him last week."

"Oh," she said. She swung the bucket, her head down.

"So that means I know you were sneaking off to town, too," TJ said. "There's something there that you want as much as Jimmy and me."

"I don't want nothing in that town," I said, worrying that he might mean the same thing he wanted.

"You got friends there, don't you?" Frances said.

"Sure." I thought about what Robbie might say to Matthew. "Not like you and TJ." The mud packed on my shoes smelled like manure.

"You ever going to tell us who it is you're meeting in town?" Frances said to TJ.

TJ seemed to be seeing something way out ahead, past Lawrence and the fields. I could see out the corner of my eye him looking at me. "Don't think I will."

Once in the field, we spent hours filling a few dozen bags of corn just good enough for hogs to eat. TJ stood and seemed to count the rows remaining. He let out a long blast of air through his nose and mouth.

"What's wrong with you, boy?" Lawrence said from the next row over.

TJ looked back at Lawrence, then turned and rolled his eyes toward the sky.

"I said, what's wrong with you, boy?"

"Nothing." A scuff on TJ's forehead, still scabbed in a long streak, met up with his new wound from the hail.

Rolling up the road, Daddy and Mama brought the wagon out, the spokes thick with mud, the old hag huffing through the mud.

"Found the rest of the hogs drowned in a ditch," Daddy said. He pointed to where buzzards circled, then floated down toward the ground.

Mama fed us our lunch as Daddy told us that the storm cut a path through the fields. It had dumped hail in some places, destroying everything it could. Other places got a dash of rain. "Rumor of a twister other side of town near Palmer Field," he said.

Frances put down her chicken and wiped her hands. "Excuse me." She walked off into the shrubs along the edge of the field. It looked as if she went off to do her business, but I saw the way she stopped eating and gagged a little when Daddy mentioned Palmer Field. She must have been worried that something bad had happened to Matthew.

After supper we picked until the last embers of yellow and purple sky bled away for the night.

The next morning, Daddy woke us as the sky had just started turning ashen. Crickets still chirped, a bat darted about catching bugs. Mama had breakfast ready as we woke up. I don't know how early she planned to leave, but her Sunday bag and hat sat ready on the chair by the front door.

"Your Mama and I'll be out to help you when I get back."

Mama turned her head toward Daddy, then went back to flipping the pancakes.

"It's Sunday. I was going to church."

"Not this week," Daddy said. "We'll haul the corn in the wagon to town to sell it and see if we can find the Old Man."

Mama stood silent, looking out the window.

By the time we finished breakfast, the morning sun stood big and bold against a white wispy sky. The heat seemed to blast down as if I stood too close to a wood fire. We went back to the fields with empty sacks. I wondered how long *White Cliffs of Dover* would stay at the Marlboro and hoped we'd get through the mess the hail left us before the movie went away.

"Going to be a thin year," Frances said.

"We got plenty of preserves and smoked meat," Lawrence said.

"But we'll be set back for all the acres we didn't get up in time. Daddy wasted half the harvest mad at the Old Man."

"Don't be talking poorly about Daddy," Lawrence said.

"It's true," I said.

"I don't care if it's true, don't be bad talking Daddy."

Lawrence walked out ahead of us, then went to the far

end of the field from where we chose to pick.

We picked quietly in the fields. Irene picked a few ears, brought them to Frances, and asked a dozen times, "Is this one okay, Frannie?"

"Yes, sweetie, it's okay. Put it in the bag."

Husks rustled and browned as the summer heat dried them. Planes flew high above us, dipping and turning as the pilots learned their lessons before going off to war. I stopped and watched the planes for a minute or two. One plane looked as if it might crash as it raced toward the ground, but somewhere still high above it pulled up in an arch and disappeared into tall white clouds.

While she examined the ears lying in the mud along one row, Frances hummed the tune and sometimes sang words to a song I'd never heard. Some of the lines said, "No love, no nothing,"

TJ sang low a song I couldn't quite understand. I felt myself growing angry that he seemed so happy. He didn't seem to care that I'd seen him go into that alley.

They always picked faster than me. I picked as fast as I could to match what seemed to be their middle pace—the pace that let them pick longer between breaks.

The water had drained off the land in most places, but the ditches flowed, still full, though not overflowing. Everywhere, dead coons, birds, rabbits, and mice, some of them squashed the way they are down on Hamlet Road when cars squish them, but hammering hail had finished these. The rest, I figured, had drowned.

Everyone seemed to hear the car at the same time. Dust didn't sprout up from the still damp roads, so we'd missed the tell-tale rooster tail that warned us of someone coming. I might not have heard the car down on Wilder if it hadn't backfired, but it did, doing its best with wartime gas.

Frances turned toward Lawrence, who had heard. He looked off toward home.

"Think it's the Marines coming to get Lawrence?" I said to Frances.

"Lord, I hope not. Why can't they just forget about him?"

"I'm sure everyone's okay down Palmer Field," I said.

"Well, I hope so," she said.

"Come on." TJ picked up a sack of corn. We hauled the full sacks to the road, water dripping out of the burlap.

Lawrence dragged his sacks to the edge of the road, then walked back toward us along the side of the irrigation ditch.

"What you think that was?" Lawrence asked everyone.

"Don't know," Frances said.

"Frannie, I have to pee." Irene had her knees pressed together.

"Renie, honey, why did you start calling me 'Frannie'?"

"I don't know. I have to pee." She bent over, turned around a few times, and then danced on her toes.

"Go on, honey. Go down to those bushes and do your business."

Irene ran off toward the hedgerow at the end of the field.

"Could be the sheriff come checking on everyone after such a storm," I said.

TJ took off his hat and wiped his forehead. "I'll go find out." He tossed his cornhusk hat onto the stack of burlap sacks. "I'll bring back dinner," TJ said over his shoulder.

"Dinner? Daddy and Mama are bringing it out," Lawrence said. "You ain't going no where. Get back here."

"Mama's gone off to church," Frances said. "Let him go, brother. We'll need food. Ain't no since in waiting on Mama to bring it out. A woman who walks to church every Sunday ain't about to miss it to pick an extra bushel or two." Frances took a rag out of her bib pocket and wiped her hands.

"Daddy said she had to go with him," I said.

"Well, may be, but I saw her rocking her way toward church not long after we made it out here."

"Come back here, boy!" Lawrence shouted. His chest rose and fell several times. He looked to Frances, then to TJ, then at me. Lawrence took off his old felt hat and slapped it against his leg. Mud on his feet cracked and fell off as he stamped them.

TJ turned and put his hands to his mouth. "I'll be back." He waved and kept walking.

"No sense in yelling, Lawrence, he ain't coming back.

Leave it be," Frances said.

"Boy!" he yelled one more time, but TJ had gone down the cracking road. "Shoot. I can't wait to tell Daddy about this one."

"Lawrence Quick!" Frances threw down the corn she had in her hands.

"What?"

"You'll do nothing of the sort." Frances put her hands on her hips. "There's too many secrets going on around this place for anyone to be telling anybody anything."

"What are you hiding?" Lawrence said.

"Don't matter what I'm hiding," she said. She pressed up against Lawrence. "What are you hiding besides running away from the Army?'

"Marines."

"It doesn't matter!" Frances screamed.

Lawrence took a step back. "What the hell is wrong with you?"

I'd never heard Frances yell like this. She had anger and hurt, a spring uncoiled all of a sudden, coming out of her mouth. Angry at Lawrence, the farm, the storm, Matthew, the world. Lawrence had already pounded on TJ worse than Daddy had ever done.

"She's right." I dropped my sack and stepped toward Lawrence.

"You back off, boy, or I'll kick your ass," he said.

"That's it, Lawrence. You beat one brother near to death, now you want to hit another one? You want to know what's wrong with me? What's wrong with you?"

"I—," he said, taking a half step back.

"—It was you, Lawrence." I moved toward him, pointing in short jabs. "Don't lie and say it wasn't. There wasn't anyone else in that alley but you and TJ. That soldier didn't do it and no one jumped him. It was you."

"I . . . I—" Lawrence stumbled back.

"—You did. I was there. You can't lie about it."

"You didn't see anything."

"I saw plenty."

"What?" He threw his arms out, palms up. "What you see?" Lawrence spread his hands like a preacher. "You

207

ain't seen nothing."

"I heard plenty." I turned away, then back. "You beat your own brother like a dog in the street!"

"You don't know nothing!"

Frances got between Lawrence and me. "Stop it. Stop it."

I took a step away, my face hot, my head throbbing. I could feel myself breathing fast. I flung my hat to the ground, turned away, and walked a few paces off.

"I . . .," Lawrence seemed to swallow some words.

His hesitation made me madder. I turned and ran to him. "You beat him until he bled!"

He backed away, stumbled over the sacks, and fell to the ground. He tried to crawl, but the burlap blocked him.

I stood above him. "You beat him, Lawrence." Spittle flew from my mouth. "You broke his bones! Have you looked at his face? There are scars. A scuffmark still on his head. You did it. A scuff mark! You kicked your own brother!"

I looked at Frances who nodded at me, tears falling from her eyes.

I walked away from him again.

Lawrence got to his knees.

"Why'd you do it?" Frances said. "What did he do? You can't stand it when someone disobeys you? You beat him because he snuck off?"

"No."

"What? Was he drinking a beer? What was it? Smoking? Kissing a girl? He broke one of Daddy's rules. What was it? What could be so bad that you'd beat your brother?" she said.

"No. You don't want to know." Lawrence got up off his knees. "You're so goddamned stupid, you know that?" Lawrence let the air out of his lungs. His face lost some of its redness and a hint of white peeked through. "You don't want to know." He leaned back and looked straight up where buzzards rose currents above the fields. He wiped the corners of his mouth.

My throat felt swollen and sore, my mouth empty of spit. "I know why he beat TJ."

"Why?" Frances said.

"Alright, God damn it. You want to know?"

Lawrence's voice made my eardrums ache.

"Yes. Yes. Yes. I want to know," Frances said, nodding. "What did he do? Tell me so I won't get the crap beat out of me by my own brother."

"I didn't mean to hurt him so badly." Lawrence took off his hat and wiped the lining and his forehead. Tears glazed over his eyes then tumbled down his high cheeks. "I didn't mean to hurt him." His tree-like body shook. "I was just mad. I caught him in the alley—"

"—So what!"

I took Frances' hand. "Let him finish," I said, my voice low.

"Damn it," Lawrence said. He looked toward Irene as she crossed a ditch, coming out of the trees. "I caught him in the alley with a another guy."

I looked up to Frances. Her face hadn't changed expressions. She raised her eyebrows. "That's it? You caught him in the alley with a guy? Gambling?"

"Jesus Christ, do I have to spell it out for you?" Lawrence turned and walked a few paces off then came back. "You so smart, Jimmy, you tell her."

"What does he mean, Jimmy?"

"He was with another boy," I said. "You go off to see Matthew, TJ goes off for the same reasons."

Lawrence pulled a rag from his pocket and wiped his face, then he bent over and held himself up with his hands on his knees. His crying burst from him like a clap of thunder.

"Lawrence? Is this true?" Frances said.

Lawrence dragged in as much air as he could, then blew it out. "I caught TJ kissing another boy."

Frances put her hand to her mouth. "Oh, my Lord."

"Yeah. It really made me mad. I whacked the boy on the head and he took off running. Then TJ stood up as if he was going to hit me so I whacked him a few times too. I guess I hit him too much."

"TJ don't like no boys," Frances said. "All the girls just love him. They love his black hair and brown eyes. I've heard girls talking about wanting to marry TJ someday. Gertrude can't help but giggle when she's around him." She turned toward me, but I couldn't look her in the eye.

"Could this be true?"

"I saw him go into the alley next to The Rendezvous last Saturday night," I said.

"Saturday night? We didn't go to town Saturday night," Lawrence said.

"That don't mean nothing," she said.

"Fran, yes it does," I said.

"We didn't go . . ." Lawrence started, then realized. "You all been sneaking off, ain't you?"

"You ain't got no room to talk about sneaking off, Lawrence," Frances spat back at him.

A crack, like a pistol shot, came from down the road. Daddy's whip snapped across the mule's back as he pulled up an empty wagon. Irene jumped down from the back. Mama wasn't with him.

"Frances, Irene was halfway down the road," Daddy said.

"She was supposed to just do her business and come back."

Lawrence wiped his face again. Frances turned away from Daddy.

"What's going on out here? There ain't no time for standing and talking. Dinner's in the back."

We stood there as Daddy put a feed bucket on the mule. Irene took Frances' hand.

"What I just tell you?" Daddy stopped and looked around him, down across the fields and up into the hedgerows. "Where's TJ?"

We looked between ourselves. Irene seemed to want to say something, but Frances pulled on her arm. Lawrence turned away.

Daddy took off his hat and looked around the fields again. "Last time I'll say it. Lawrence, you're in charge out here. Where's TJ?"

"He went back to the house looking for dinner." Lawrence stuffed his hands into his overall pockets.

"When?" Daddy said.

"Not long ago. About the time we heard a car. Did you hear it?"

"I heard it. Drove past the house toward the spring and McCormick's fields. Army car."

"You didn't pass TJ?" Frances said.

"No." Daddy's eyes stretched open as if seeing something for the first time. He took the feed bucket off the mule. "So he left after the car went by?" He climbed back into the wagon and pulled on the reigns for the mule to turn the cart around. "Damn boy. Knows damn well I'd bring the food out. Rip his hide apart. Get on there, go on!" He snapped the whip at the mule. As the wagon completed its turn on the narrow road, we all ran to get aboard. "Stay here, damn it."

"We'd better come." Lawrence put Irene in the back. As Daddy pulled off, Frances and I ran, Lawrence taking our hands and pulling us into the back.

Daddy drove the wagon hard, splashing through mud and not slowing at corners. We held onto the sideboards, Irene bouncing up as we came out of the ruts.

27

"**W**here's the boy?" Daddy said, stomping into the kitchen. Mama's hat and bag sat on the table. She sat at the table rubbing her legs.

"Which boy?" Mama said. Then she looked past him and blinked a few times as Lawrence and I came through the door.

"TJ. Where is he?"

"I haven't seen him, Luther. What's the matter?"

"I don't know, but I'm tired of him sneaking off so much."

Frances turned and whispered to me, "He knows."

I whispered back, "He knows something."

"Oh, Lord," she said. "We'd better find him before Daddy does."

Daddy turned toward us. "You thought I didn't know?" Mud streaked across his face. "Ain't nothing I don't know happens on this farm." The house felt cool. The smell of rotting flesh came from the backyard.

Daddy went out into the yard, we followed. Flies flew thick in the air. One of the hounds wallowed in the sty gnawing on a dead hog.

"Daddy." Frances ran to catch up. "Daddy!"

He turned. "What."

"We'll help you look."

I looked beneath the house while Lawrence went off toward the barn. Frances walked down to the vegetable patch. Daddy went back into the house. I could hear each door slamming open. By the time he'd come out, Lawrence had swung open the barn door, it rattling and squeaking before banging against the wall.

Daddy stood on the stoop with his hands on his hips. "Where is that boy?"

"Don't hurt him none." Mama stood just inside the door, her hand on Daddy's arm.

He stepped off the stoop and walked toward the path that led to the spring. I knew that's where I'd be if I didn't have to work the fields or look for TJ.

"Let me run ahead and check for you," Frances said as we passed the barn.

"Get behind me," Daddy said.

Lawrence ran up. "Nothing in the outbuildings."

Daddy walked yards ahead of us as fast as his long legs could carry him. "TJ! Where are you boy? TJ!"

Halfway down the path to the spring, I saw a green U.S. Army car through the trees. On its door a white star shone, parked behind the grove of pines and oaks next to the deep water. It gleamed in the afternoon sun, a reflection of the trees lifted off the roof as if a tiny grove had sprouted roots in the green paint.

Daddy had not cleared the trees ahead of us when I heard the first shouts. It sounded like someone needed help, but then there came a laugh.

Daddy ran toward the spring. I ran as fast as I could, Lawrence and Frances somewhere behind me.

Reaching the edge of the spring, we came up behind Daddy who stood with his hands on his waist. In the water, two heads bobbed about. TJ and the boy, the soldier, Tony. From the slight rise at the edge, I could see their arms swaying back and forth beneath the water. The boy reached out and pushed TJ down. TJ's body seemed to glow white in the dark water.

"Luther!" Mama called from somewhere up the path as she hobbled toward us.

Daddy's breathed heavily. Sweat soaking the back of his shirt. Lawrence stepped toward the spring his fists clenched, but Daddy put out his arm stopping him.

"Luther." Mama came into the clearing. "Whatever

he's done, don't be hurting that boy none."

Daddy looked back toward Mama. "I'll handle my boys any way I want." He picked up a stone and tossed it into the water, splashing the boy.

The boy let go of TJ's head and spun around in the water. "Oh, God." His white smile dropped off as TJ's black hair popped up from below.

"Daddy." TJ swam toward the edge. He seemed to almost leap from the water, the boy quickly behind him. Frances turned away from their naked bodies. They both got on their underpants. TJ slid into his overalls. The boy kept whispering "Oh, God. Oh, God." He slipped on his pants, but couldn't seem to untangle the belt and suspenders.

TJ's bib dangled around his knees. His hard chest heaved up and down as he took quick breathes. Trying to slip his shirt on, TJ never took his eyes off Daddy, but his mouth whispered something.

Daddy walked toward them a few yards, then stopped. "What're you doing boy? Come here."

TJ stood, frozen, except for his efforts to get his shirt on. When he did, he left it unbuttoned.

"Run," Frances said, her hand covering her mouth, her words not loud enough for Daddy or TJ to hear.

I didn't know who she meant, TJ or the soldier. I wanted to run. I wanted to be anywhere but there at the edge of the cool spring. I wanted to be in London or Paris or New York or Hawaii or home in bed. Anywhere but there. I didn't want to watch how TJ might try to explain this. I didn't want to see the hurt that would cover Daddy's face. I didn't want to see what the soldier would try to do. I didn't want Mama to see.

"Luther." I tried to turn Mama away, but she pushed me aside, her strength greater than I thought she had.

Daddy stepped toward TJ a few more yards. "Come here, boy."

The soldier kept pulling on the knot that bound the belt and suspenders wrapped around his legs. I could see the white edge of the soldier's boxers. His stomach had sharp ripples of muscles showing through his tanned skin.

"We're just swimming, Daddy." TJ looked up at the sun.

I didn't see Lawrence move until he passed Daddy running toward TJ. "You liar." Lawrence struck TJ in the shoulder. TJ fell back onto his butt.

Daddy and I moved forward, but Frances went faster. She got into the fray before Lawrence could land another blow on TJ. She pushed him back. TJ bounded to his feet. Daddy caught him about the waist and picked him up.

"Now hold on there." Daddy squeezed TJ, shaking him like a doll. "Hold on."

Frances pushed Lawrence away, her hands pressed against his chest. "Lawrence, I love you. You're my brother, but so help me, you'd better leave TJ alone."

"What's going on here?" Daddy put TJ down, but stood before him.

"Get out of my way, Frances. That boy needs another lesson taught to him."

"Lawrence," Mama said. "Stop acting crazy, boy!"

"Don't ever touch me." TJ tried to get around Daddy, his fists tossing out toward Lawrence. Daddy caught a hold of TJ's wrist. TJ pulled it away.

"Jesus, Lawrence. You've beat him bad enough already. That's your brother. Look at him. He's your own flesh and blood. You want to hit him? Just how much of Daddy do you have in you?"

"Frances! Don't bad mouth your father like that," Mama said.

"You're the one who beat TJ in town?" Daddy stepped toward Lawrence. "You lied to me? You hurt your brother that bad, Lawrence? What's wrong with you, boy?"

Frances stood between the two of them, her back to Daddy. She kept pressing on Lawrence's chest.

I went to TJ. "What are you doing?"

"We were just swimming," he said.

"You weren't," I said. "It ain't just swimming when you're in the water with . . . .." I didn't know what to call Tony.

"You liar." Lawrence pushed Frances aside and rushed past Daddy, but Daddy turned and slapped him on his head.

Lawrence stopped. "Jesus, Daddy, don't you see? You think they were just out swimming? Your son is

215

sleeping around with other boys. Look!"

Daddy turned toward TJ and the soldier.

"Lawrence," Frances said, disappointed.

"Christ, Frances, it's here in black-and-white. There they stand." Lawrence pointed to TJ and Tony, then turned and walked down to the spring.

Daddy walked back to where the two of them stood. "Is this true? I see with my eyes the two of you swimming about. Okay. Is this true?"

TJ looked back at Tony. His pants still not fastened right. The suspenders coiled in and out and around the belt, the belt laced through its hoops, but somehow tangled in the material of the pants.

"Jesus, boy. Jesus Christ."

Mama walked forward, then stopped. Then she walked forward again as if each step was the only step she'd ever take again.

"You son of a bitch." Daddy stepped toward Tony, but TJ got between them. "Get out of my way, boy." TJ gripped Daddy's arm so tight that his knuckles turned white.

"No, Daddy."

Daddy tugged at TJ's grip.

"TJ," I said. "Better do what he says."

"No." Daddy seemed to take a step back, though he didn't move his feet. TJ let go of Daddy's arm. Daddy looked them up and down, then toward Lawrence.

The boy's face had turned bright and crimson, but he didn't seem afraid. TJ trembled a bit. So did I.

"TJ, honey, tell your Daddy it isn't true." Mama walked up and put her hand on Daddy's arm. "Tell him."

TJ looked at Mama and I knew he couldn't. I knew he could convince Mama and Daddy that they'd just been swimming to get out of the heat. Mama and Daddy would have believed it because they wouldn't want to believe anything else. He could have said that Lawrence lied because brothers sometimes said mean things. He might have even said that Lawrence hadn't been the one who beat him in town that Saturday night. Instead, he said nothing.

"Oh, dear Lord." Mama's hand covered her mouth.

"Mama," Frances said, reaching out for her, grabbing her hand. Mama pulled away.

Tony looked from face to face. Everyone quiet. Somehow, I think, he believed that things were calming down. He extended his hand to shake Daddy's. "I'm Tony," he said.

TJ grabbed the boy's arm as if to pull it back.

I moved forward. "No!"

Daddy swung out his right hand and smacked the boy on the head.

A snap echoed off the spring.

The boy took a step back. His buckle caught between two rocks. The suspenders pulled tight. Tony twisted and the belt tripped him. He fell sideways, his arm extending.

TJ's hand still rested on the boy's arm. The boy's skin scrapped through TJ's grip.

Mama reached out as if she wanted to catch him.

Just like that.

It took a second—half a second—the time for part of a breath.

His head landed on a jagged rock and opened up. I'd seen watermelons fall off a cart and crack the same way.

TJ looked down.

Lawrence and Frances moved forward. I followed.

TJ fell to his knees and touched the boy's head.

Daddy stepped forward. "Jesus Christ."

TJ sprung at Daddy's chest, hands catching him in the shoulder, tumbling him to the ground. Daddy's cheeks went pale as he fell backwards. TJ sat on Daddy's chest, slamming his hands into his face, head, chest, arms, once, then again, and again. A dozen blows fell before Lawrence yanked TJ away. Daddy scrambled to his feet.

Mama crouched next to Tony. She pulled her apron off and pressed on his bleeding head.

"Give me your shirts, boys," Mama said.

I yanked mine off and gave it to her. Her apron had already turned red with blood. She balled up my shirt and pressed it on top.

Daddy moved toward TJ, but Lawrence stepped before him pushing Daddy back by the shoulders. Tears streaked down Lawrence's face.

"Get your hands off of me, boy," Daddy said.

"Leave it be," Lawrence said.

"Leave it be? You've shown me the light here, boy, and you want me to leave it be? Get out of my way!" Daddy moved toward TJ, fists ready.

Lawrence stood before Daddy. "Don't you touch him."

TJ pulled off his shirt, knelt next to the boy, and added the tattered cotton cloth to the dampening apron.

The boy's eyelids opened, but only the whites showed. "I need some rags," Mama said. Blood slipped down her arm dripping off her elbow.

"Tony? Tony? You'll be all right. Mama's like a doctor. She'll take care of you." Blood seeped through the cloth and onto TJ's hands.

"Hush, child." Mama said.

"Enough, Daddy. It's enough." Lawrence pushed Daddy back.

Daddy looked down at what was going on. He seemed to deflate, and then turned away. Lawrence yanked his shirt off, tearing the sleeves on the overall's suspenders. Frances snatched it away from him.

Daddy sat on the ground, first facing the spring, then turning towards us. A mark on his forehead trickled a little blood and his eyebrow looked swollen. Blood seeped from his nose. "My nose," Daddy said, "Nobsey, my nose." His shirt had a long streak of red and brown running from collar to stomach. He pulled out his kerchief and put it to his face.

"This boy's hurt bad, Luther."

Tony's hand shot up and grabbed TJ's arm. His muscles hardened showing the veins, his fingers gripped. TJ pried the fingers from his, but the hand didn't change its shape. Tony sucked in short breaths.

"Mama," TJ said. He sat on his rear. A moan exploded from TJ's mouth. "Ma."

Tony's open mouth made no sound except rattling breaths.

28

*T*J had Tony by the legs and Lawrence had him around his chest. I did my best to support the middle of his body, but the three of us running up the path back toward the house didn't work too well.

"Put him in the barn," Daddy told Lawrence

"You're going to be okay," TJ said to Tony. "Mama can fix anything."

Lawrence readjusted his grip on the boy. "Daddy—"

"I said put him in the barn!" Daddy held his head back as much as he could, dabbing at his face with a kerchief.

Mama came up behind us as fast as she could. "Luther—"

"—Put him in the goddamn barn!"

"Boys, put him in my bed." Mama passed us.

Frances had run ahead. She stood on the back stoop with what looked like all the rags we had.

Frances stepped aside as Mama went up the steps. "Where's Irene."

"She's okay. She's in our room."

Lawrence couldn't get up the steps backwards. Frances took one arm and I took the other and helped Lawrence pull the boy up the stairs.

They put Tony on the bed. Blood seeped onto the patchwork quilt that Grandma had made for Mama.

"I'm going for help," Lawrence said.

Mama, Frances, and TJ clamored into the bedroom. Daddy, Lawrence, and I went into the kitchen.

"You ain't going nowhere!" Daddy grabbed Lawrence's arm.

Lawrence pulled his arm away. "Don't touch me ever again." Lawrence's teeth clamped down tight. He looked toward the room and called louder, "He needs help. I'm going. Alright, Mama?"

Daddy reached for Lawrence's arm, but Lawrence pulled it away before Daddy could get it. "Ain't no one going anywhere. Boy, goddamn it, you're going to listen to me. Or—" Lawrence grabbed Daddy by his blood-soaked collar and pushed him up against the sink. The biscuit pan fell off the narrow counter and banged against the floor.

"—Or what? You'll dash my brains out, too?" Lawrence leaned in to Daddy, glanced at Mama's bedroom, then at me. He lowered his voice. It rasped like the rustle of dry leaves. "I'm telling you, ever lay a hand on me, Mama, or anyone else ever again and I'll kill you."

"Luther!" Mama said, standing in her bedroom doorway. "Lawrence!"

"I'm going for Doc Kinney, Mama." Lawrence turned away from Daddy and headed for the front door.

"No, Lawrence." Mama stepped away from the door, reaching for Lawrence. She looked back toward the bedroom and lowered her voice. "Ain't no one going for help. They'll charge us with murder."

"Us? It was Daddy who did it."

"And if your father is sent to prison or lynched, then it's all of us who suffers. I ain't saying what has happened ain't wrong, because God knows it is. I ain't saying that, Lawrence. You go out that door and we're all finished."

"I'll take care of everyone, Mama."

"I know you can, but don't you think those Marines are going to come and get you some day? Then what? It's your father, Lawrence. Your brothers' and sisters' father. The Marines haul you off and your father in jail, we'll starve. We'll die out here in these fields."

"Don't be defending me, Nobsey."

"Luther, you need all the defending anyone can give. Lawrence ain't all wrong. I'd feel a heap better if Doc

Kinney was out here. I just don't think it would do a whole heap of good."

"Mama!" Frances called from the bedroom.

"I'm coming." Mama pulled Lawrence close, her voice very low. "Stay here, Lawrence, but yell out that you're going for the doctor. At least we can give him a little hope." She went back in. "We're going to need more rags. Frances, pull the linens off the beds if you have to. Jimmy, fill some buckets with water. Sit them in here."

"Mama!" Frances looked at the boy's head and then raised her eyebrows.

"Doctor's on his way," Mama said.

When Lawrence looked at me, I shrugged.

"Mama, I'm taking the mule and wagon. Be back as soon as I can." Lawrence went out the front door, mounted the wagon and drove off.

I knew what Mama meant about giving them hope. The boy's eyes, still rolled back, leaked blood about the edges. Frances took a clean pile of rags in one hand and switched the old ones out as quickly as she could. The side of the boy's head showed a long, deep gash, the shape of his head odd and off kilter. The doctor could use a plane to get here and it wouldn't be soon enough.

"Oh, God," TJ said. He turned away from the bed and collapsed against the wall.

I ran outside, two buckets in each hand, and took to pumping water into the pails. When I came back, Mama dropped some of the rags into the buckets.

"Add some lye soap to them and bring them back," Mama said.

Lawrence pulled the buckboard into the barn, the door squealing as he shut them.

TJ stood up. "Is the doctor here already?"

"It's too soon," Frances said. "Keep the pressure on those rags."

TJ sat down and added a dish rag to the pile of reddening cloth.

Daddy went to the back door. Lawrence came through it and sat at the kitchen table.

"By the time Doc Kinney gets here, it'll be too late," TJ said.

I went out back and tossed the red water into the yard. It seeped away from the house, down toward the barn. I filled the buckets, adding a bit of lye from a tin next to the pump. When I came back in, Daddy had gone out front.

A streak of shining blood stretched from the back door to Mama's bedroom. Footprints smeared the blood around, tracking it to the front door and into my room. The mattress in Mama's room had turned red.

The boy moaned, then inhaled as if the whole world had to fill his lungs. His skin looked white, his lips blue.

I sat the lye water buckets down next to Mama expecting her to tell me to dump and fill the other ones, but she didn't.

In the living room, Lawrence said, "That boy's going to die, isn't he?"

"I think he's pretty much dead already." I imagined, like the pumpkins crushed by the mule one fall, that the insides of the boy's head felt loose and pulpy and seedy.

Lawrence and I went out the back door and walked around front. Daddy sat on the stoop, his nose stuffed with cotton. Blood caked his face in crimson splotches. His eyes stared off wide; his lips hung low. Raw spots of red crept along his hairline where he'd rubbed his hands a hundred times.

Frances and Mama came to the door. The front of their dresses, maroon and brown from neck to hem, seemed to glow next to the dingy wood of the house. Their hands had turned red. Streaks of blood crossed their faces, noses, foreheads, and cheeks.

The boy had died.

Daddy stood and Mama shook her head. "He's gone."

Daddy reached for her. The two hugged and cried. Lawrence sat on the bottom step looking out across the barren cornfields. I went into the room, Frances behind me.

TJ had the palm of his hands pressed against his eyes. Frances knelt beside TJ and put her arms around him. They rocked back and forth. Irene came over and joined them, her tiny hands patting both of their backs. Stripes of blood crisscrossed her legs.

Tony's eyes were closed. I've heard people say how peaceful the dead can look. This wasn't peaceful. His head was tilted back as his body reached for that last bit of air. His skin was pale where it had been tan when we first saw him at the spring. His lips were the color of a moonless stormy night. His fingers clinched the leading edge of the quilt.

Rags covered the floor spreading pools of liquid. The sheets were brown and red and dark. Above the bed, on the white washed walls, a red streak where a hand had slid. The stench of hog rot and piss and black, dark waste covered the smell of Mama's cooking and the fresh cut hay and the rain approaching from the west.

From the bedroom window, I saw Daddy kiss Mama on the forehead, pull himself away from her, and walk down the dirt road. Dark clouds gathered in the distance for a late afternoon assault.

"Luther!" she called. "Where are you going?"

He shoved his hands deep into his overall pockets and watched every step he took as he walked toward the approaching storm.

In the distance, past the farms, lightning jumped from cloud to cloud. Thunder skimmed the surface of the corn for miles, then rattled the window panes inside the dark house.

I dumped the crimson water from the buckets. It flowed a red stream under the house and down toward the wrecked chicken coop and pigsty. Another stream meandered toward the corn and cotton fields. Flies drank from the dark liquid. Buzzards sat on the sty fence, others inside pulling at the dead hogs.

I came back inside and sat next to TJ. He took the dog tags from around Tony's neck. Pulling one off, he tucked it into one of Tony's pockets. The other tag, on its long beaded chain, went around TJ's neck. "I think his mother lives in New York," TJ said, as if explaining what he'd do with the tag.

He then put the heel of his hands back over his eyes and let out a long, bellowing cry. TJ sat there and cried as loud as his lungs would let him. His anguished moans bounced from wall to wall. The dogs under the house let out a whimper. I don't know how many times the two met that summer, I only know that TJ cried as if he'd known the boy a very long time. We all cried.

Then he went calm. Like the still air that comes a moment before a twister, TJ quieted   .

29

"Come here." Mama said from her bedroom. "Jimmy, Lawrence, Irene, come in here."

We had scattered. Frances stayed with TJ, the two rocking. TJ quiet and still, not moving, his glare fixed on something distant that it seemed only he could see. Lawrence sat on the back stoop, his hands locked together and under his chin. Irene leaned against the Zenith while looking through the house into the room. I stood on the front porch watching the roads and the distant sheets of rain falling. Somewhere beyond the curtain of gray water, the sun shined. I thought I saw Daddy's head bouncing above the hedgerow at the end of the cotton field.

"Come in here."

Lawrence got up. He groaned and his hands rasped across his face. His feet shuffled across the floorboards.

I went in and picked up Irene. She felt stiff at first, coming into my arms like a plank. Then all of a sudden, she wrapped her legs around my waist and buried her face against my neck. "It's okay, Renie."

She whispered into my ear, "That people's dead. Ain't he, Jimmy?"

I kissed the side of her smooth face. "He's dead, Renie. It'll be okay."

I leaned against the pinewood chest. Lawrence stood in the doorway.

Frances sat beside TJ, her hand on his knee, patting it. "What are you doing, Mama?" She somehow hadn't noticed that Mama had washed Tony's body and had pulled up the ends of the sheet and covered him preparing to sew it shut.

"I'm getting this boy ready for a proper burial down in the cemetery."

"We can't do that." Frances got up. "We have to go get the Sheriff. Somebody."

"We can't, Frances," Lawrence said.

"You shut up." Frances pointed at Lawrence. "Just shut up. Mama, listen to me, we have to get the Sheriff. That boy's dead. Daddy killed him."

"It was an accident." Mama pulled the sheet across the boy's body.

"Accident or not, he's dead."

I readjusted Irene's weight. Whichever way I moved, she moved so that her face turned away from the bed. I said, "Daddy didn't mean to. Tony tripped over his belt."

"Jesus. My whole family's gone crazy." Frances pulled at her hair where it looked as if blood had clumped it together. "Mama, you've tried to teach us right from wrong our whole lives. Never mind the church, you taught us good and bad and evil. This is bad, Mama. We can't just let it go. Bury the boy in that little plot and forget about it? He has a family somewhere. The Army will want him back. If we hide this it will be evil."

TJ hadn't moved. His bent knees supported his arms. He looked straight ahead, across the top of the bed and the body, toward the wall.

Mama stopped sewing and looked up at Frances. "What about us? What will happen to us if they lynch your Daddy? He's your father, Frances. You're old enough to go out on your own, but what about me? What about Jimmy?"

"I can take care of myself."

". . . What about your baby sister? Who'll put food on the table for her? I'll try my best. I'll do whatever it takes, but I don't know if it'll ever be enough."

"The Marines might come for me. Won't be no one to tend the farm," Lawrence said.

"If it was an accident, they won't lynch Daddy. We can run the farm." Frances pulled harder at the crusty blood in her hair.

226

Mama put down the thick black thread and silver needle. She pushed herself off the bed and came to the chest I leaned on. When I moved aside, she took out some newspaper pages from the top drawer. I could see pictures of Negro men hanging from ropes off of trees and telegraph poles. "Look here, Frances. They lynch men in this country."

Frances took the pages and turned from one to the other. "All these men are Negroes, Mama."

"Keep looking." Mama knelt down again and took to sewing the gap.

Tony's skin looked almost clear. I didn't know how much blood a person had in their body, but it seemed that all of it had seeped out of him across our farm and onto the bed.

"You talking about Cherokee Bob here?"

Mama nodded while licking the end of the thread. "Read the piece with it."

"'Columbia. Lynching. Sheriff's Deputies report that a mob assaulted them and wrestled the prisoner, Cherokee Bob, from their safekeeping. Before the Deputies could regroup and put an end to the mob's thirst for blood, the Indian was lynched. Cherokee Bob had been accused of killing Corporal Ray Luck from Camp Jackson during a car crash outside of Columbia. The Sheriff commented, 'While the law should have been allowed to run its course, justice ultimately has been served.' No one from the mob has yet been identified.'" Frances slapped the paper against her leg.

"You see them pictures? You want that to happen to your Daddy?"

"But right is right, Mama," Frances said. "This ain't right. It ain't right for these people to lynch someone. Why is it right for Daddy to kill this boy and we just bury him? Are we supposed to just forget about it?"

"I suppose we'll never forget it, but what's going to happen to us if your Daddy is lynched? Okay, even if they don't lynch him. He's certain to go to jail for some time. Huh? He's a good man. I know he's hard on you, but it takes a hard man to raise you kids and run this farm."

"She's right," Lawrence said. "Say they don't hang

him from a tree. Say it goes to trial. He'll still be in jail for months, then maybe prison. Meanwhile, I'm likely going off to the Marines. Ain't none of you able to keep up the farm. Heck, who'll even tell Old Man Patterson he's cheating us?"

"We can get another farm." I put Irene down. She turned and faced the wall. "There's always land that needs someone tending it." I didn't know which side I was on. It was an accident. It was the belt. The boy fell. Daddy had struck him, but not a hard slap. We'd all had a slap or two like that around the farm. Certainly not a slap that itself would kill anyone.

"But you got to know how to do it."

"Then we'll move into town." Frances' tone sounded defeated. "Get jobs. We'll get by."

"Frances. We can't live without your father. Once word of this gets out, no one in these parts will give any one of us a job. Even if there was land, we couldn't get an acre to grow a garden. Without the crop, the Old Man will likely kick us off this piece here. You understand?"

I didn't know who sounded more right. Lawrence paced between the kitchen and the bedroom door. Mama ran the thread along the seam, in and out, fast.

Frances looked at each of us. "So we just kill a boy and walk away?"

"What are you saying, Mama?" I said.

"We'll move to Baltimore. Get a fresh start. George will help us."

Lawrence stopped pacing. Frances slumped into the chair next to the bed.

"Really?" I said

Her face looked serious and solid, her tears dried, her color back and strong. I knew she meant it and inside of me a part leaped about wanting to go, right then, at that moment. To walk out the front gate with a stick and all my stuff tied into a bindle and walk up Wilder Road and not look back. Then I looked at Tony's face, a fly landing on it. Mama fanned at it and the fly flew off. Another part of me inside, near my heart, seemed hot and I felt it move as if it crashed against a tree. I imagined a woman in New York City standing on a street corner in a yellow print frock looking both ways up the street, waiting for her son to come home.

TJ stood up, his eyes still wide and unblinking. Then he rubbed his face as if bringing it back to life. His face had turned pale, his lips showing a tinge of blue. "Mama's right."

"TJ? That's your friend lying there dead."

"She's right, Frances. Look at it anyway you want, we're finished here."

The front gate slapped shut. I went to the bedroom window and pulled the curtain back. Blood marred the sheer material. "It's Daddy."

He clumped into the house and came to the door. Lawrence stepped into the room.

"Lawrence." Daddy raised his hand as if he wanted to put it on Lawrence's shoulder, but then didn't. "Will you go get the Sheriff? It's Sunday, so you should ask the deputies to call him."

"I already told you, Luther, he ain't going nowhere," Mama said, closing the last thread over Tony's face.

30

Daddy made a stretcher out of the quilt off of my bed and two hoes. Lawrence and I ran ahead to the cemetery to begin digging a grave. Wind blew the clouds in and the first drops of rain fell.

I put the spade into the ground. It sunk easily through the thick layer of leaves.

Lawrence tapped me and pointed to the nearest headstone. "Too close to Grandma and Grandpa."

We moved further over, away from any stones that we could see. I shivered as I thought about digging down and coming across the bones of some long-buried relative.

"What about that?" I pointed to the green Army car that had a thin sheen of water flowing off the roof as the rain fell harder.

"Damn." Lawrence tossed down his shovel and we both ran over to the car. "Let's push it into the spring."

The keys dangled from the ignition. I started it and flipped on the headlights. I had to back it up and then squeeze it past some trees and a boulder before stopping at the edge of the spring. It rested on a flat piece of rock.

Lawrence came up behind. I joined him. "One, two, three." We pushed and slipped on the smooth rock, but the car rolled. The front wheels went over the edge, then the underbody caught. It hung there for a moment.

"Push." I'd stopped, but Lawrence kept going. Then, sparks leaped in a long stream from the rock as the car scrapped forward. The back wheels rolled as they met the edge of the rock. Cold water flipped off the bumper and showered my face with droplets. The car sank away from us in the clear water. White bubbles burst to the surface. I felt an odd pride in seeing the last of the car, headlights glowing, taillights red, disappearing into the dark depths.

We went back to shoveling where the roots grew thin. I looked around at the two-dozen stones that stood guard over the little cemetery and wondered how far back the graves went.

Before long, we dug the shape of a grave into the ground. TJ and Daddy carried the stretcher down and sat it next to the growing hole. Tony's nose poked up forming a tent beneath the white material.

I climbed out and Daddy lowered himself into the hole to help dig. He and Lawrence dug fast. Their bodies rocked as they flung the heavy clay and mud and dirt from the hole. Rain hit the trees, bending the branches and filling the hole with mud. The cold rain smelled of the ocean, salty and thick.

Mama, Frances, and Irene gathered there and watched us finish. Mama had her Bible, the raindrops slapping against the open pages. Frances had two pieces of bare wood nailed together to form a cross.

When they'd dug the grave three and a half or four feet deep, Daddy hit slate, a spark flying off the spade. Mud slid in faster than Lawrence could throw it out. The ground turned slick and slippery. The drops pounded the surface of the spring. Daddy climbed out. Lawrence stood in the hole and received the white and red mummy from off the stretcher.

Mama said "The Lord's Prayer" while the rest of us stood there quietly listening to the splattering of rain against leaves.

When Mama closed her Bible, TJ took to shoveling the wet dirt back in.

When I picked up a spade to help, Mama tapped me on the shoulder and shook her head.

We all walked off a distance, under the trees, the rain dumping from the sky, and watched TJ fill in the grave by himself.

31

We stood beneath the chestnuts, pines, oaks, and magnolias while the rain fell in heavy waves, reminding me again of the beach. For a moment, an image of me standing on a Paris street corner spying on the Nazis came to mind, but I pushed it aside. A hot feeling lingered inside of me that we'd done something wrong, but it seemed way below, as if I stood atop a hill and could see into a valley.

I watched TJ fill the hole. It seemed to take a very long time. Our hair matted to our heads. Water ran down our faces. Irene shivered, wedged in Frances' arm. TJ tapped the surface down with the shovel, then knelt in the mud, rain pouring down on him, his head bent.

A flash of lightning with a jolt of thunder crashed into the McCormick's field on the other side of the spring. Irene yelped.

TJ got up and walked back toward our house. As the trees rocked back and forth in the wind, I could just make out the brown side of the barn. Frances went out from beneath the trees and put the cross into the ground near the head. Then we all walked back toward the farm.

As we came up to the back stoop, the squeal of two sets of car breaks came from the road out front. Mama, Frances, Irene, and Daddy went into the house. Mud fell off their legs and feet onto Mama's floor.

"Someone's here." I walked around the house, Lawrence behind me.

Just outside the low fence, Pastor Myers' Army Plymouth idled, the rain steaming off the hood. Behind it, a Jeep with black letters reading "Military Police" on a white background, parked behind Myers' staff car.

I stopped and felt myself running down into that valley. "MPs, Lawrence."

The rain lightened. As Lawrence and I came around the corner, everyone except TJ stood on the front stoop.

Pastor Myers pulled himself out of his car. He no longer had the metal frame on his leg, but he walked with crutches under each arm.

"Jimmy, go down and help Pastor Myers." Mama waved me on.

"Mrs. Quick. Mr. Quick. Jimmy."

The Jeep's windshield wiper flipped back and forth flinging the rain about. Its canvas top sagged beneath a puddle of water. Inside, darkness filled the cabin.

I opened the gate for Pastor Myers.

Then the doors to the Jeep opened and Matthew and Frankie stepped out. They wore white helmets and white armbands with "MP" on them in black.

"You two?" I said. I couldn't imagine how they knew, but somehow they did and they were here to take Daddy. I wondered if they'd take Mama, too.

Frances came down off of the stoop and ran past Pastor Myers.

"Frances," Mama said. "Get back here."

Mama's voice seemed to say what I worried—that Frances might tell what happened. She had her opportunity. The law, in one fashion or another, not the Sheriff, but the law, had arrived at our doorstep.

"Matthew." Frances balanced herself on the muddy road as she ran toward the Jeep.

Everyone watched Frances. She passed Matthew and ran off down the road a few yards.

"Where are you going, Frannie?" Matthew said.

"Looks like she's got some beef to fix with you." Frankie tossed his head toward Frances indicating that Matthew should go to her.

"Who's that?" Daddy said.

Mama nudged Daddy in the stomach. "None of your

business, I'd say."

Pastor Myers stopped at the bottom of the stoop. He coughed, drawing everyone's attention away from Frances. "Well, I'll get right to the point. We've come to take Lawrence back."

Mama smiled. "That's why you're here?" She looked crazy with her hair stuck to her head and a wide grin on her face.

Pastor Myers blinked a few times. "Yes, Ma'am. Well, I wanted to see how you were faring after the storm, so when I got a notice from the Marines about Lawrence, I thought I'd better come out. I knew that some of your children knew Matthew and Frankie, so I brought them along. Army regulations: Two MPs or the local sheriff when we come to get . . ., well, ..."

"A deserter." Lawrence stepped forward. "I'm here, Pastor Myers."

I turned back toward Frances and Matthew for a moment. She yelled at him, but I couldn't make out the words. Matthew seemed to be pleading for her to calm down. He touched her arm, but she pulled it away.

Daddy stepped down off the stoop. "I'm sorry, Pastor, but Lawrence ain't going back to the Marines."

Pastor Myers' forehead wrinkled. "I don't understand. I know he was scared. That's what it is most of the time. But he signed up and the draft pulled his number."

Mama slipped a little on the step as she stepped down. Daddy and Pastor Myers reached for her. She took Daddy's hand. "We've lost everything, Pastor. More than everything. Even the hogs and chickens were killed by the storm."

TJ came from around the corner of the house.

Pastor Myers turned toward him. "Afternoon, TJ."

TJ bowed his head a bit. "Pastor." Then leaned up against the house. He put Tony's dog tag under his shirt.

"Yes, Ma'am. I'm sorry this happened to you."

"Pastor, we need Lawrence here," Daddy said. "The War Department says he's essential on the farm. We've got a lot of rebuilding to do."

"Is there any way we can just let him stay?" Mama said.

Pastor Myers rubbed the back of his neck. He looked puzzled, as if he'd rehearsed, but none of it seemed to be going like it should.

Frances and Matthew walked back toward the Jeep. Matthew went up close next to Frankie and whispered. Frankie nodded and looked our way, then nodded some more. Frances leaned against the Jeep, folded her arms, and seemed to stare down at the muddy road.

I knew she'd told. Matthew and Frankie were planning how they'd manage to arrest Daddy. They had Colt 45's at their sides, and I figured if Lawrence had anything to say about them not taking Daddy, they might just need them. *Damn her.* The image of the Negro men hanging from the end of ropes, their heads sideways, necks stretched, hands tied behind them came to me.

Matthew finished and Frankie shook his hand. I didn't know what that meant. Then Matthew came through the gate with Frances behind him. I stepped in front of Matthew. "Hey, Jimmy." He looked back toward Frances for a second.

"Pastor Myers, I'm sorry, but we went out to find Lawrence at the Quick place and didn't find anyone. Think we can try again in a couple of days?"

"What are you talking about, Corporal?"

"It's a real shame how that storm tore this farm up. Lots of work to be done. Who knows? Maybe this family will have to move to another farm, or something."

Pastor Myers looked around, out across the barren fields. The rain had stopped and the sun forced its way through the thick clouds again. From beneath the house, two of the hounds clamored out, then ran toward the sty to eat on dead hog.

"What was that again?" Pastor Myers said.

Matthew looked back to Frankie. "I'm sorry, but we went out to the Quick's place, but didn't find anyone. We'll try again in a few days."

Pastor Myers nodded his head.

Matthew turned and gave Frances a quick kiss on the lips. "I'll be seeing you around, deb."

"Not if I see you first, drone." Frances smiled and watched Matthew walk.

Rick Kemp

Matthew patted me on the head as he passed me by. "How's the battle going?"

"Good," I said.

"Attaboy." He walked on. "I'll see you around, Jimmy boy."

She hadn't told.

Matthew and Frankie got into the Jeep. It spun up mud as they pulled away and raced toward Wilder Road.

Pastor Myers held out his hand to Daddy. "Then, I wish you well." They shook hands. So did Lawrence.

Mama hugged him. "God bless you."

He held her away for a moment and seemed to look deep into her. Too long, I thought. "And with you, Sister Quick."

He kissed Irene on her forehead. Frances kissed him on his cheek.

He shook TJ's hand, then put his finger under the beaded chain. "Where'd you get dog tags?"

TJ straightened up. He looked past Pastor Myers right at me. "Just found them in town."

I helped Pastor Myers back to his car. His foot caught a rock that bounced across the road. "Can you get me that one, Jimmy?"

I fetched the rock, smooth and pale green, for him. He tossed it in the air, then put it in his pocket. "Thank you."

When he got into his car, he rolled the window down and took my hand. "Did you hear the Allies have entered Paris?"

"No, I hadn't heard that yet."

"Won't be long, now." Pastor Myers waved, got into his car, and drove off.

236

32

Bennettsville, South Carolina August 21, 1944

Mama and Daddy went off in the wagon to call Uncle George from the phone at the cotton gin.

Uncle George got there the next day with a Ford truck and a man named Jerry to help us load whatever we could. "Would have been here earlier, but that damned U.S. 1 has got so many cars on it," Uncle George said.

We took the Zenith, but not the windmill. The hailstorm had broken the fins and Uncle George assured us he could get someone in Baltimore to hook it up for electricity.

When he said that, we all stopped our packing and looked at him until he said, "What?"

"Electricity?" I said.

It seemed not one of us had even thought about that. From then on, someone would ask him a question every few minutes about running water, churches, ball games, the harbor. He knew about a house for us--one that he owned standing empty between renters. "It's near the train station, not far from downtown and the harbor. Just down at the corner is a church that Novaline can go to."

"Train, train, train, train," Irene said, moving around the yard like her favorite toy.

Daddy shoveled a few remaining dead chickens out of

the yard, their heads dangling over, bobbing about. He tossed them onto the rubble of the coop and tool shed, then dumped kerosene on them and lit it. The feathers curled, the beaks popped when they got too hot, it smelled like burnt supper.

"Burn the hogs where they lay," Lawrence said to Daddy.

We cleared out a few tools from the collapsed shed: some hoes and shovels, rakes and axes, hammers, screwdrivers, and saws. We left the scythes and corn planters, the burlap sacks, egg crates, milk cans, and buckets.

Lawrence put the dozen or so kerosene lanterns we had on the back stoop. "Save two. You might need them in Baltimore if the electricity goes out." Lawrence lit all but two. Frances carried out the cast-iron skillets and pots, then the butter churn and Mason jars. They brought out preserves and emptied the smoke house of meat. Jerry and Uncle George carried out the kitchen table, the chairs, the bed frames, and the pinewood chest. Mama packed photos and papers into crates.

I carried a lantern down to the barn. When I opened the mule pins and slapped them on their rears, they trotted out and into the fields, breathless in their hee-hawing.

Ham didn't go as easily. I milked her, then dumped the cream onto the ground. It seeped down the alley and under the boards out into the fields. I had to pull on her hard, most her life kept in that barn. Her eyes looked wild and frightened. She must have thought slaughter time had come, what with the smell of rotting flesh all around her. When she saw the fresh weeds at the back of the yard, she sauntered over to them and ate.

I took a lantern by its handle, flung it around a few times, and let it sail into the loft. It crashed and burst, catching the dry hay up there afire. In seconds, the roof caught and smoke lifted high into the sky.

"Come on, now. We got to hurry. Town folk will see the smoke and send out the fire brigade." Mama carried out Daddy and her belongings in two Pepsi crates.

I ran back to the house and found my carpetbag sitting in the middle of my empty bedroom. The only other thing left was the well-worn mattress propped against the wall. I checked to be sure I'd put my dozen or so *National Geographics,* seashells, photos, arrowheads, and other stuff into my bag.

In the living room, Big Ben still sat on the mantle. I stuffed it into my bag, then rolled up the little rug that had sat before the radio. The edge of it caught on the nail head that still stuck up.

The chicken coop and tool shed, the pigsty, outhouse, smokehouse, and barn now burned hot and red. Flames jumped into the sky. A light breeze brought pollen floating through the air and bent the smoke out toward the empty fields.

TJ flung a lantern into Mama's bedroom. I tossed one into my room. Daddy sent one through the front door. Lawrence let another one go through the living room window. Smoke poured from the windows and the eves glowed red.

Frances sat up front with Uncle George and Jerry. Mama and Daddy sat on our couch that stretched across the back of the truck, Irene asleep on their lap. Lawrence stood at the front of the truck's bed, rocking with each bump. TJ and I rode on the back edge of the truck. Our feet dangling off, swaying back and forth.

Long streaks of cloud pointed toward the horizon. The sky reminded me of a picture I'd seen in *National Geographic*—one from Africa or South America or just someplace else--orange, violet, gold, silver. Buzzards circled above riding the shimmering currents from the rising heat. Behind the house, the morning sun grew big and red out of the horizon.

Acknowledgments

My thanks go out to many people. Particularly, this novel would not have been written if it hadn't been for the support and encouragement that Maribeth Fischer gave me. I am also grateful to Fred D'Aguiar, Evelyn Mayerson, Sandra-Jackson Opoku, Bob Antoni, Edwidge Danticat, and Mark Farrington, as well as my colleagues Laura Albritton, Brad Bertelli, and Lisa Hartz for sharing their insights and expertise. In Bennettsville, South Carolina, many thanks to the Bennettsville Historical Society and Chamber of Commerce, Bill Kinney at the *Marlboro Herald Advocate*, and Karen Lewes at the Marlboro Theater.

Red Sun in Morning

www.ingramcontent.com/pod-product-compliance
Lightning Source LLC
Chambersburg PA
CBHW060133130626
46556CB00006B/2335